The Fangover

ERIN McCARTHY

and

KATHY LOVE

BERKLEY SENSATION, NEW YORK

THE BERKLEY PUBLISHING GROUP
Published by the Penguin Group
Penguin Group (USA) Inc.
375 Hudson Street, New York, New York 10014, USA

Penguin Group (Canada), 90 Eglinton Avenue East, Suite 700, Toronto, Ontario M4P 2Y3, Canada
(a division of Pearson Penguin Canada Inc.) • Penguin Books Ltd., 80 Strand, London WC2R 0RL,
England • Penguin Group Ireland, 25 St. Stephen's Green, Dublin 2, Ireland (a division of Penguin
Books Ltd.) • Penguin Group (Australia), 250 Camberwell Road, Camberwell, Victoria 3124, Australia
(a division of Pearson Australia Group Pty. Ltd.) • Penguin Books India Pvt. Ltd., 11 Community
Centre, Panchsheel Park, New Delhi—110 017, India • Penguin Group (NZ), 67 Apollo Drive,
Rosedale, Auckland 0632, New Zealand (a division of Pearson New Zealand Ltd.) • Penguin Books
(South Africa) (Pty.) Ltd., 24 Sturdee Avenue, Rosebank, Johannesburg 2196, South Africa

Penguin Books Ltd., Registered Offices: 80 Strand, London WC2R 0RL, England

This book is an original publication of The Berkley Publishing Group.

This is a work of fiction. Names, characters, places, and incidents either are the product of the author's
imagination or are used fictitiously, and any resemblance to actual persons, living or dead, business
establishments, events, or locales is entirely coincidental. The publisher does not have any control over
and does not assume any responsibility for author or third-party websites or their content.

PUBLISHING HISTORY
Berkley Sensation trade paperback edition / November 2012

Library of Congress Cataloging-in-Publication Data

McCarthy, Erin, 1971–
The fangover / Erin McCarthy and Kathy Love.—Berkley Sensation trade paperback ed.
        p.   cm.
ISBN 978-0-425-25323-6
1. Vampires—Fiction.   2. New Orleans (La.)—Fiction.   3. Paranormal fiction.
4. Erotic fiction.   I. Love, Kathy.   II. Title.
PS3613.C34575F36   2012
813'.6—dc23
                                                        2012031877

PRINTED IN THE UNITED STATES OF AMERICA

10   9   8   7   6   5   4   3   2   1

Dear Reader,

We've been good friends for ten years and took our first trip to New Orleans together six years ago and have been back together many times since. We've made friends on Bourbon Street, we've heard a lot of Journey, seen many a weird thing, and shared a lot of laughs. So when we talked about collaborating on a book, it made sense to combine three things we both love: New Orleans, vampires, and a sense of the absurd. Because really, what could be more absurd than vampires waking up from a forgotten night of debauchery with missing fangs, a priest in the bathtub, and a drunk parrot who sings Barry White?

While we conceived the story idea and time line together (not to mention our awesome chapter headings) Erin wrote Wyatt and Stella's story, and Kathy wrote Cort and Katie's. We hope you'll enjoy our fun romp into hungover vampires as much as we enjoyed writing it, and if you're ever in New Orleans, stop by Fahy's and have a drink. Just don't tell the bartender you know us.

Cheers and Happy Reading!
Erin and Kathy

Praise for the novels of *USA Today* bestselling author
ERIN McCARTHY

"Steamy . . . Fast-paced and red hot." —*Publishers Weekly*

"A runaway winner! Ms. McCarthy has created a fun, sexy, and hilarious story that holds you spellbound from start to finish."
—*Fallen Angel Reviews*

"The searing passion between these two is explosive, and the action starts on page one and doesn't stop until the last page. Erin McCarthy has written a fun, sexy read." —*Romance Reviews Today*

"This is Erin McCarthy at her best. She is fabulous with smoking hot romances!" —*The Romance Readers Connection*

Praise for the novels of *USA Today* bestselling author
KATHY LOVE

"Love has a way of expertly blending poignant narrative with wonderfully lovable flawed characters . . . She adds a suspense-filled, supersexy plot to keep her readers' hearts racing in more ways than one." —*Booklist*

"Supercharged with sexual tension, mind melding, and suspense . . . Love delivers, with her usual fast pace and witty style."
—*RT Book Reviews*

"A fast-paced, humorous book that dishes out satisfying romance as well as lighthearted laughs." —*Love Vampires*

"Kathy Love has done the impossible: come up with an original idea for a vampire romance. A bloodsucker's delight." —*The Best Reviews*

Chapter One

THE NIGHT AFTER

HOLY crap on a cracker. Wyatt Axelrod's head hurt. Big-time. He pried his eyes open and groaned as the ceiling came into focus. He felt like his neck was broken and he was paralyzed from the waist down. He moved a leg and an arm. Still working, which was a good thing, but damn, even that small movement made the blood vessels in his head threaten to burst.

He wasn't sleeping in his bed. He was in a chair. And there was the most god-awful screaming coming from the other room. Righting his head and leaning forward, swallowing hard, he realized he was in his bandmate Cort's apartment. Saxon, their keyboard player, was lying on the floor, holding his own head, blonde hair falling into his face.

Wyatt didn't remember coming back to Cort's. He didn't remember leaving the riverboat they were having Johnny's wake on. He didn't remember much of anything from the night before, and that was a first. A scary first.

"What the hell happened last night?" he asked.

No one seemed to know. As Cort and Saxon blathered on and on about who the hell knew what, Wyatt checked his jeans pocket. He still had his phone and his wallet, fortunately. But he also still had a headache, which the shrieking wasn't helping. Asking his friends what the awful noise was, he contemplated standing.

No one had the chance to answer his question before a woman came running into the room, looking more than a little hysterical. Wyatt felt his eyebrows raise as he recognized the mortal washboard player from the day band at the bar where their band worked. What the hell was Katie doing here?

"I woke up in someone's room . . ." she was saying to Cort, who had somehow mustered the energy to stand.

Wyatt knew what that meant—someone had hooked up with Katie. He didn't think it was Saxon. He knew it wasn't him. So it was either Drake or Cort, and he had no interest in watching this very awkward morning after moment go down. Besides, speaking of hookups, he wanted to know where Stella was. The last thing he remembered was having a bit of an argument with her on the deck of the riverboat. He didn't want to fight with Stella. He wanted to make love to Stella, all night long, like a classic rock song. He was head over ass for her, and now he was worried.

He opened his mouth to ask if anyone had seen her when Katie beat him to the punch.

"I seem to be a vampire," she said, her voice shaky, eyes panicked.

Wyatt cursed.

That sound?

That would be the shit hitting the fan.

48 Hours Earlier

"Ugh, it's disgusting in here," Stella Malone said as she stood in the middle of her brother Johnny's apartment and gestured to the floor. "Who just dumps an ashtray in the middle of the room?"

Wyatt knew his buddy Johnny was a two-pack-a-day vampire, but he didn't think even he could create a pile of ash that high. With a piece of paper in it. And a necklace.

Oh, shit. He glanced toward the French doors a few feet away. The drapes were pulled open, and Wyatt knew for a fact that the New Orleans sun beat in those windows during the day.

It couldn't be.

If he had a heartbeat, it would have been racing by now. As it was, his stomach was churning, the bag of blood he'd had an hour ago sitting like an anchor in his gut. Johnny wouldn't do it.

It could have been an accident. A horrible, careless accident.

Wyatt pulled the piece of paper out of the ash carefully and shook it off.

"It's so typically Johnny to just run off without telling anyone where he's going," Stella said.

"Oh, actually, he left a note." Wyatt scanned the piece of paper and cursed.

"What? What does it say?" Stella snatched the paper away from him, kicking some of the ash as she moved toward him, a little gray cloud rising up to her ankles.

It seemed appropriate. Wyatt kind of wanted to kick Johnny himself. How the hell could he kill himself? It was selfish, stupid, so not like Johnny that Wyatt was reeling.

"Stella . . ." Wyatt tried to take the note back, thinking he could break it to her more gently. "Maybe you should . . ."

Too late. She gasped. "Oh, my God. This is a suicide note." It fell out of her hands, fluttering down to the ash pile. She suddenly seemed to realize she was standing in her brother's remains and she jumped back. "How could he do this?"

Wyatt shook his head, bewildered. He'd known Johnny for forty years and he'd never thought of him as anything but happy-go-lucky. "I don't know, sweetheart. I didn't see this coming at all. He seemed fine. I just saw him last night." When Stella had told him Johnny wasn't answering his phone, he hadn't thought it was any big deal. He'd figured she was overreacting, but he had agreed to come check on Johnny with her.

It seemed her worry had been well founded.

Reaching down, he picked up the note and scanned it again.

To Whom It May Concern,

I have walked in darkness far too long.
Today I will step into the sun.
And die.

Don't grieve me. But if you throw an Irish wake, which you really should, please don't let Saxon do backup vocals on any Boston songs. He sings like a cat in heat.

Cheers,
Johnny

P.S. Stella, the fifty bucks I owe you is in the cookie jar.

"He was fine. This is insane." Stella grabbed the note from him again. "And To Whom It May Fucking Concern? Really? That's how he starts a suicide note?"

"It sounds like a bit of last-minute humor. You know Johnny." Wyatt was still in shock himself and he honestly had no clue what to say to Stella, how to calm her down. It had been a long time since any vampire he knew had died. He had watched hundreds of humans leave this life, but he'd gotten used to the idea that he and his vampire buddies were exempt from death. Immortal was immortal, right?

Except when you threw open the blinds and went sunbathing.

"Yeah, I know Johnny. I've spent my whole life being the responsible one while my brother screws around and does whatever he feels like." Stella crumpled the note and threw it at the wall in a fit of fury. "How dare he? How dare he just kill himself without even saying good-bye? Without talking to me about whatever was bothering him?" With an exclamation of frustration, she kicked the coffee table. "I'll give you To Whom It May Concern. Concern this."

Wyatt's gut told him to just let Stella have her rant. She started swearing and spinning around, tossing Johnny's lamp on the floor with a resounding crash. She threw the pillows from the couch in the direction of the kitchen and knocked over a breakfast bar stool. It was almost as shocking as Johnny's suicide. Stella was one of the most controlled women Wyatt knew. She was never late to work. She paid her bills on time. She drank her blood delicately, in a glass. She never swore. Ever.

And now she was cursing with a creativity that astounded him, her eyes blazing with fury, her finger bleeding from the lamp she'd shattered.

Finally, she seemed spent, her face crumpling. She gave one final kick, right through Johnny's ashes. She seemed to instantly regret it, her heavy breathing the only sound in the room as she bent to try to cup his ashes back into a pile, then thought better of it.

She burst into tears as she stood back up, fingers flexing.

Wyatt moved toward her. "Oh, Stella, sweetie, I'm so sorry." He wrapped his arms around her and pulled her into his chest. She let him, which showed him she was really a hot mess. Stella didn't like to be touched—not by him, anyway. She thought of him as the goofy guitar player. Fine for friendship, but nothing else. And she'd never let him get particularly close to her.

For years—okay, decades—he'd had a crush on her. But she was out of his league and he knew it. He was just a dusty old cowboy-turned-vampire guitar player, and she was all that was class and intelligence.

If he could be there for her in any way, hell, he was grateful. He held her and murmured words of comfort in her ear, his hand rubbing up and down her back. It was so damn hard to process the fact that Johnny was gone. It was surreal, mind-boggling. So he focused on the feel of Stella in his arms, the soft floral scent of her hair, and the sound of her sobbing as it slowed into snuffled crying. He was glad she hadn't found Johnny alone.

"I'm really sorry," he told her again. "But eternity is a long time. Maybe Johnny was just tired of the ride."

"I don't understand," she said, her words muffled against his chest. "I need a glass of wine. My stomach is upset."

Wyatt wasn't sure that alcohol was the best thing for her, but he kissed the top of her head and moved to Johnny's sparse kitchen. He found vodka and rum, but no wine. He poured some vodka into a glass and brought it to Stella. She tossed it back in one quick motion.

Holy shit. Wyatt wiped the tears off her cheeks, debating whether he should suggest they clean up Johnny or if he should wait and let her take the lead. She was a control freak, so chances were she'd want to handle it, but he was a little concerned he might wind up with Johnny on his boot if they left him there too long. There was something seriously unpleasant about the thought of walking around with his best friend stuck to him like old gum.

"Can I have another drink?"

Wyatt hesitated, but she looked up at him, so vulnerable, eyes glazed with shock and pain, that he couldn't say no. "Sure."

He went back to the kitchen, feeling the need for a drink himself, Stella on his tail. She kept glancing back to the pile of ash, almost as morbid as an actual body lying there would have been. "I just don't understand," she repeated.

"That's the rub, honey. Some things we're just not going to be able to understand." Like how he could be looking at Stella and thinking how beautiful she was when they were in the midst of tragedy. Or that her body looked particularly enticing in her jeans and V-neck T-shirt. But he was. Which made him a sick, sick man, and eternally grateful that she couldn't read his mind.

Of course, he always had those thoughts around Stella. Maybe he was just conditioned to be aware of what she was wearing and how much he wanted to play hide the salami with her that even death couldn't distract him.

Now he definitely needed a drink.

Wyatt poured her another finger of vodka, and one for himself. She downed it then just took the whole bottle out of his hand, clearly going for efficiency. He felt his eyes widen as she chugged half of it. Who chugged vodka? His throat burned just watching her. "Stella. Babe. I think that's enough." He reached for the bottle.

She evaded his hand. "He left me. He just left me here. All alone. By myself."

The pit in his gut had nothing to do with the alcohol and

everything to do with the fact that for a very long time he'd been crushing on Stella, and it broke his goddamn heart to hear her so torn up, so quiet, so sad.

"You're not alone. I'm here." He brushed her auburn hair back off her cheek. Stella's Irish heritage was evident in her hair coloring, and the dusting of freckles that popped even louder against her pale, smooth vampire skin.

"I've never been alone, Wyatt. I'm scared."

"You're not alone." He cupped her cheeks, moving so that his body blocked hers up against the counter. He wanted her to feel that he was physically there, not going anywhere. He wanted to reassure her.

"You won't leave me?" she asked softly, her green eyes glassy with grief and alcohol.

"No, I won't leave you." He wasn't sure what she meant by that, but he was willing to offer her anything that she would take. It was no secret to him that he'd been finding excuses to spend time with Stella for years. Hell, that was half the reason he stayed in the band, because Stella was the sound tech and he got to see her five days a week. It was very possible he was actually in love with her, if he wanted to get technical about it.

But Stella had never given him the time of day. Or night, more accurately.

Until now.

Now she was gripping the front of his shirt and staring up at him with such woeful eyes he would have done anything she asked.

"Kiss me," she said.

"Uh . . ." For a second Wyatt wondered if he'd slipped at work and hit his head on an amp and he was unconscious. This had to be a dream. Well, a nightmare and a dream. Johnny was gone.

Dead. Stella wanted to kiss him. The whole world had tilted on its side.

None of this could be real.

Only he hadn't gone to work since it was Monday and their night off from playing on Bourbon Street.

He didn't think he was dreaming.

And if he thought about it too much, his head might actually explode, so he decided not to think at all. He was just going to obey.

Kiss her. He could do that.

He leaned down, eyeing her small lips with a predatory satisfaction. He'd been waiting forty years for a crack at her mouth.

Stella wasn't really sure why she had asked Wyatt to kiss her. It was just that she felt so lonely, so shocked, so horrified. So drunk.

Her brother was dead. After eighty-five years of hanging out undead together, her taking care of him, suddenly he was gone. Just gone. He was never supposed to be gone. They were going to live forever. But he hadn't. She couldn't comprehend it. She couldn't think about it. At all.

Wyatt was looking at her with such compassion, his muscular body close to hers as he brushed her hair back off her head. Stella had never really thought of him as much more than a slightly less annoying version of her brother. But now he looked like a perfect way to ignore what was really happening.

Plus, she was drunk.

It had been years since she'd tossed back that many shots in such a short amount of time. In combination with her shock, it had gone straight to her head. Why that meant she would ask Wyatt to kiss her, she wasn't sure. But she had, and he was clearly going to oblige her, and that seemed like it all made sense to her.

She'd never noticed how intense his eyes could be. Or how perfectly pristine his fangs were.

His fangs were out.

That meant he was aroused.

By the mere idea of kissing her.

Which aroused Stella.

Wyatt was a good-looking guy. He had caramel-colored hair that skimmed his shoulders and a seductive mouth. Which was now on hers, kissing her with more finesse than she would have thought possible. Wyatt and Johnny had been two vampiric peas in an undead pod. Both jokesters, both happy-go-lucky, though truthfully, Wyatt was way more thoughtful and far less selfish than Johnny. She'd never thought of Wyatt as being a ladies' man either, like her brother had been, though how Johnny had ever managed that was still a mystery to Stella.

Yet for never having a girlfriend that she could remember, Wyatt sure in the hell knew how to kiss. His lips were taking skilled possession of hers, warm and confident. It was the kind of kiss that made you want to keep kissing, for hours and hours or until you were naked, whichever came first. Stella gave a soft moan and opened her mouth.

But Wyatt pulled back. "That better?"

Yes and no. She nodded. "Do it again."

He hesitated. "Are you sure?"

Instead of arguing with him, Stella just went up on her tiptoes, buried her fingers in his hair, and went at his mouth with her own. She was definitely not as smooth in her moves as he had been but it was effective. Within seconds, his tongue was sliding between her lips and tangling with hers. A sharp kick of lust between her thighs had her running her fingers over his hard chest and down to cup his suddenly obvious and quite impressive erection.

He tore his mouth off of hers, breathing hard. "Stella."

"What?" She bent over and unzipped him, drawing that hard length out of his jeans.

"What are you doing?"

Forgetting. Distracting herself. Trying to feel alive, when for the first time in eight decades, she felt the weight of mortality. In a hazy fog of alcohol and grief, desire sliced through the murkiness and gave her something to hold on to.

Her nipples beaded as she enclosed her mouth around his swollen cock. She figured that was a good enough answer to his question.

"Holy shit. Ahh." His words were strangled, and he gripped her shoulders with enough pressure to cause bruising. "Damn, that feels so good."

It did. It felt like she was back in control. As his breathing deepened, she stroked faster, feeling her own body respond. It had been years since she'd had sex. Probably since the '80s, if she wanted to get technical about it. Mortals never seemed able to satisfy her and they moved in such a small world of vampires, there hadn't really been any men she'd been interested in. Now she was wondering why the hell she hadn't tried a little harder because this felt delightful. Vibrant.

Wyatt had a perfect penis, the kind that filled her mouth so completely she couldn't help but imagine what it would do to another part of her.

He must have had the same thought because suddenly Wyatt was pulling back, pushing her off him and against the kitchen counter. Popping the button on her jeans, he stared at her intently. "Can I?"

Part of her insanely wanted to correct his grammar, another part of her was touched that he would ask, that he would give her an opportunity to say no. But the rest of her just wanted him inside her without any hesitation or interruptions.

"Yes. Yes." She unzipped her jeans herself to lend credence to her words.

"Oh, Stella," Wyatt groaned. Bending over, he took her mouth again, his tongue doing a delicious slide into her mouth while he took her jeans down to her knees in one swift motion.

Then he bit her bottom lip, hard enough to draw blood. He lapped at it, breathing deeply in through his nose as he took in her scent. It was Stella's turn to moan. The last time someone had bitten her, she'd been wearing bell bottoms and a mohair vest, and that had been by a nutjob trying to become a vampire.

This was much better. This was electric. Each lap with the tip of Wyatt's tongue, taking in her tangy blood, was an erotic jolt between her thighs. His thumb skimmed over her clitoris and she felt frantic, fumbling with her fingers to grab him, guide him to her. Wyatt was way ahead of her. Before she could even voice her desperate need, his cock thrust inside her with such impact that she was actually lifted up onto her tiptoes.

She let out a startled moan. He swore. And she shivered in delight as he started to move in and out. Wyatt put his hand on the small of her back so that she wouldn't slam into the counter as he picked up speed, gritting his teeth, eyes boring into her.

"You're so tight. You feel so good," he told her.

There was no way she could actually speak. She was too busy trying not to shatter into a thousand pieces and drop to the kitchen floor. Her senses were being assaulted: the feel of his grip on her hip, the lingering smell of her drying blood, the rustle of his jeans, the hot blast of his breath on her. And most of all, the thick pounding of his cock into her slick, warm wetness.

"Oh, oh," was all she could manage before she completely lost it and came with a startled shout. It was amazing how good it felt, how overwhelming and all-consuming it was. There was nothing but her body and his, and tight ecstasy.

Wyatt stopped pumping for a brief second, then resumed as his orgasm joined hers. Together they gripped and groaned and stared deep into each other's eyes. It was a moment so intense Stella shook her head slightly in disbelief at the raw, deep connection she felt with Wyatt.

Then he pulled out and she came back to reality. As he ran his fingers through his hair and wiggled his ass a little to get his stuff back into his jeans, Stella felt her cheeks flame. What the frickety frack was that? She had just had rabbit sex with her brother's best friend thirty minutes after finding her brother's body—or what was left of it.

She was appalled. She was speechless. She was still feeling the effects of the vodka. And she was wishing that her body didn't feel so goddamn satisfied.

What she finally managed to say was, "Sorry."

Which said nothing.

It seemed to confuse Wyatt. He frowned as he zipped his jeans. His jaw worked, like he was going to say something, then changed his mind. "I'll, uh, just call the band and let them know what's going on."

Right. Yeah. They needed to deal with the situation at hand. "Okay, thanks."

"We could plan a wake for tomorrow or the night after. Probably tomorrow since we don't have to work. We could use the riverboat where we played that gig last Mardi Gras."

Stella wasn't sure if it was the alcohol or the reality of her brother's death, but she just felt numb, incapable of thinking. So she nodded, and let Wyatt handle it all. "I need to get out of here."

"Go ahead, that's fine. I'll take care of everything."

Fumbling to pull up her own jeans as she walked, Stella lost her footing. Going down on one knee, she caught her fall.

With her hand in Johnny. Pulling it back, she stared in horror at the layer of ash now coating her skin. Seriously? Could this night suck any more?

Johnny didn't even own a dustpan. So she wasn't even sure how she was supposed to clean up his final mess.

Wyatt's firm grip on her waist yanked her out of her pity party. Actually, it yanked her right off the floor and upright.

"It's okay. You're okay."

Um, no she wasn't. Her brother was dead. She was a random slut. And she was the clumsiest vampire ever. "I'm all alone, Wyatt," she repeated, the tears returning. Johnny was dead. What the hell.

"You're not alone." Wyatt leaned in, brown eyes dark with desire, and something else. "I love you, Stella."

Oh, yeah. This night could get worse and that was it. Why would Wyatt say that? And why did him saying those words strike a fear almost greater than death in her heart?

"Thanks," she said, in what was arguably the lamest response ever. "I have to go."

And she bolted. Like a slutty, ash-covered coward.

Maybe she and Johnny weren't so different after all.

Chapter Two

THE WAKE

(Or What They Remembered of It)

WYATT was grateful that he'd played "Carry On Wayward Son" approximately nine thousand times in his years playing with The Impalers on Bourbon Street, because he was completely distracted at Johnny's wake.

Johnny was dead and he'd slept with Stella.

He'd told Stella he loved her and she'd run away.

He wasn't even sure why he'd said that. He had meant it more in the way of reassurance that she wasn't alone. That he cared about her. He did love her. He wasn't exactly sure to what extent, but he totally did.

But what kind of crap-ass timing had that been? Her brother was dead, they had just spontaneously screwed, and oh yeah, I love you.

He would have run from that.

So basically, everything sucked and he wanted to crawl into a coffin and sleep for a century. He hadn't slept in forty-eight hours and his eyes felt like sandpaper with an overlay of crushed glass.

He had actually even reached up to wipe something off his cheek at one point during his eulogy for Johnny and had discovered it was a blood tear. Never in his whole 150 years of life had he been so mortified. Except for when he'd told Stella he loved her and she'd said thanks and left. There was that.

How could Johnny have committed suicide? And how could Wyatt have blurted out some weird random vow of love to his sister over his ashes?

Stupid. Stupid, stupid. Now he was standing onstage at Johnny's wake in a haze of grief and liquor, staring out at the crowd of vampires who were mingling, talking, drinking, dancing in remembrance of a life, if not well lived, at least fairly long lived.

Wyatt's eyes followed Stella, worried about her. He'd been happy to handle all the arrangements of collecting Johnny and planning the wake, to lessen her burden. He'd also been quite happy to stick his dick in her. Who did that? He was absolutely disgusted with himself. The only thing he could say in his own defense was that he hadn't experienced the death of a friend in a very long time. Clearly, he didn't know how to do grief anymore. He just knew how to do Stella.

Now he was playing by rote, wondering if she had enjoyed their five-minute encounter as much as he had. She seemed to have been into it while it was happening. He was positive she'd even had an orgasm. He'd felt it, that tightening around his cock, that shiver of her inner muscles, and the catch of her breath before she had called out . . .

Wyatt shifted his guitar in front of his newly sprung erection. Yeah, he was a sick bastard.

A bastard who didn't want to be there. He'd never been big on funerals or wakes. Back in his mortal days out West, someone died, you dug them a hole, and kept on riding. There was none of this fuss and bother, and the good thing about that was you had the luxury of ignoring your feelings. You didn't have to stand around and acknowledge that you felt lousy that you'd lost someone important to you. You could just stuff your grief down inside and never deal with it. It was the man's way of handling death.

Saxon was showing off on the keyboard, adding unnecessary notes left and right, and Wyatt wanted to hit him on the head with his guitar. He also wanted to whisk Stella off and spend a few days naked with her until this whole thing blew over.

Then he wanted to find a way to convince her that they really should be a couple.

He settled for flicking a guitar pick at Saxon, bouncing it off his shoulder, but the satisfaction was short-lived when the keyboardist didn't even notice, too busy flinging his long hair back over his shoulder.

Then Wyatt saw Stella. She was standing by the bar, a glass in her hand, which she drained with one smooth tilt of her head. She looked pale, even for a vampire. The dusting of freckles on her pert nose was visible from across the room, and there was a droop to her shoulders, which he imagined was from lack of sleep. Every minute or two, a vampire approached her, offered a few murmured words, sometimes a hug. Stella nodded, gave tight smiles, stiffly accepted embraces. But the whole time she clung to the bar, leaning on it, gesturing to the bartender, Jacob, to fill her empty glass no less than four times.

In all the years Wyatt had known her, she'd never been a drinker. Now twice in twenty-four hours, he'd seen her tossing them back. Apparently she didn't know how to deal with grief any better than he did. But at least she wasn't crying. Wyatt couldn't take it when women cried. He found himself promising everything from diamonds to puppies to unlimited oral sex just to get them to stop. Wait. Maybe he should offer Stella that anyway—the oral sex, not a puppy.

His erection throbbed again. He needed a drink himself.

What he wasn't going to offer Stella was a look at the second note he'd found from Johnny in the cookie jar shaped like a bust of Elvis. Going off his suicide note, Wyatt had checked for the fifty bucks referenced after he had cleaned up Johnny's ashes. But there weren't cookies or cash in the jar. Just another note from Johnny that read, "Stella, you're a sucka. You know I'm broke as a joke. Love, your brother."

So Wyatt had put Johnny in the cookie jar. He figured that was fitting.

"Yo, dude, I need a break," Saxon said over his shoulder. "I lost my ChapStick. And this is harshin' my mellow."

Wyatt didn't even bother to ask what exactly was bothering Saxon. He just nodded and turned to Cort. "Five?" he asked.

Cort nodded and at the end of the song, they put down their instruments and picked up their drinks. It was a nightly ritual they were all familiar with. They had been playing together for years and while Wyatt could do without yet another set crammed with Journey, Bon Jovi, and Lynyrd Skynyrd, he enjoyed watching the crowds. It beat the hell out of playing some glittery game of baseball.

Setting down his five-string Spector bass, he went in search of Stella and another beer. He wanted to make sure she was okay. The beer he just needed in order to survive another hour of this weird night.

He didn't have to look far. With a wave at Raven, a pretentious vampire who played in a rival band on Bourbon, Stella barreled across the room toward him, a little unsteady, clutching her purse strap. For years, she'd been wearing a uniform of tight jeans, combat boots, a variety of rock T-shirts, and a banged-up cross-body bag in worn brown leather. You'd think it was her baby the way she always cuddled it to her breasts. He had to admit he was just a little bit jealous of that leather bag.

"How are you doing?" he asked her, reaching for her hand, wanting to touch her.

She ignored the question and his reach, leaving his hand floating in midair. "Do you have Johnny's blood vial?"

"Um . . . no." Caught off guard he let his hand drop. "I left it on the breakfast bar."

Frowning, she said, "I was just at Johnny's apartment. It wasn't there."

"You probably just missed it." It was a small necklace, a tiny skull filled with a drop of Johnny's blood. He could see why Stella would want to keep it, but it would be easy to have looked around the room and not have seen it. "So how are you holding up?"

STELLA FELT INCREDIBLY impatient with the way Wyatt was talking to her and looking at her. Like he thought she was going to collapse in a screaming, kicking heap on the floor of the *Natchez*. Which, granted, he might have reason to believe given her behavior the night before, but she was fine. Damn it. So she'd had a meltdown, what of it? It wasn't every day you found your brother lying there like last night's campfire. What was she supposed to do, toast a fucking marshmallow? She had cried a little. Screamed. Thrown a lamp or two. Had sex with Wyatt. What woman wouldn't?

Her cheeks burned a little. Okay, probably most women wouldn't have done that, but she hadn't been thinking straight.

She regretted it. For the most part. Ignoring the fact that her nipples were suddenly pert, Stella shook her head. "I looked on the counter. It wasn't there."

"We can go there later and look for it. It couldn't have walked away."

There was nothing she'd rather do less than go back to Johnny's empty apartment, but she wanted that necklace. It had meant everything to Johnny and if it were lost she would freak out. How it could just disappear was a mystery to her, unless someone else had been in the apartment at some point, which of course made no sense. She was the only one with a key. "What did you do with his . . . you know. Ashes."

Wyatt hesitated. Then he gave her a sheepish look. "I put them in the Elvis cookie jar."

"Seriously? That's just weird."

"Well, it was a good, solid container. With a lid. The head really locks into that jumpsuit collar."

Oh, my God, was she really having this conversation? "I'm going outside." She wanted out on the deck, in the fresh air. The March air was still crisp at midnight, not wet and oppressively hot the way it would be in another six weeks. The riverboat they had rented for the wake had a wraparound deck, and as she pushed open the door and stepped out, cool air greeted her. That was better.

Leaning over the railing, she took a deep breath, waiting for the tears to come. They kept showing up at random intervals when she was least expecting them. But there were tears now.

"It's hard to believe he's gone."

Shit. Wyatt had followed her. Where had he gotten the impression that she wanted his company? She was embarrassed to be around him. She had yanked down his zipper in what was arguably the strangest move she'd made in her whole life. For no apparent reason, at the absolute worst time. It was mortifying.

Not wanting to look at him because she felt so pathetic and just not herself, Stella just said, "Yeah." She wasn't sure what else to say. She'd ranted and raved the night before and now she was just tired and numb and she wanted Johnny's necklace and her bed. She wanted to wake up and have everything be normal again, her brother spending money he didn't have and toying with the affections of mortal women, while she went about her business never knowing how large Wyatt's penis was.

Was that too much to ask for?

"So, about last night."

Oh, no. He was going to bring up the unbring-upable. She refused to comment, gripping the railing as tightly as possible without breaking her fingers.

"I know that what we, uh, did, was sort of unexpected, but the thing is, it's something I've actually thought about a lot. It's something I would like to, you know, repeat."

Could someone please arrive and jam ice picks in her ears? Stella couldn't deal with this. Like she really, really couldn't cope. Part of her was, of course, flattered that he was admitting he'd been attracted to her. Part of her was intrigued by the idea of going another round with Wyatt.

But mostly, she was just horrified and mortified and petrified.

This so wasn't the time or place to talk about their inappropriate dick-stick session.

"I really can't talk about this right now." Stella finally forced herself to look at him, lifting her purse off of her shoulder. It was irritating her skin for some reason. Wyatt looked . . . soulful. It was unnerving.

"I don't mean it to be disrespectful. What I'm talking about is us, you know. Us dating, trying out a relationship. This isn't about sex."

It wasn't? Now she was thoroughly freaked out. "There isn't an us."

"I just want to establish—"

"No! No establishing!" Tension whipped through her like a hurricane and she gripped her bag in her hands, suddenly wanting to pummel him until he went away. Until all of this just went away. Gone.

"But—"

"Gah!" she shrieked.

Wyatt's eyes went huge. "Okay, damn, calm down. We won't talk about anything important, how's that? We'll talk about the weather. It's a nice night, isn't it?"

Okay, now he was being petulant. It wasn't her problem. Even if she felt a tiny bit bad. A lot bad. It wasn't his fault that this was lousy timing. It wasn't his fault Johnny was dead and Stella had thrown herself at him.

Feeling contrite, she said, "I've had better nights. But thank you for being here for me. I do appreciate it."

His stiff shoulders relaxed. "You're welcome. Let me know if you need any help with Johnny's apartment."

Yet another thing she didn't want to think about. Going through Johnny's stuff. Which reminded her. She reiterated, "That necklace wasn't there, Wyatt. I would have seen it."

"It has to be there. But what are you going to do with it anyway? Take Johnny's blood and clone him?"

Oh, no he didn't. "Excuse me?" she asked, her voice steely and unnatural even to her own ears.

"It's there," he insisted.

Stella followed up on her earlier impulse and whacked him on the arm with her purse.

"What the hell? What's the matter with you?"

"You're the matter with me! How could you even say something like that to me?" She hit him again, for good measure. Her purse tipped on its side and all its contents spilled all over the deck of the boat. "Shit!" She started chasing a rolling lipstick.

He bent over to help her and she held her hand up. "I've got it!"

Wyatt hesitated a second, but then he just shook his head. "Fine. You know where to find me if you need me."

Stella sat back on her butt on the deck, deflated, watching him stomp off. He had a valid question. What the hell *was* the matter with her? She was pissing off the one person who was offering to help her. The other guys in the band had given her condolences but not a single one had offered to help with the arrangements for the wake or with Johnny's effects. Just Wyatt. And she was shrieking at him like the banshees her mother had always told her about back in Ireland when she was a little girl.

After she cleaned up her purse mess, she should probably apologize. Or at least buy him a drink. Grappling around, she found her wallet, her keys, her compact. It was a bitch to apply makeup as a vampire because her skin was so pale, but she'd perfected the art of touch-and-go. Light powder, a swipe of nude lipstick. That was everything except her phone. Looking around, she didn't see it. Fabulous. Her cell was gone.

Then she saw it had rolled along the deck, fallen off the edge, and down onto a dirty corner of the lower deck, which was closed off for their event. Stella sighed. Just what she needed. She knew she couldn't reach it. Her options were to find a staff member and see if they would let her down onto the lower level. Or she could morph into bat form and snag it.

If she hadn't consumed a large quantity of alcohol she might have reasoned out that option two wasn't really much of an option as bats are generally not equipped to hold cell phones. She realized this a minute later and did what any drunk vampire would do—she tried to morph back on the tiny landing, promptly fell, and wound up face-first in the Mississippi before she was even sure what had happened.

It was cold. Wet. Dirty. And smelled like rotting fish and grease. Without hesitation, she went back into bat form, terrified she might swallow some of that seriously unhygienic river water. Granted, it wasn't Dublin at the turn of the century, which had been a complete cesspool, but she was convinced there was a fair amount of funky in the Mississippi. As a vampire, she wasn't going to catch a skin disease, but that didn't make it any less gross.

Being in bat form wasn't necessarily her favorite thing. She couldn't even remember the last time she'd done it. Probably in the '80s right along with her last sexual activity. She'd been in a phase then involving teased hair and a love of spandex. Sometimes it had been nice to escape high-maintenance fashion and fly around.

Now she just wanted back to herself.

Only when she tried to morph back on the deck, she couldn't.

What the hell.

She tried again.

Nothing.

It would seem she was drunker than she had realized.

Fabulous. She got to fly around until she sobered up. Just what she always wanted to do. Maybe she could lick some coffee to speed up the process.

When Wyatt reappeared on the deck a minute later, calling her name, she hid, suddenly embarrassed. She didn't want him to see her like that. Which was stupid, but she was stupid. That's what had been established in the last twenty-four hours. She was a big old idiot.

Besides, he would wonder why she didn't change back and as a bat she couldn't exactly tell him.

"Stella?" He stopped on the deck and looked around. When he spotted her purse, he swore.

He picked it up.

And that was the last thing Stella remembered that night.

Wyatt put Stella's bag over his shoulder, calling her name again. He was worried. She never went anywhere without that purse. And there was nowhere to go on the deck but in the water. Leaning over, he scanned the river. No sign of her. But her phone was a few feet down on a ledge, and he reached for it, snagging it with one hand.

Leaning over made his head spin. Damn, he felt weird. Drunk, but a strange kind of drunk.

Woozy.

Climbing up onto the railing, because it seemed like the thing to do, Wyatt yelled, "Stella!" at the top of his lungs, suddenly feeling like he might have lost her forever. *"Stella!"*

And that was the last thing Wyatt remembered that night.

Chapter Three

A PARROT, A PRIEST, AND
THE SLIGHT PROBLEM OF AN EXTRA VAMPIRE

R**EALLY?** Damned sirens again?

Cort groaned, determinedly hauling the covers over his head.

Couldn't these damned humans make it through one day of partying without the medics coming to deal with some idiot who drank seventeen hand grenades and now had alcohol poisoning? Or was it a couple of macho superegos who'd gotten into a bar-room brawl, probably over a woman they both just met that night.

The siren wailed again as if to answer. Hell, no. They couldn't manage that. But this was Bourbon Street—what did Cort expect?

He tugged the blankets tighter around his ears, but that didn't help. In fact, it was starting to sound like the incessant wailing was coming from inside his apartment rather than down on the street below.

Shit, sleep wasn't going to happen with this racket going on. Letting out a low growl, he shot upright, only to clasp his head as a ripping pain threatened to split his skull.

"What the fuck."

He remained totally still, trying to figure out what the hell was wrong with him. Then after several seconds, he carefully parted one eyelid, then the other.

The colored lights from Bourbon Street glared brightly through the windows, and he winced as another wail ricocheted off the walls of his apartment.

Shit, he knew what was wrong with him, even though he wasn't sure how it could be. He hadn't experienced one of these in nearly two hundred years, but even after all that time, there was no forgetting the blinding pain in his head, the roil of his stomach, and the feeling he'd just eaten flour straight from the bag.

"Shiiit, I have a hangover."

Cort lifted his head from his hands, pretty sure he hadn't said this realization aloud. He squinted across his room only to discover he wasn't sleeping in his room, but rather on the living room couch under . . . a woman's coat?

He looked in the direction from where he thought the comment had come. A heap near the window moved. As the shadowy figure slowly sat up, Cort made out long, golden hair and almost angelic features.

Saxon. His band's keyboard player.

"Oh, dude, my head."

Cort wasn't always sure about the newest bandmate, but in this instance he had to agree. Shit, his head hurt, too.

Of course, it made sense the keyboard player might have a headache. Saxon was a relative baby in vampire terms, and he still had some lingering human weaknesses. But Cort's vampire constitution was far beyond mundane ailments like a hangover.

Another wail echoed through the room and agonizingly through Cort's throbbing head.

Okay, obviously not. This was definitely a hangover. Damn, he needed some blood, but getting up off the couch, lumpy as it was, and heading to the fridge seemed like far too much work.

"What the hell happened last night?" came another groggy, miserable voice from the worn, oversized chair in the corner.

Cort saw Wyatt, The Impalers' bass player, slumped forward in the chair, his hands sinking into the tangle of his long, dark hair. Cort didn't answer, but he did try to search his aching brain. What the hell had happened?

"Dude, all I remember is dust in the wind," Saxon said, collapsing back into a heap.

"What does that even mean?" Cort asked, not bothering to hide his irritation with Saxon's cryptic comment. Leave it to Saxon to quote classic rock in some misled attempt to be deep. The mentally challenged should never, never try to be deep. Especially when he felt this damned shitty.

Saxon lifted his head and frowned, which gave him the appearance of a wounded angel. "It means all I remember was dumping Johnny's ashes over the side of the riverboat."

Johnny's ashes. Johnny's ashes. Shit, Johnny Malone was dead. That's where they'd all been last night, on a riverboat, giving him his final send-off. Saxon was being literal. Damn.

How could Cort have forgotten Johnny's wake? The loss of their bandmate had been rough on all of them, from the newest to the oldest member. Cort fell somewhere in the middle.

"That's all I remember, too," Wyatt said, then groaned as another wail filled the room. "What the hell is up with that noise?"

This time there was no denying that the sound was getting closer. Not to mention, this time the piercing screech was followed by the sound of footfalls and a frenzied commotion of someone tearing down Cort's hallway.

Cort, Wyatt, and Saxon all sat upright as a woman dashed wildly into the room. She stopped just inside the doorway, her hair wild, her eyes huge, and her whole body heaving with panicked breaths. Her terrified gaze moved over each of them, but no one spoke. Only her uneven breathing reverberated through the room

Finally Saxon made a snorting sound and stated, "That was unexpected."

Cort frowned, even though he didn't totally disagree, but then he returned his attention to the woman, who he was starting to recognize behind her tangle of honey-colored hair.

"Katie?" he said tentatively.

She made a small noise, which he wasn't sure was agreement or just more panic, but he didn't need her to confirm. He knew it was Katie. He'd spent enough time watching her to recognize her even in this disheveled state.

Katie Lambert, the washboard player from the day band at the bar where The Impalers played at night. He couldn't say they were friends exactly, but he certainly knew her. They'd spoken many times, and he was always aware when she'd stay after her set was done and watch them play. She was hard to miss with her pretty, pixielike face and infectious smile.

Hell, he could even admit that a couple of times he'd imagined what it would be like to take her to bed. Okay, more than a couple—more like dozens. And dozens.

But that still didn't explain what she was doing in his apartment. Looking like . . . damn, what had happened to her?

Even though he was in pain and really didn't want to move—maybe ever—Cort eased himself off the couch and started toward her, his movements slow, partly because of feeling like shit and partly because she looked like she might bolt if he approached her too quickly.

"Katie? Are you okay?" he asked softly.

She stared at him, her eyes frantic and glassy. He wasn't sure she'd even heard him, then she shook her head.

"Not really."

Her response was oddly calm, given all the screaming she'd been doing—unless that hadn't been her.

Dear God, please don't let there be more than one hysterical woman in his apartment.

Cort pushed that horrifying thought aside. "What's wrong? Do you know what you are doing here?"

Maybe she knew what clearly none of his friends did, but she quickly dashed that hope.

"I don't know," she said, her voice reedy. "I woke up in someone's room, but I have no idea how I got here."

In someone's bedroom. That meant either his bed, or his roommate, Drake's, and truthfully neither option sat well with Cort.

"But—but I seem to have a larger—problem," she said, her usually upbeat and happy voice trembling.

"What?" Cort's stomach churned, this time not at the threat of losing his lack of lunch, but because obviously something awful happened to her. And he might have been there and didn't even remember what it was.

She hesitated, then straightened as if bracing herself. She swept the mass of blonde hair away from her very pale face and looked at each of the men in the room, then back to Cort.

"You are going to think I'm absolutely insane," she said. "But I seem to be"—she paused, clearly not knowing how to go on, but finally she just blurted it out—"I think I'm a vampire."

Cort was certain she expected some sort of reaction to her statement, but he highly doubted it was the one she got.

"What the hell," Wyatt said. "We've always said no crossing over coworkers. We don't shit in our own backyard."

"I didn't do it," Saxon said, shaking his head adamantly, his eyes wide. "Man, I didn't do it. No way, dude. Nooo way."

"I sure as hell didn't do it," came a raspy voice from behind Katie, which caused her to jump and scurry over to stand beside Cort.

Drake walked into the room, looking no better than the rest of them. In fact, he looked almost as distraught as Katie.

"Dude, do you remember what happened last night?" Saxon asked.

Drake shook his head, his strange expression not fading. Hell, maybe Cort looked the same way.

This was beyond weird. They'd all blacked out. They all had hangovers. And clearly someone had broken a cardinal rule and crossed one of their human acquaintances. He looked toward Katie, who seemed to be getting paler by the moment.

Quite possibly, she'd been turned into a vampire against her will.

He suspected he was becoming as pale as she was.

This was bad.

Damn, he couldn't have been the one who bit her. It went against everything he believed in. But he could admit, at least to himself, he'd wanted Katie enough to think about biting her. He'd thought about having her in every way possible—but all he'd allowed himself to do was think about it. Hell, he hadn't even asked her out. His vampirism always stopped him.

But apparently that isn't a stumbling block anymore, he thought wryly.

But wow, she was a vampire. What if he had bitten her? No, he just wouldn't have done that.

"Well, like I said, I didn't do it," Saxon repeated, as if he'd read Cort's mind. "I'm all about safe sex." He pulled a condom out of his jeans pocket. "See."

Wyatt glared at the youngest band member. "What the hell does a condom have to do with crossing a human over? What, do you put them on your fangs?"

"No," Saxon said, making a face like that was the dumbest thing he'd ever heard. Clearly he didn't listen to himself. "I have a motto: Keep 'em sheathed."

Everyone stared at the dopey keyboard player.

"Get it? I keep my fangs sheathed and my . . ." Saxon glanced down toward his crotch. "Brown sugar sheathed."

Cort grimaced. "What does that even mean?"

Saxon made his *you're so dumb* face. "I'm talking about my *penis.*" He whispered the last word.

"I know that," Cort said, getting impatient with this whole situation. "But you aren't black."

"You don't have to be black to have a . . . you know."

"Oh for Christ's sake," Wyatt growled, "why even bother, Cort?" He stood and strode over to the window. "We need to figure out what happened last night."

"And I need to find my damned fang."

Now it was Drake's turn to gain everyone's attention.

In response he curled back his lips to reveal a gaping, black hole where his fang should be.

Cort, Wyatt, and Saxon all gasped. Holy crap. Having one fang was like having one testicle. You could still get the job done, but you didn't want anyone looking too closely while you did it.

"That sucks, dude," Saxon said.

"It really does," Wyatt agreed.

Cort opened his mouth to also agree—fang loss was no laughing matter—but Katie spoke first, her voice high-pitched and bordering on hysterical.

"Wait, wait, wait," she said, raising a hand to stop them. "You are all vampires. You've all been vampires? As long as I've known you?"

Wyatt nodded as if that should be pretty obvious. Saxon gave her a hang-loose sign—because, well, he was stupid.

"I'm half the vampire I used to be but, yes," Drake said.

Cort gave her a pained, apologetic smile, but nodded.

"So it must have been one of you that made me this way?" She tilted her head to show them two already healing puncture wounds, then she bared her teeth like Drake had just done to reveal two white, sparkly, and brand-spanking-new fangs.

"Show-off," Drake said wryly, but his dry sense of humor was met by a glare from Katie.

"Perhaps not the best timing for that joke," he conceded.

"Maybe it was one of us," Cort said, only to be cut off by the adamant denials of the others, but he raised a hand to stop them. "But since none of us can remember, it's hard to say."

Katie stared at him for a moment, then said slowly, "So there are more vampires in the Quarter than just you guys?"

Before Cort or any of them could answer, a sudden whoosh and flapping sound echoed through the room, followed by a high-pitched squeaking.

Katie squealed, too. "A bat!" She ducked closer to Cort.

"Now, who the hell is that?" Drake asked, frowning up as the black winged creature circled the room wildly.

"*Who?*" Katie said, looking up at Cort with wide, wary eyes. "That bat is a person?"

"Well, not a person exactly, but maybe another vampire," Cort said.

Her gaze shifted to watch the bat, her expression a combination of disbelief, dismay, and fear.

"Although sometimes a bat really is just a bat," Cort added, hoping that might calm her. It didn't seem to.

"I bet that's Bob," Saxon said with certainty. "You know how he always gets stuck in bat form when he gets drunk."

Cort didn't know, and he suspected none of them knew. Hell, Cort wasn't even sure who Bob was.

"Bob?" Katie said. "Bob the bat." She laughed, and Cort was pretty sure she was getting hysterical again. It was startling to see the always smiling, always sweet Katie totally falling apart, but discovering you are a vampire definitely did that to a person. In fact, he'd seen worse reactions. Much worse.

He slipped an arm around her, expecting her to pull away, but to his surprise, she sagged against him, the laughter dying on her lips.

"It's okay," he murmured to her.

"No, I really don't think it is," she murmured back.

"What the hell is Bob doing?" Wyatt said, ducking out of the way just as the bat swooped toward him. The bat made a sharp turn and dove toward Wyatt again. "Saxon, call your stupid friend off me."

"He's probably still drunk," Saxon said.

"I don't care," Wyatt said. "He's going to get caught in my hair."

"Bob, stop it," Saxon cried at the circling bat.

Katie laughed again.

All of a sudden the flapping sound grew louder, and something red flapped into the room, joining Bob in his frantic race around the ceiling.

"What now?" Wyatt asked, peering out from under his arms, which he had folded protectively over his long hair. "What the hell is that?"

"Wait, this one is a what and not a who?" Katie asked, staring up at the flying blurs.

A what and not a who. Why did Cort suddenly feel like he'd been dropped into a Dr. Seuss book? At least that would explain why nothing was making sense this evening.

Even though he knew it was probably a lost cause to try and understand this new turn of events, Cort squinted to make out what had just joined the bat.

And as expected, his deduction only added to the confusion of the evening. "I think, I think that's a . . . parrot."

As soon as he said the word *parrot*, the bird flew down from the ceiling and landed on Cort's shoulder, the shoulder of the arm that was around Katie. Katie screamed and jerked away. The parrot lifted its crest and cawed in shrill response.

"Crazy train . . . crazy train," the bird squawked in a weird falsetto voice.

Katie squealed again, then fell back into her hysterical laughter. Yeah, this was all going very, very strangely.

"Rad, dude, a talking parrot." Saxon nodded, approaching the bird.

The bird eyed him with skeptical, beady, black eyes. "Jenny, I've got your number," it said, then cawed loudly and ruffled its feathers.

"I don't think that bird likes me," Saxon said, looking wounded again. He ran a hand through his tangle of surfer-blonde hair.

"What happened to your forehead?"

Saxon frowned, touching the place where Cort stared.

"What is it?" the mussed blonde asked, looking around at all of them, panic clear in his eyes. "What *is* it?"

Wyatt leaned in to inspect the large pinkish mark. "It looks like a burn. In the shape of a cross."

"A burn? From a cross?" Saxon hurried off to the bathroom to inspect.

"Okay, this is officially crazy," Wyatt said, watching Saxon leave. "Cross burns. Parrots. Fledgling vampires. Craziness. Oh, and let's not forget idiots trapped in bat form."

Wyatt looked up at Bob the bat, if that was actually who the bat was. It no longer flitted around the room, but now hung from the dusty chandelier in the center of the living room ceiling. But it did shriek loudly at Wyatt's comment.

The bird cawed again, nearly deafening Cort.

"I think it's safe to say that none of us have a clue what happened last night," Drake stated.

"Except I'm definitely a vampire," Katie said slowly, and Cort noticed she was no longer staring at the parrot, but rather her hand. "*And* apparently I might be married as well."

She lifted her left hand to display a gold wedding band. A gold wedding band that had "Hers" etched onto it. The rest of the guys, including Cort, reluctantly looked down at their own hands. Oddly he wasn't terribly surprised when he saw that he, too, had a golden band glinting on his left hand.

And, of course, etched in the band was the word "His."

"Are we *married*?" Katie asked, her voice pitchy again, hysteria creeping back. This time, the same sensation was creeping up on him, too.

Married. Damn, he'd never even managed to ask this woman out on a date. They couldn't possibly be married. This was crazy.

"That probably means you crossed her over, too," Wyatt pointed out.

"No, it doesn't," Cort said automatically, even though he wasn't sure. "And I'm sure I didn't marry her either."

He was even less sure of that, what with the matching rings and all.

"I didn't marry you," he repeated to Katie as if saying it again would somehow make it true.

Katie rightfully didn't look convinced, and for just a moment, Cort could have sworn an emotion akin to hurt flashed in her dark blue eyes, but he couldn't be certain.

"Damn, I feel rough. I need some blood," Drake said, but before he could leave the room, Saxon returned, blocking his exit.

"It is a cross burn. That's really messed up."

"Just chalk it up to one crazy-ass night," Drake said, moving around him. "At least you have all your teeth."

"I have a permanent scar, dude," Saxon said, distressed, lifting his bangs. "You know wounds from religious relics take forever to heal."

Drake shrugged and left the room.

Drake was never long on sympathy.

"It doesn't look that bad," Katie said, the hysteria somehow gone and replaced by genuine empathy.

Amazing. She'd just discovered she was undead, and she was still being her kind, generous self.

"Thanks, man," Saxon said, smiling appreciatively.

Well, at least his troubles seemed soothed. Too bad all their problems weren't so easily dismissed.

"But we should probably try to figure out what happened," Saxon said. "You know, retrace our steps or something. But first maybe we need to assimilate what we do know."

Cort raised an eyebrow. Who'd have guessed that the out-there surfer dude would be the one trying to act the voice of reason. Maybe the burn had seared some sense into him. And despite his typically odd choice of wording, Saxon was right. They needed to try and piece together what they knew. Maybe that would jog their memories.

"Okay," Cort said. "The last thing I remember was being on the riverboat. We took a break and headed to the bar for a drink."

"That's the last thing I remember, too," Drake said as he strode back into the room, with a wineglass filled with blood. "I remember toasting Johnny with Raven."

"Raven," Cort said, realizing the way he said the man's name sounded much like Seinfeld when he addressed his unpleasant neighbor, Newman.

But the truth was, Cort did not like Raven. Raven was a vampire, too, except he fancied himself as some sort of Goth prince of darkness. Cort found him pretentious, self-indulgent, and frankly outright silly.

He tried to find the poser vampire amusing since he really was rather pathetic with his outlandish clothing, tattoos that tried too hard to be deep, and then there was his harem of women. Raven had a group of women who actually agreed to let him feed from all of them. They were sort of a combination sister wives/all-you-can-eat buffet.

But what really had Cort gritting his teeth about the jerk was that Raven had recently taken notice of Katie. Cort hated the idea of Katie being involved in that. Or involved with Raven, period. Or any other male, for that matter.

Wait, what was he thinking? He certainly hadn't made any moves to get her himself.

Well, except for maybe last night. They were now wearing matching wedding bands. That was a move. A big one.

But there had to be a simple and reasonable explanation. It had to be some sort of joke or something. He couldn't imagine, no matter how gone he was, that he'd get married like this.

But then again, he'd vowed to never cross over another mortal, not without their absolute consent, and even then he wasn't sure he'd do it. Immortality was a blessing and a burden. At least it had been for him.

"I vaguely remember going out onto the deck to talk to Stella," Wyatt said, frowning. "Where is Stella? I would think she'd be with us."

Bob the bat chose that moment to swoop down from the chandelier, buzzing close to Wyatt's head again.

"Saxon! Call off your moronic buddy," Wyatt shouted, his hands going back up to protect his hair.

"Bob, you so need to chill," Saxon said toward the ceiling, but the bat had disappeared into the other room.

"If we are done with this little trip down amnesia lane, I'm going to get some more blood," Drake said testily, then unconsciously fiddled with the place where his fang had once been.

"Wait," Cort said, "so we all blacked out around the same time." He then turned to Katie. "Do you remember anything?"

Katie was staring wide-eyed at Drake's now empty wineglass. It probably was unnerving to watch someone sip blood like it was a fine cabernet. Or maybe she was longing for a glass herself. If that was the case, that desire was probably freaking her out even more.

She tore her gaze away to look at Cort, narrowing her blue eyes as she tried to focus. Yeah, she was definitely fighting a craving.

"I remember coming onto the riverboat to give you all my condolences about Johnny." She squinted more. "You were all doing shots, making toasts to him. Cort—you asked me to join in. I did a couple, but then said I couldn't do any more. So you decided to go back onstage and play Johnny's favorite song."

"'Freebird,'" all of the remaining bandmates said in unison, except for Saxon who said, "'Jessie's Girl.'"

They all stared at him and he shrugged. "I'm scarred, man. What do you want?"

"Do you remember anything more?" Cort asked Katie.

She nodded slowly.

"I think I remember you"—she looked at Cort—"pulling me up onstage to sing along, and then . . ."

She thought a moment longer, then shook her head. "Then that's all I remember."

"I think I should go to Stella's place and check on her," Wyatt said, clearly concerned for their sound woman.

But before Wyatt could even hit the hallway, a low, muffled groan came from farther down the hallway.

Wyatt spun back to them. "Did you hear that?"

"I totally heard that," Saxon said. "Maybe it's Bob coming back into human form."

Another groan sounded, this time louder.

"That doesn't sound like Bob though," Saxon said, tilting his head. "He's from Boston."

Cort was pretty certain that you couldn't tell a person's accent from their moan, but as usual, it didn't seem worth the effort to point that out to Saxon.

"Let's just go check," he suggested instead.

Carefully all five of them moved into the hallway, creeping forward as if they expected someone to jump out at them. As if they weren't all vampires who could easily defend themselves from well, just about everything.

Except memory loss, apparently. And it turned out, memory loss was very unnerving. None of them were acting like themselves.

First they peeked into Drake's bedroom, which was cluttered with a large assortment of leather clothing and guitars, but appeared empty otherwise. Next they all looked into Cort's.

The bedding was a tangled mess, and random clothing littered the floor, but it, too, seemed empty.

"This is where I woke up," Katie said. "Or rose. Or whatever I do now."

Yeah, well, whatever she wanted to call it, being in his room also seemed to imply that whatever happened to her last night, Cort had been involved.

Drake gave him a pointed look, clearly thinking the very same thing.

"Oh, you aren't off the hook yet," Cort murmured to his roommate, only to see Katie shoot them both a dirty look.

They sneaked farther down the hallway, then came to a dead halt as another moan echoed toward them. Very close now.

"The bathroom," Drake mouthed.

Cort and Wyatt nodded. Saxon did his usual hang-loose sign, and Katie's eyes were huge

They all hesitated until Cort nodded and stepped forward. They moved as one behind him. When they reached the bathroom, Cort couldn't see the source of the moaning. Not at first. But then after a few moments, he realized there was something or someone sprawled in the bathtub, the shower curtain half over him—her—it—whatever.

Cort squinted, certain he couldn't be seeing what he thought he was seeing. Even with his excellent vampire vision.

"That looks like a priest," Wyatt said, confirming exactly what Cort was telling himself he was absolutely not seeing.

"Why would there be a priest in your bathtub?" Saxon asked.

"That's the million-dollar question, isn't it?" Drake said, but gave Cort and Katie another pointed look.

"Huh?" Saxon said, clearly lost.

"Actually, I think the bigger question is how you didn't notice him while you were in here," Cort said to Saxon.

Saxon lifted his hair from his forehead again, jabbing his thumb toward the ugly, red burn. "I was a little distracted."

"Let's wake him up. Maybe he knows something," Wyatt suggested, shouldering his way into the bathroom. He flipped on the light, but the priest didn't rouse.

"He seems drunk or something. Maybe we should let him sleep it off," Cort said, his first instinct being that he didn't want to know what this priest might have to say. But then he realized he—and Katie—needed to know the truth.

He glanced at Katie, who worried her bottom lip, clearly as nervous about what the priest might say as he was.

"Don't do that," Cort said softly. "You could nick yourself with your new fangs."

She stared at him for a moment, but stopped.

"Try to wake him," Drake said, gesturing to Wyatt.

Wyatt stepped forward, only to stop again. "He has Stella's purse."

"What?" Drake said.

"He has Stella's purse. Why would he have that?" But Wyatt didn't wait for an answer. He reached down and tugged it out from underneath the priest's limp arm. The man's hand flopped to the bottom of the tub with a *thud*.

"This isn't good," Wyatt said, staring at the tatty old messenger bag like it was one of Stella's limbs rather than just an accessory.

"I have to go look for her," he said, again shouldering his way past the rest of them.

"Shouldn't you wait and see what this guy has to say?" Cort called after Wyatt, who was already striding toward the door.

"Call me if he tells you anything." The apartment door slammed.

"He's too tense, man. It makes me weary." Saxon sighed.

"You make me weary," Drake said, then pushed Saxon into the bathroom.

"Hey! Dude," Saxon muttered.

"Wake him," Drake said again, gesturing toward the unconscious priest.

"Why me?" Saxon said. "I've already got battle scars. He could throw holy water on me or something."

"Just do it," Cort said, getting impatient.

Saxon hesitated a moment longer, then nudged the priest's leg with his Vans-clad foot. The priest didn't respond.

"Wake up, Father," Saxon said and prodded him again. Nothing.

Saxon turned back toward them and shrugged. "What do we do now?"

"Three for one. Three for one. Craaazy. Craaazy."

Everyone gaped at the parrot, which quite honestly Cort had forgotten was still perched on his shoulder. Clearly his memory still wasn't working quite right. Who forgot about a large red bird on their shoulder? The same guy who very possibly forgot that he bit a woman then married her. Or vice versa.

"The bird must be talking about Krazy Korner. They have three-for-one specials," Drake said, as if they all didn't know that very well. "Maybe we were there last night? Maybe someone there remembers something."

"That could be," Cort agreed, although he wasn't sure following the ramblings of a tropical bird was their best strategy.

"Going to the chapel and we are going to get married," the bird said in its strange singsong voice.

"The chapel," Drake said, seeming encouraged by the bird's comments. "You two need to go to the all-night chapel on Burgundy."

Cort gave him a doubtful look. "Really? We are going to wander around the French Quarter because a crazy bird is saying random things? He's probably just repeating phrases he's heard."

"Crazy train. Crazy train," the bird called.

"Do you have a better idea?" Drake said.

"But what about the priest?" Cort said.

"Like you said, he's drunk or drugged or something. And I think the bird is a good lead. We can come back and see if we can wake the holy guy after we check out these places," Drake said.

Cort wanted to argue, when was a talking bird ever a good lead? But Katie touched his arm, her fingers pale against the sleeve of his black shirt.

"We need to try to find out something," she said. "And a chapel seems like a good start." She lifted her left hand and wagged her fingers. The gold band flashed in the light.

As if he needed a reminder.

Cort's gaze moved from the ring to her pale face. A wave of protectiveness rushing over him again. She deserved answers. After all, even if they weren't married, her whole life was changed. She didn't have a life anymore . . . she had an eternity.

He nodded, but then turned to Drake. "You take the parrot." He jerked his shoulder toward his bandmate. The bird ruffled its feathers, but didn't budge.

"I'm not taking the parrot," Drake said, eyeing it dubiously.

"You were the pirate," Cort pointed out.

"I wasn't a pirate. I was a convict on a penal ship, which

eventually turned to piracy. But that doesn't really make me an actual pirate, per se," Drake said.

"Penal." Saxon chuckled. "That's funny."

"Fine," Cort said. "We'll take the bird, but you have to take Saxon."

Drake hesitated, glancing at the bird, then their blonde bandmate thoughtfully.

He sighed. "Come on, Saxon. Let's go to Krazy Korner."

"Okay," Saxon agreed readily, oblivious to the fact he'd just barely been chosen over a bird as a search partner.

They both headed to the door.

"Well, I guess you are stuck with me and the bird," Cort said.

Katie nodded, but didn't say anything. She still looked as if she might get hysterical at any given moment. She didn't seem like she needed to feed. Her color was good and her eyes didn't have that dark, glazed look they got when vampires were hungry. This seemed to be just natural hysteria, for which he couldn't blame her.

They followed the other two out of the apartment, but once they reached the street, Drake and Saxon went in one direction, while Cort and Katie needed to go the other way.

"Call me if you find out anything," Cort called after his bandmates.

Drake waved in response without looking back.

Cort sighed, then fell into step beside Katie.

"Why do I have the feeling we just sent Shaggy and Scooby off to find clues?"

Katie smiled vaguely, but he could see she was lost in her own thoughts.

"Jinkies. Jinkies," the parrot called.

Jinkies, indeed.

Chapter Four

WINGING IT

STELLA watched all the guys leave Cort and Drake's apartment with a sense of total disbelief from where she hovered by the ceiling. What the hell had happened last night? Granted, she had to admit she was grateful Cort was whisking the shrieking washboard player out of the room because Katie was about to shatter her eardrums. But the fact that Wyatt was going off in search of her, Stella, when she was right there in the room was a frustrating irony for a self-proclaimed control freak.

Never in eighty-five years of her undead life had Stella found herself trapped in bat form. Saxon did it all the time but Saxon smoked too much of the wacky weed. Stella never even drank, if you didn't count the last two nights, and she swore once she was walking on two legs, she never was touching the stuff again.

Stiff from hanging upside down off the chandelier all night, Stella took another turn around the apartment, doing a kitchen flyby in search of blood to drink. It seemed logical to her, given the deep thirst she was feeling, that she was dehydrated, and once she had a pint, she would be able to morph back. But Cort didn't have anything in his kitchen but a pile of mail and Victoria's Secret catalogs. She tried not to throw up in her mouth. Sometimes it wasn't a lot of fun being the only girl hanging with a bunch of boys—in fact, most of the time it involved a lot of eye rolling on her part. The question was why she stayed.

The real answer was she had stayed because she loved her brother. She loved New Orleans. She loved rock. And if it meant she had to organize their blood bags for them and soothe their ego-induced spats, she had.

Overcome with melancholy in the suddenly super quiet and empty apartment, Stella rested on the counter, her wings heavy. How the hell bats didn't get tired of the damn things she didn't know, but then again she'd frequently asked herself how men could stand walking around with testicles and yet they seemed pretty happy with them. It was just a matter of what you knew, she figured.

A snore cut through her musings.

She remembered there was a mortal guy in the bathroom. There had been a whole lot of yelling to that effect earlier. Apparently they'd left him there.

Perfect. Breakfast.

Stella flew into the bathroom and eyed the priest passed out in the bathtub. He didn't look like a real priest. He looked too young. Too good-looking. Not that men of the cloth couldn't be hotties, but she hadn't seen any lately. You know, with all the time she spent in church. Stella mentally eye rolled herself. Settling on his shoulder, she went for the open ribbon of skin between his collar and neck and bit.

It had been a long time since she'd fed off a live mortal. It wasn't really de rigueur these days in socially acceptable vampire circles. It was more for rogue types and newbies. But she had to wonder why they had ever stopped, because truth be told, it tasted divine. Salty, warm, delicious. It slid over her fangs and down her throat with satisfying ease. Though it wasn't as good as sex with Wyatt, it was a close second, reminding her of the pure physical and emotional joy she'd gotten as a mortal child licking a stick of candy.

So good she didn't realize that her donor had woken up from his snooze until a sharp pain hit the side of her head and she lost contact with his flesh, tumbling down onto his crotch. Yikes. Wincing as he started yelling and waving his arms, Stella was horrified to find she was morphing back. When the hell had she lost control of the ability to morph? But she clearly had, as last night and now proved. While she was grateful to be back in human form, she wasn't loving that she was sprawled across a stranger in Cort's bathtub.

Or that he had seen her transformation.

His eyes were huge, his breath coming in rapid little anxious bursts. His fingers inched up to his neck and when he pulled them back covered in blood from her feeding he said, "Holy shit."

That about summed it up.

"It's okay," she said, in the most soothing voice she could muster. Every vampire had the ability to influence humans, but Stella's had always been slight. She was a veritable weakling when it came to talents primarily because Johnny had turned her as a fledgling himself. It had never particularly bothered her because she had always wanted to live as normal a life as possible, but at the moment she could have used some memory wipe mojo.

Maybe he hadn't really seen what had just happened.

"Oh, my God, you're a vampire," he said, gazing from the blood on his fingers to her and back again. "That is the shit."

Or maybe he did. "I don't know what you're talking about." Stella pushed on his very muscular chest and sat back away from him.

"You were a bat and you were biting me and OMG you just turned back into a beautiful woman vampire."

Well, that was nice to hear considering her hair was a wreck from the wind and the dunk in the river. But it was irrelevant. "I'm not a vampire."

"Yes, you are. Bite me, please, Dark Angel."

Oh, no. He was tenting that priest robe, his eyes rolled back in ecstasy, his hand reaching for hers. This was creepy. "I'm not going to bite you."

"You already did."

"No, I didn't. There was a bat in here biting you and I came and swatted it away. It flew into the other room. I hope your rabies shot is up to date." Stella hauled herself out of the tub and away from Boner Boy. "Who the hell are you and why are you dressed like a priest?"

It was New Orleans. There was probably a festival of some kind going on. Maybe there had been a showing in the CBC of *The Exorcist* or something. So truthfully, the costume didn't really matter. What mattered was that she was now realizing that she was at Cort's with no purse and no cell phone and Wyatt was who knew where with both.

"I'm a dancer at Bounce."

Ah, a stripper at the gay bar. That suddenly made so much more sense, though she had to question the political correctness of his outfit. "You strip as a priest?"

"It was tarts and vicars night," he said. "Tranny crowd. The tips aren't as good, but hey, it's a living. I'm Benny, and I'm straight. Who are you, besides my darkest desire?"

Stella sighed. Curses on all the vampires in pop culture. It made being turned suddenly sexy.

"I'm Stella. And you need to leave."

Benny struggled to sit up, his erection no longer on full display, which was an improvement. "What happened last night? My head is killing me and I don't remember anything after I left work."

That made two of them. "I have no idea."

"Do you think we had sex?" he asked hopefully. "Did you imprint on me?"

"No!" she snapped, losing patience with Benny, the vicar stripper. "Look, I need to go find my friend and I can't just leave you here alone. No offense, but you need to go."

"Is my cross bothering you?" Benny fingered the cross hanging around his neck. "It's not real. It's a prop."

Was there such a thing as a fake cross? A cross was a cross. The shape never changed, no matter the material. "It doesn't bother me. What's bothering me is that I lost my purse and my cell phone and I want them back now."

Ignoring her denials, Benny still tucked the cross into his robes. He flung a leg over the side of the tub and heaved himself out. "Do you need me to help you? I could totally help you. What, do you need to, like, file a police report? Were you mugged? God, it's too bad I wasn't with you. I would have kicked the ass of anyone who messed with you, my goddess." He slapped a fist into his opposite palm to give force to his vow.

Stella raised an eyebrow. Being called a goddess was a first.

Hopefully it was a last as well. "No, I don't need to file a police report, but thank you. I just need to find my friend. If you wouldn't mind lending me your phone, I'll give him a call."

"Sure, of course, right, absolutely." Benny lifted his robes.

Stella's jaw dropped. He wasn't wearing anything but a Speedo under all that fabric and he was either hauling home a brand-new pack of tube socks in his drawers or he was hung. And then some.

Most women would have been attracted to all that hard thigh muscle and tightly packed junk, but Stella wasn't interested. The only penis she really cared to see was Wyatt's.

The thought gave her pause. She did? She did. Wow. That merited analysis later.

"Sorry," Benny said with a sheepish grin as he pulled his phone out of his butt crack. "I don't usually leave work without changing but I was going straight to a party last night and it was only two blocks up Bourbon. What the hell happened to me in two blocks? Alls I can say is I hope I had a good time."

Stella shook her head, not at all sure she wanted to know what had happened. "I have no idea." Gingerly taking the phone, she held it with the end of her sleeve. There was no way she was putting that up next to her face.

Hitting Speaker with her knuckle, she paused. What the hell was she going to dial? She didn't have Wyatt's number memorized. She didn't have anyone's number memorized. They were all in her phone. With Wyatt.

Not helpful. "Shit." She hung up the phone and handed it back to Benny. "I don't know his number."

"You could go to his place."

"That's true. I could do that." Without a purse, she didn't have any money but Wyatt's apartment was only ten blocks or so. Getting back to her place if Wyatt wasn't at his was a bit more of a problem. Maybe Benny could give her a ride. "Did you drive to work?" she asked him.

"Oh, hell no. Too expensive to park and finding a spot on the street is like digging for gold in a diaper."

Stella didn't even know what that meant but she supposed it didn't matter. Benny put his phone back in his sack. "So how are you getting home?"

"Cab. I live in Harahan. How about you?"

"I live uptown. Can I borrow a buck for the streetcar?" She would happily show up at Bounce and tip him when all of this was said and done.

"Sure. If you bite me again."

Really? "No. Stop asking."

"I want to be a vampire, too." He flexed his muscles. "I'd never have to work out again."

"That's shallow. And there's no such thing as vampires."

"My Dark Angel, I know the truth. I'll give you a dollar and my devotion."

Benny was getting a weird look on his face. Stella was afraid to look at the lower portion of his robe. "Let's just go."

She went into the living room and almost ran into Saxon. "Ack! Saxon, what are you doing?"

He held up a tube. "I was going out looking for clues, you know, about what happened last night, but I forgot my lip balm. Can't think with cracked lips."

She could ignore the stupidity of that because she was happy to see him. "Where's Wyatt?"

"Don't know. He went looking for you. Guess he didn't find you." Saxon laughed, then stopped short. He grimaced as his gaze shifted behind her. "You!"

"Who, me?" Benny asked, looking behind himself.

"Yes, you! You cross-wielding freak! Dude, that was seriously not cool."

"Uh . . ." Benny looked a little scared. "Are you a vampire, too?"

"Duh." Saxon pulled his bangs to the side and pointed to his forehead. "Yes, crosses burn vampires."

"Holy shit." Stella gaped at the wound on Saxon's smooth vampire skin. "Why hasn't that healed? How did you get that?"

"Your little boy toy laid a crucifix on me. Totally not funny, man. Now I have to grow my bangs out forever and get a forehead tattoo. Who has a forehead tattoo? Like no one."

"He's not my boy toy." Stella moved away from Benny. She'd had no idea a cross could actually hurt a vampire. That was an old wives' tale. Maybe. But now she wasn't taking any chances. She didn't look good with bangs.

"How do you know it was me?" Benny asked. "I'm not the only guy in the Quarter with a cross."

"You're the priest."

"Benny, you should just go," Stella said, her head starting to pound. "Saxon, can I borrow ten bucks?"

"No can do, Stella-roo. I think I must have gone to the casino last night because all I have in my pocket is a receipt for condoms."

What? "You always buy condoms at the casino?"

"No. Why would I do that?"

"I don't know! Let me borrow your phone."

"It doesn't work. I forgot to pay my bill again." Saxon wrinkled his nose. "I'm leaving. It smells like cheese in here. See you later."

"If you see Wyatt, tell him to bring my purse to work tomorrow night, okay?" She supposed she could live twenty-four hours without her cell phone. Worse came to worst, she would just get it at the bar when they all showed up for their usual Thursday-night gig.

"No problemo. Catch you later."

Saxon was gone with a wave and Stella pointed Benny toward the door. "Time to go."

"I'm going where you go."

"Fine." Only because she might need to use his phone again or get that streetcar money. Not that she could get into her apartment without her key. What a total disaster.

"Can I hold your hand?" Benny asked.

She'd rather go tanning and die. "No." Stella pulled the door to Cort's apartment shut behind them.

"Can we stop for a daiquiri? I feel dehydrated. I think you took too much blood."

She'd taken like a thimble's worth, but she wasn't about to argue with him. It made her feel a little sheepish to be strolling around with her unwitting blood donor. Though Benny unconscious was a lot more desirable than Benny awake and gazing at her in total mortal devotion.

"Sure."

As the sounds of Bourbon Street hit her when they stepped outside, Stella sighed.

It was going to be a long night.

WYATT WAS OFFICIALLY freaking out. Stella wasn't anywhere. No one had seen her since the night before, when he had gone out on the deck with her. Granted, no one remembered a damn thing after the wake, which was weird in and of itself, but it seemed like someone should have noticed Stella at one point or another.

Stella was noticeable. Wyatt noticed her all the time. Like every second of every night when they were at work. He even knew when she went to the restroom, that's how constantly aware of her he was. He could tell her what T-shirts she'd worn for the last five nights and if she'd worn her hair in a ponytail or not.

But he supposed not everyone was the same way. You know. Like in a totally unrequited, pathetic crush.

Pacing in his apartment, he gripped Stella's purse and tried not to panic. He would go ask around and see if anyone had seen her the night before. According to his phone, it was midnight, around the time everything went fuzzy in his memory the night before. He knew a lot of the bartenders, sound guys, deejays, and band members on the street, and they all knew Stella. If she had been out and about, someone who knew her might have seen her.

So he took to the street, her phone and his in opposite pockets. Maybe she'd call him. Or herself. Because that made sense. Not. But it was his only plan.

He lived on Burgundy and Conti, and as he headed toward Bourbon, he popped his head into a few local bars on the way. No one had seen Stella.

Cutting the corner close at the daiquiri shop, Wyatt glanced in, annoyed as usual at its neon flashing lights and sparkly floor. Too much stimulation for a vampire, though he supposed that hadn't been factored into their decorating.

But he forgot all about the floor when he saw a tan, built guy in nothing but a banana hammock. Which in and of itself wouldn't have caught his attention, because it was a common enough sight on the street, but it was who the dude had his arm around that made him stop suddenly in his tracks.

It was Stella.

A guy bumped him from behind. Wyatt barely managed a

mumbled apology as he stood rooted in the doorway, shocked. Speechless. Furious.

Stella was sipping from a giant cup and talking to the bartender. The musclehead next to her stood there, his hand possessively rubbing the small of her back, his taut butt cheeks flexing in his orange Speedo as he shifted.

Wyatt felt sick. Even worse, he felt jealous. He hadn't felt jealous in about a hundred years, and he had certainly never felt jealous of a pinhead with a waxed chest. But he could still feel Stella's mouth on his cock and the thought of her with anyone else, especially this mortal show-off, made him see red. He needed to punch something.

He settled for taking a deep breath and calling, "Stella!"

She was already turning around, clearly sensing him. "Wyatt, oh my God, I'm so glad to see you."

That soothed his battered ego a bit. He started toward her, eyeing the almost-naked guy as he turned around.

But then Stella followed up with, "Please tell me you have my purse and my phone."

That was a little deflating. "Your purse is at my place. I have your phone in my pocket."

Sighing in relief, she held her hand out. "Thanks."

That was it? Thanks? Wyatt had been worried sick for the last three hours. "Where the hell have you been?" he demanded.

Instantly, she bristled. "I was in the room with you guys the whole time. You all thought I was Saxon's friend Bob."

"That was you?" He'd never known Stella to morph into bat form. "Why didn't you just come back and tell us?" He spoke in code, very aware of the mortal standing next to her. The mortal who smelled like baby oil and dried blood.

Blood? Wyatt homed in on the man's neck. There were bite

marks on him. Bite fucking marks. She couldn't have. She wouldn't have.

"I couldn't," Stella said tightly. "I was stuck."

"How do you get stuck?" Wyatt asked. Stella just wasn't the type to get stuck in bat form. "And who is this?" He thumbed a finger at her buff sidekick, who was just standing there sucking on his drink straw. With bite marks on his neck.

"I'm Benny."

"He's been helping me since you all left me without any means of communication or a way to get to my apartment or into my apartment!"

She was seriously going to cop attitude with him? Wyatt was floored. "I was worried about you! I wasn't going to just leave your purse laying on a riverboat deck. You're never more than an inch from your purse. I thought you were kidnapped or mugged or fell off the boat or something."

Just the thought of any of those made his shoulders tense and his skin tight, even knowing that she was safe now.

"I did."

"Did what?"

"Fall off the boat."

It took him a second. "You fell off the boat?" Well, that explained her leaving her stuff on the deck. She hadn't meant to. It also explained her morphing. It didn't explain her getting stuck or who the hell Benny was and why she had bitten him.

"After that I have no idea what happened. The night is a total blank. Then when I woke up, Benny here was in the bathtub and he let me borrow his phone but I couldn't remember your number and I didn't have any money."

Wyatt eyed Benny. "You're the priest?" He could honestly say he would have never realized this was the same guy. This dude did not look like a priest to him now that his eyes were open and his robe was missing. Maybe he'd never really looked like a priest. Wyatt had been more focused on the fact that he'd had Stella's purse than anything else

"No. I'm a stripper who dressed like a priest for tarts and vicars night." His hand came up and waved around. "How the h-e-double-l I wound up in your friend's bathtub, I have no idea. The last thing I remember was leaving work. Then nothing until I opened my eyes and saw the most beautiful creature on the face of the earth." He gazed adoringly at Stella.

Fortunately, she ignored her admirer. "Okay, so how is it possible that you, me, Benny, Saxon, Cort, and Drake all don't have a clue what happened last night? That's basically impossible."

That was really strange. Something else occurred to him. "Hey, have you been to Johnny's?"

"No, why?"

"Because I was there looking for you and the place looked like it had been tossed. I just figured you'd been there looking for the necklace." But if she hadn't been there, who had? The relief he'd felt at finding Stella was replaced by worry. Something was going on.

"No." Stella bit her lip.

"Did Johnny piss anyone off lately?" Wyatt racked his brain for anything his friend might have said that would have indicated someone might be out for him. "Did he owe any money?" That might explain his suicide, too. Maybe he'd gotten himself in some kind of trouble?

But Stella shook her head. "Not that I'm aware of. He wasn't acting any differently."

"Who's Johnny?" Benny asked.

Wyatt struggled not to be annoyed. "Stella's brother. Can we

give you a ride home or anything, Benny? We appreciate you helping Stella out but she and I have a few things to take care of now."

"I don't have time to go home, but thanks, bro. I have to be
back at work for the late shift tonight, in an hour." Benny slurped
his drink. "You live in the Quarter, right? Can I grab a shower at
your place?"

Wyatt wished he knew who the hell this guy was and why
Stella had bitten him. He figured he had been fairly patient. Now
he was expected to let the guy bathe at his house?

"Of course you can," Stella said, shooting Wyatt a warning
look. "Come on, let's go so you're not late."

Apparently she expected him to just go along with it.

Apparently he was going to.

Wyatt followed Stella and Benny as they walked out of the
daiquiri shop, heads bent together, whispering like a couple of
middle-school girlfriends. He felt left out. Bitter. Jealous. His head
was still throbbing a bit from whatever they had drunk the night
before. He was starting to feel like they'd been slipped a roofie.
But all of them? How was that possible?

Heading down Conti behind them, he brooded. Some might
even call it pouting. But he preferred smoldering. He raised his
hand in a wave to Raven, who played at the Famous Door across
from them and probably was on a set break. They weren't friends,
given Raven's odd proclivities of gathering a harem of mortal
women around him and doing animal blood sacrifices. It was
showy and, in Wyatt's opinion, cruel. But Raven had never given
him reason to get into it with him. They had an unspoken agreement to politely tolerate each other.

Raven had been at the wake the night before. Wyatt wondered
if he remembered anything from that night. He called to Stella to
hold up, then jogged across the street.

"Hey, man, what's up? Thanks for coming last night."

"Sure." Raven tilted his shaved head, the dagger tattoo trailing down his cheek glowing in the neon lights of Bourbon Street. "That sucks about Johnny. Didn't think he would do himself in, man. Still can't believe it."

The thought made Wyatt's throat tighten. "Me either." He wasn't sure how to broach the subject, so he asked, "Did you see Stella around last night?"

Taking a drag on his cigarette, Raven shrugged. "I saw her at the wake for a minute or two. I see her now with some douche bag across the street. What's up with that?"

Like he needed to be reminded. "I don't know."

"You should shorten her leash, Axelrod. I wouldn't let any of my girlfriends disrespect me like that."

Wyatt suddenly couldn't remember why he thought he needed to be polite to Raven. "Stella isn't my girlfriend." Unfortunately. "And I don't need your dating advice."

Raven's eyebrow shot up. "Hit a nerve, huh? Maybe you need to take a look at your life. Be a little more careful."

What the hell was that supposed to mean? "I'll do that," he told Raven wryly. "Catch you later, man."

Pretentious prick. With a stupid tattoo.

Fast walking, he caught up to Stella and Benny.

"Are you a vampire, too?" Benny asked him as they turned onto Burgundy.

Wyatt shot Stella a sidelong look. She shook her head slightly. "No. There is no such thing as vampires."

"Alright, play coy. I know the truth. And I'm going to convince Stella to turn me. We're meant to be together."

Wyatt almost lost his lunch all over the cobblestones. He would put Benny in a box and ship him to Antarctica before he let Stella cross him over. Meant to be together. Please. Benny had absolutely nothing to offer her in the way of intelligence or conversation or understanding. He knew nothing about her.

Unlike Wyatt, who had forty years of knowledge of Stella. He knew her. Knew how to make her happy.

Feeling his mood grow even stormier as they got back to his place, he was actually grateful to show Benny the bathroom and hand him a towel. He shut the door on the grin Benny was sporting across his tanned cheeks and stomped back into his living room. He tried to control his frustration but it took all of three seconds before he lost it on Stella.

"Did you actually bite that idiot?" he asked her.

She had sat down on the couch and was riffling through her purse, which he'd left on the coffee table. She shot him a look of defiance. "I was stuck in bat form. I needed to feed and it's kind of hard to open the fridge when you have wings. Benny was there, passed out, and I seized the opportunity. It's not my fault he woke up."

If he were feeling rational, he would see the logic in what she was saying. But Benny had muscles Wyatt didn't even know existed, and he wasn't capable of letting it go. "He saw you. He wants you to turn him. Please tell me you won't do that."

"Now you're just being insulting. Why would I do that? Do you honestly think I want him hanging around tonight even, let alone for eternity? You've lost your mind." She slapped the flap of her purse closed, set it back down, and glared at him. "I'm just trying to make the best of a shitty situation."

"You need to wipe his memory and get rid of him." That was the bottom line.

"He helped me. I'm not going to just wipe his memory. No one will believe him and he doesn't remember anything from last night either, so I feel bad for him. He's like a sweet Labrador, you know? Somehow he got sucked into our night and God only knows what could have happened to him. Look at the washboard player. She woke up a vampire because apparently we can't hold our liquor."

Wyatt glanced toward the bathroom, the sound of the shower reassuring him that Benny couldn't hear what they were saying. He felt completely indignant. Insulted. Blown off by Stella.

"I have no problem holding my liquor. I could drink your buff dog under the table."

So there.

Chapter Five

EVERYBODY HATES A DRUNKEN BIRD

KATIE didn't know what was weirding her out the most—that she was a vampire or that she was potentially married to Cort, or that she was trying to find out what happened last night based on the comments of a talking parrot.

She knew being a vampire should win, hands down. Vampires really existed, and she was one of them. That should be a totally astonishing and scary realization—but for some reason, it really wasn't.

She had to be in shock or something. She was a *vampire*. A real, live—wait, was she alive still? Maybe she was dead. Okay, she could admit that was a weird concept, but for some reason the whole idea of being married to Cort was the thing foremost on her mind.

How was she supposed to process all of this, period? She certainly couldn't process it all at once, that was for sure. She needed time to think. She needed . . .

"I need a drink."

Cort stopped his determined stride, turning to look at her. The parrot fluttered its wings at the sudden stop. Both man and bird studied her for a moment.

"Are you alright?"

"What do you think?"

"Katie," he said, taking a step toward her, but she backed away. She didn't want him too close to her. Not right now. She knew full well that his nearness would just serve to confuse her more.

Of course that wasn't a new sensation. She was very accustomed to that particular feeling. She'd been experiencing it since the very first time she'd met him.

She'd just finished the last set of the day with her zydeco band, Beau and the Bayou Band, and she'd decided to stay for a drink with her favorite bartender, Jacob. A usual day on Bourbon. Until Berto Cortez had walked into the Old Opera House, tall and lean and mussed in a perfectly sexy way. She'd been instantly attracted to his swarthy, Mediterranean good looks and charming smile. But she'd especially loved his dark eyes that managed to look sleepy and intense all at once. He'd strolled up to the bar and introduced himself to her and Jacob, telling them that he was the new lead singer of The Impalers and to call him Cort.

From that very first meeting, she had been in serious lust with him, even though she never acted on her feelings. For the last three years, they'd talked only on an amicable level, two musicians working on Bourbon Street at the same bar. Never had Cort been anything but polite and friendly, no signs of attraction. Certainly no signs of lust.

And now they might be married. She might be married to Cort the vampire. And she was a vampire herself. This was nuts.

"A drink is probably a good idea, actually. A little hair of the dog," Cort said, and she wasn't sure if it was because she looked like she needed it, or because he himself did. Not that it much mattered, she just wanted some time to process what she knew before they found out anything more.

Katie knew she was a happy, sensible person. She also knew people considered her a good girl. Not prone to drama, or excitement of any kind, really. Downright boring, some might say. In fact, she'd always hated the lack of excitement in her life. That's why she'd left her dull, small-town existence to play in a zydeco band in New Orleans. Wild, decadent, dangerous New Orleans. But even with this big move, she'd still managed to have a pretty humdrum existence.

Until now. Now she'd managed to find excitement in spades.

Maybe she didn't really want excitement after all. But she did want that drink.

"Let's go here," Cort said, pointing to a small bar across the street.

In all her time living in the Quarter, she couldn't recall ever noticing this place, not that she cared where they went as long as she could get a very, very stiff vodka and tonic with extra lime.

They walked up a couple of dirty, concrete steps and through the open door of the small, dimly lit room. A few patrons were scattered along a glossy wooden bar, each of them seeming to be there alone, focused on their drinks rather than finding companionship.

That worked for her. Katie walked to the end of the bar and slid onto one of the wooden stools. Cort took a seat beside her, his shoulder brushing hers briefly as he situated himself.

The parrot hopped down from his shoulder to his forearm, then down the bar, waddling a few steps, before whistling loudly.

The bartender looked in their direction instantly

"Jack and Coke. Jack and Coke," the bird chanted in its strange voice as the man approached.

"Well, the bird certainly knows how to get service," Cort said, shaking his head.

Katie probably would have been amused on any other day, but all she cared about at the moment was ordering her own drink and trying to understand what was happening to her.

"Grey Goose and tonic. With extra lime," she told the bartender. "Actually make that a double. Please."

From the corner of her eye, she saw Cort raise an eyebrow, but then he said, "I'll have the same."

"And the bird?" the bartender asked, eyeing the parrot dubiously.

"You heard him," Cort said. "Jack and Coke."

"Jack and Coke," the bird repeated.

The bartender shrugged as if that was a fairly reasonable request and left to fix their drinks. As soon as he was out of earshot, Cort turned toward Katie.

"I think we need to talk, don't you?"

She didn't answer, not even sure where to start. Instead, she studied the gold band on her finger. This was just way too freaking surreal.

"Come on, Katie. Talk to me. What are you thinking?"

She decided to just go with the truth. "I don't even know where to start."

Cort chuckled, although she could tell it was more out of awkwardness than actual amusement. "I have to agree with you on that one."

She didn't say anything for a moment more, trying to decide which of the zillion questions whirring in her head was the most important.

She sucked in a calming breath, then met Cort's gaze directly.

He watched her with those sleepy, sexy eyes of his, and for a moment, she was lost.

God, what a cliché. What was her damned problem? She had just found out some of the strangest, most traumatic, and frankly most insane things she could imagine, and yet she still managed to find herself distracted by his gorgeous eyes.

Wait. He was a vampire. Didn't vampires control people with their gazes? Hypnotized them or something? Was that what he'd been doing to her? Was he doing it now?

"Stop it!"

Cort looked around, clearly figuring she must be talking to someone else. When he realized no one else was around, aside from the bird, which stared at them with beady eyes while bobbing his head, Cort's gaze locked with hers again.

Her insides leapt. He was doing something.

"Stop doing that with your eyes."

"Doing what?"

"Making them look that way. Hypnotizing me, or whatever your kind does," she said.

"What? I'm not doing anything. These are just my eyes."

She opened her mouth to tell him that couldn't possibly be true, that no regular gaze could affect her so, but before she could get the words out, the bartender returned with their drinks. They all, bird included, reached for their drinks, but before Katie or Cort could even get the glasses to their lips, someone shouted behind them.

"You two!"

Both of them turned to see who this man was yelling at.

A short, stocky man with chest hair curling out from the collar of his silky shirt barged toward them. And he was clearly not happy.

"I thought I told you two that I did not want you or that damned bird back in my bar," the man yelled, his voice thick with a Cajun accent.

Cort immediately stood, towering over the other man, but that didn't seem to intimidate the short guy.

"Listen, buddy, I've never even been in here . . ." Cort stopped. "Wait, we were here last night?"

"That's what I said. And you will never be here again. Go." The man gestured wildly toward the door, revealing sweat stains under his arms despite the cool weather. "And take that evil creature. *Now*."

The parrot squawked loudly in seeming protest.

Cort still didn't move, except to shoot the bird a warning look. The parrot returned its attention back to its drink, pecking at one of the ice cubes.

"Listen," Cort said, his voice calm and even, "I'm sorry about whatever happened last night, but we honestly don't remember it. Could you tell us what happened? Please."

The man's angry grimace didn't ease at Cort's remorseful apology. "My wife sure as hell won't ever forget what happened."

Just then, as if his words had conjured her, a woman, a very, very buxom woman with platinum blonde hair, appeared from behind the bar. Heavy gold jewelry adorned her ears, wrists, and cleavage.

"What are they doing back here?" she demanded in a voice that could only be described as grating. This was clearly the wife in question.

The garish woman stopped short and gave a sharp scream as she saw the parrot, which seemed oblivious to the reaction it was getting. It again poked at the ice cubes in its cocktail.

"We're really sorry, ma'am," Cort attempted again with an apology, but he got even less chance than he did with the husband.

"Get that thing out of here. Leave! Leave now!" she cried.

As if the bird understood, it stopped and turned toward the screeching woman. It began to waddle toward the couple in what Katie could swear was meant to be an intimidating swagger.

The woman squealed again and leapt behind her husband, her hands going protectively to her ample bosom.

"Trosclair, make them leave!"

The man pointed at the door again, and this time Katie caught a whiff of his armpits even though he wasn't close to her. Sweaty old onions. That was definitely the odor.

She grimaced. Apparently vampires did have a heightened sense of smell. Ick.

"We will go," Cort said, raising his hands in surrender. Whether because of their demands or because of the smell, Katie wasn't sure.

"We just wanted to know what happened," Cort said even as he reached for the bird.

The parrot attempted to peck Cort, clearly not pleased to be taken away from his drink, but it did hop onto his arm and crawl up the sleeve of his black shirt back to his shoulder.

"It's not our job to remind drunks what they did," the man known as Trosclair said, positioning himself so he could herd both Cort and Katie out of the bar.

They both headed toward the door with Trosclair and his wife following, still pressed to him.

Once they reached the street, the barkeeps stopped in the doorway.

"Don't come back," Trosclair repeated.

"We won't," Cort assured them. "But really, all we want to know is what happened."

"Well, I'll tell you this much, jokester," Trosclair said in his thick accent. "You should be ashamed of teaching your pet to expose a woman's breast like that."

The wife nodded adamantly, her hands still clutching her already half-exposed chest.

With those final words, both Trosclair and his wife disappeared back into the darkness of the bar.

"Jokester?" Cort said with a confused frown as if that label was the weirdest part of what just happened.

Katie stared at him for a moment, then actually found herself laughing, this time a genuine laugh rather than her earlier ones tinged with hysteria.

"I just hope it was the bird he was calling your pet and not me," she said.

Cort smiled, too. Damn, he was so gorgeous.

Katie's smile slipped and again her eyes glanced to the wedding band on her left hand.

He caught her action, his own smile fading. "I guess we should just head to the wedding chapel and see what we can find out there."

Katie nodded. She still had lots of questions, but maybe it was best to find out about the rings first.

They started walking down the cracked, stained sidewalk.

After a few moments, Katie said, "So who do you think was more traumatized by exposing that woman's breasts, the woman or the parrot?"

Cort's surprised laugh warmed Katie.

"I think that one might be a draw."

"Jack and Coke," the parrot cawed. "Jack and Coke."

Katie laughed, too.

Chapter Six

BENNY NEEDS TO JET

STELLA stared at Wyatt. Was he for real? That's what he was worried about? His manly ability to hold his drink or not? She would honestly never understand men. Eighty-five years and they still managed to surprise her with their inability to ever see what was really important. She felt like a mother who'd never given birth. Instead, she was emotionally rearing a whole band of vampires. Maybe that was why she didn't want to just toss Benny out into the street. She felt responsible for him as well now.

It was a heavy burden, one she admittedly had placed on herself. If she had any intelligence whatsoever, she'd leave them all to their own devices. They'd starve to death with a bag of blood in their hands.

She fought the urge to sigh. "No one is doubting your studly shots-drinking ability. I'm just saying that something weird happened last night and this guy got dragged into it. Let him take his shower and head to work and back to his own life without you challenging him. Is that really so hard to do?"

"I'm not challenging him. There's no challenge there."

"I suppose you're not acting jealous either?" For all she despised jealousy, she had to admit that somewhere deep in her girlish heart, she appreciated that Wyatt felt something for her, whatever that might be. He cared about her. As a friend. That felt nice, especially now that Johnny was gone.

"Jealous of what? That guy?" Wyatt scoffed, tossing his hair back over his shoulder as he jerked his thumb in the direction of the bathroom. "I think you swallowed too much of the Mississippi and it's chemically altered your brain. There is no way in hell I'd be jealous of that guy."

"So you're denying that you've been acting like you might lift your leg and pee on me at any given moment?" She was definitely feeling like a fire hydrant.

His mouth dropped open. "That's ridiculous."

Stella just raised an eyebrow. The way his jaw was working and his fist was opening and closing, she figured she'd hit the nail right on the head. Wyatt was seriously annoyed that she was with Benny. Well, not *with* Benny per se, but that he was around her. The thought gave her a fair amount of satisfaction. She gave him a slow smile. "So you're saying you don't want me to bite you, too?"

Watching the way his expression changed from astonished and embarrassed to smoldering with a deep, hot desire aroused Stella. She had just wanted to tweak him, but she'd done more than that. She'd reminded them both of the passion that had exploded between them two nights earlier with just one little kiss.

Wyatt moved closer, stepping in between her legs. Suddenly his jeans, sporting a prominent erection, were at eye level. His hands went into her hair, directing her to look up at him. "Oh, I want you to bite me. And you're right. I am jealous that you bit Benny. Very, very jealous."

Stella swallowed. When you play with fire . . .

"You don't have any reason to be jealous. I only did it out of necessity."

"Doesn't mean I don't want to feel your fangs in me. Doesn't mean I don't want to see that pleasure cross your face." Wyatt popped open the button on his jeans and exposed his hip. "Just take a little nip."

Licking her lips, Stella stared up the length of Wyatt to his dark eyes and back down again to his smooth, muscular hip rising above the black waistband of his briefs. It was very tempting. Vampires weren't supposed to feed off of each other and she was a rule follower.

But this wasn't feeding.

This was foreplay.

If she bit him, her mouth so close to his cock, she wasn't going to be able to resist taking a suck. Dragging his blood with the tip of her tongue over to his erection and flicking along the length of his hardness.

The same thoughts were probably running through his head, because he thrust his hips toward her in an unmistakable invitation.

Stella figured it would be inhospitable to turn down his generous offer. Opening her mouth, she bent her head over his flesh, drawing the scent of Wyatt into her nostrils. He had an earthy, masculine scent that tugged at her inner thighs. She already knew what his flesh tasted like, now she was going to draw his blood into her.

As she punctured his flesh, he moaned, and she closed her

eyes in ecstasy. It occurred to her that this was an intimate act, more so than sex in some ways, but she wasn't able to stop, to pull back at this point. Not when it tasted and felt so amazing. The sweet warmth of his blood rushed past her lips and down her throat like honey.

Oh, damn, that was good, good, good. Stella sighed through her nose, her sex wet and throbbing, her fingers gripping his hip tighter.

Suddenly Wyatt made a low sound in the back of his throat, and he pulled her away from him and up. He was strong, like all vampires, but usually he wasn't so commanding. Now she had no choice but to stand up at his urging. He kissed her, the taste of his blood still on her tongue, mingling with the deliciousness of his lips, the pressure of his body pressed against hers exciting and a little bit scary.

She wasn't sure where this sudden passion between her and Wyatt had come from. Or maybe it had always been there and she had ignored it. She didn't know. All she knew at the moment was that they were wearing too many clothes.

Grappling with his shirt, trying to lift it, only to have it catch on the thick chain necklace with a gun dangling from it that Wyatt always wore, Stella didn't hear the shower turn off.

She had forgotten Benny altogether until he spoke behind her. "Stella." His voice sounded crushed.

Oh, no. Wincing, she pulled away from Wyatt. While she wasn't thrilled with Benny's infatuation for her and her fangs and didn't intend to encourage it in any way, she didn't want to crush the poor guy either. When she had been mortal, fresh off the boat from Ireland, she'd had a substantial crush on a banker in Chicago. He'd married an heiress and left her heartbroken.

Only not that Benny really liked her. He was more into the idea of vampirism, but still. She didn't want to hurt anyone ever, and she clearly had.

"Benny, how was your shower?" she said in a cheerful voice as she turned, licking the last remnants of Wyatt's blood off her lips behind her palm.

Wyatt made a sound of amusement, his T-shirt falling back into place over his chest.

"It was obviously long enough for you to get busy with rocker boy here."

Resenting that she was feeling guilty and more than a little sheepish, Stella frowned at him. She could make out with whoever she wanted. She wasn't married. She wasn't dating anyone. She was over a hundred years old and perfectly capable of making good decisions. Most of the time. Barring alcohol and impulsive bat-morphing incidents.

"What Wyatt and I do isn't really any of your business," she told him as gently as she could.

"I thought I was special," Benny said glumly, hands on hips above his orange Speedo.

If he asked what Wyatt had that he didn't have, Stella was going to walk out. "Wyatt and I have known each other for a long time, Benny. He was really good friends with my brother and my brother just committed suicide."

"Holy shit, that sucks. I'm sorry, Stella. That's awful."

It was. Stella's throat tightened and she was digging her fingers into her palms. "Thanks."

"So, he's like comforting you? Okay, I get that. I nailed my girlfriend after my dad's funeral. Made me feel alive, you know?"

Actually, she did know. The way Benny put it was a little

crude, but there was totally truth to it. It was why she'd unzipped Wyatt the other night. "I definitely understand. It's really hard to lose someone."

"Dude." Benny held his fist out for Wyatt to knuckle bump and to her surprise Wyatt did. "Take care of her, you know what I'm saying? Stella's a cool chick."

"I will, thanks, man."

Now that they had worked out their little man issue, Stella felt superfluous. If they started back thumping and one shoulder hugging she was going to throw up in her mouth. Thankfully that didn't happen.

"I'm heading to work now," Benny said. "If you ever need anything, let me know. You know where to find me. If you ever get thirsty just look me up. Anytime, my goddess."

Again with the goddess thing. She didn't think she liked it. It made her feel ridiculous. "Thanks, Benny, I will. I appreciate it."

Benny looked reluctant to leave, his little mortal heart still bruised, but she figured in the end it was better that he'd seen her kissing Wyatt. There hadn't been time for him to really get attached.

"Thanks for looking out for Stella," Wyatt added.

It seemed to be enough to send Benny out the door. With a final look of longing and a wave, he left Wyatt's apartment.

Stella sighed. "Geez. What a night. I'm exhausted." She dropped down onto the sofa. Wyatt had a shotgun apartment on a quiet street. Well, quiet for the Quarter anyway. The front of the little yellow house was flush against the sidewalk, and closed up with shutters. The living room spilled into the kitchen, which led to the bedroom. Beyond that was a courtyard, but she'd been out there only once, when Wyatt had thrown a party. He was much tidier than Johnny had been, with a wide array of electronics and a cool collection of black-and-white photos hung on the wall. It was comfortable to be sitting there with him, away from the chaos of Johnny's death and waking up with no clue as to what was going on.

"You probably need to feed." Wyatt moved into his kitchen. "I think we were all drugged, which means we've got to be dehydrated, despite your little nip on Benny. And me."

Stella sat straight up, peering over her shoulder as he went into the refrigerator. "So you seriously think we were drugged?"

"How else would we all black out?"

He'd mentioned that earlier, but she'd been so focused on Benny and the news about Johnny's apartment being torn up, that she hadn't really thought the implications through. "I don't know. But who would want to drug us? And why?" In his lifetime, Johnny had irritated a person or two, but Stella didn't see how that could be relevant to any of this.

Wyatt came back with two blood-filled wineglasses. Stella's mouth watered. She was hungry. Gratefully, she accepted one and took a drink. It wasn't nearly as exciting as taking a sip from Wyatt's hip but she clearly needed it. Instantly her head felt a little clearer. "Oh, that's good, thanks."

"I just can't think of any other explanation. Something weird is going on." Wyatt sat down next to her.

Stella was acutely aware of his presence. "So what should we do?" This wasn't her thing. Her thing was organizing the band. Making sure they were on time and well fed. She was a vampiric den mother. Not a detective.

"We need to ask around. See what the hell went down last night. Then go back to Johnny's. I wasn't looking for anything but you when I was there before, so maybe you'll notice something that will clue us in."

The whole thing made Stella's head spin. "Until two days ago, nothing seemed abnormal at all. Now I feel like my world has imploded. This is just crazy. Like I can't even process it." She set her glass down on the coffee table, aware that her hand was shaking a little. Maybe she sounded a little hysterical but she avoided conflict. She normally acted as the mediator, and even that was never huge drama. Drama made her itch, and vampire politics made her sick.

"It's okay." Wyatt set his glass down, too, and took her hand.

The words were starting to sound familiar coming from his lips. He'd been there for her since they had found Johnny on the floor in an ash pile. And she'd yelled at him at the wake, which was really sucky of her.

"Hey, I'm sorry about being a bitch at the wake. You've been really sweet about everything and I just lost it on you."

Wyatt shook his head. "Nah, it's cool. That was totally bad timing of me. It wasn't the place to bring up the fact that I dig you."

He dug her. He was sticking by that statement. Wow. She wasn't sure what to say. Stella looked at Wyatt reflectively.

Damn, he was good-looking. She had always thought he was, but she'd managed to ignore it. It was impossible to do that when he was sitting a foot away from her on his couch looking compassionate and strong. Had his hair always been that perfect caramel color, like the sun had kissed the brown tips? Which was, of course, impossible since he was never in the sun. So it was all natural. All him. All gorgeous. She wanted to run her fingers through it while he went down on her.

The sudden turn of her thoughts shocked her, and she went for her glass again so she didn't have to look at him. "I don't know why. I'm a total nag." Johnny told her that on a regular basis. Or he *had* told her that.

"That's true."

Stella gawked at him. "What?" She had expected him to deny it. Or had wanted him to deny it, anyway. Of course, that's what she got for dangling a hook like that. A tin can instead of a fish. The truth instead of smoke blown up her ass. There was something to be said for a man who wouldn't lie to her.

"But you nag because you care, don't you? Not because you want to be right or want to drive everyone crazy."

No, it wasn't a drive she had to make her friends and family insane. She just wanted things to run smoothly. Everyone to be safe and healthy. If Dr. Phil were there he would probably tell her she was displacing her unfulfilled desire to be a mother or some shit like that. Hell, maybe she was. She had wanted to have kids but she and Johnny—okay, mostly Johnny—had fallen into a bad crowd back in their mortal days. Growing up piss-poor in Ireland, the riches to be had in Chicago in the Roaring Twenties had been enticing.

Unfortunately, they'd mostly been illegal, too. Johnny had found himself in the rough crowd and at the wrong end of a mobster's bullet spray. He had woken up a vampire and before she could say "all that jazz," he'd turned her, too. Twenty-two and her mortal life was over.

"I honestly don't mean to nag. I just want things to . . ." How did she describe it? She went for humor. "I just want everyone to live long and prosper."

Wyatt grinned. "No one can fault you for that."

"I care about all of you guys in the band, even when you drive me nuts. Though you personally don't really drive me nuts." She thought about the way he kissed her. "Well, actually you do drive me nuts but in a, you know, good way. A sexual way."

She probably didn't need to be that specific, but once she started babbling, she couldn't seem to stop. Going for another sip of her blood, she banged her teeth with the rim of the wineglass. She sighed. She was such a dork. It was a fact.

Wyatt gave her a low, slow grin that did strange things to her insides. "I drive you nuts? Sexually?"

Duh. "Yes."

"That's good to know. Because you drive me nuts. Sexually."

He was leaning closer to her. That was good. "Oh," was her brilliant response.

"Want to drive each other nuts right now?"

There were probably mysteries that needed solving and Johnny's possessions needed cataloging, but what was another thirty minutes? Wyatt's hand landed on her knee. Or an hour.

"We could do that," she said breathlessly. Who the hell did that voice belong to? She'd never heard herself sound like that before. Next she'd be giggling and getting a purse pooch.

"Where should we start?" Wyatt's thumb moved in a circle on her knee, over and over, a slow, steady touch that made goose bumps raise on her skin underneath the denim of her jeans.

The problem with not having had sex in three decades (before the other night, that is) was that she didn't really know how to play the seduction game. Then again, she'd coughed up that weird girly voice, so maybe she needed to stop thinking and just go with it. "You're definitely heading in the right direction," she told him.

"Should I go north?" His hand started to slide up her thigh.

"That works." Stella studied his lips, so close to hers. She wanted to be kissing him again. She honestly had forgotten how lovely making out with someone could be until twenty minutes ago.

Instead of waiting for him to kiss her, Stella decided to take matters into her own hands and move in on Wyatt. Going with her impulse, she buried her fingers in his thick, wavy hair. It felt as good as it looked. A man shouldn't have hair that sexy. It was just criminal. His eyes darkened as he realized her intent, his feathery touch moving closer and closer to her inner thighs.

Stella let her eyes drift closed as she dropped her lips onto his. It was amazing how easy it was to kiss him, how naturally their mouths fit together, how comfortable she was taking the lead and teasing her tongue inside him. Within seconds, their kisses heated up, an urgency entering their movements as their tongues dueled with each other. Stella's nipples thrust forward against her bra, and she felt a warmth spreading throughout her body and coalescing in her most intimate spot. Remembering the thrust of him into her against the counter, Stella gave a soft moan. Her body was aching to repeat that particular pleasure.

Wyatt's thumb finally reached the apex of her thighs and rubbed over her jeans right where her clitoris was. She lifted her right leg onto his to bring herself closer to his touch, wanting more of the delicious sensation. He took the obvious invitation and cupped his hand so that he was touching her from the seat of her backside to the zipper of her jeans. It was a simple touch, but intimate and dominating, one that heightened her arousal. Instinctively, she started rocking onto his hand, wanting harder contact.

"Stella," he murmured, nipping at her bottom lip.

Oh, that was such a mistake if he wanted to take this slow. It sent her desire into overdrive, but maybe that had been his intention. Going onto her knees, she yanked her shirt over her head and tossed it to the floor so that when she kissed him again, her breasts were up against his rock-solid chest. Good, but not quite good enough. Reaching back, she undid her bra and sent that sailing. She wanted her flesh against him, her tight nipples brushing on the cotton of his T-shirt while his tongue plunged into her with hard, possessive kisses.

Chapter Seven

ROLL WITH IT, BABY

WYATT hadn't seen the night going down this way, but he was going to roll with it. As Stella stripped off her bra, he stared at the smooth, creamy perfection of her small breasts, her nipples tight little dusky buds just begging to be sucked. Stella was a tiny woman, and Wyatt knew she'd been raised in poverty and malnutrition in Ireland at the turn of the last century, so everything about her was petite. He was glad she wasn't mortal because he'd be worried about gripping too hard, pumping too fast, hurting her in some way. But he didn't have to worry about bruising or hurting her, and she was acting like she wanted it hard and fast.

Hallelujah.

He took one nipple into his mouth and suckled it, tweaking the other one with his fingers. Her response was to rock down onto him, her legs on either side of his. Part of him wondered if she would pull away as fast as she had the first time, but he wasn't going to worry about that enough to halt what they were doing. He hadn't expected to be in this position again without a lot of time, finessing, and alcohol. But here they were and he was going to take full advantage. Holding on to her tiny waist, he continued to suck and nip at her, loving the way she gave him such clear signals that she was enjoying his touch. When he tugged her nipple forward, she gasped in delight, her fingers digging into his skin. She didn't seem to have any worry about hurting him. That was a serious grip she had going on.

"Take your shirt off," she said, her voice breathy and eager. "I want to feel you against me."

He couldn't argue with that. Wyatt jerked his shirt off over his head, the chain and silver gun pendant dropping back down onto his chest. That necklace and a tattoo on his hipbone were the only remnants of his gunslinger days. Stella bent over and kissed his shoulder blade while he palmed her nipple. His eyes drifted shut at the soft, worshipful touch. Damn, this was a fantasy sprung to life for him.

Her teeth wrapped around his necklace and she tugged lightly on the chain before letting it drop. "I've always liked your necklace, though it's not exactly politically correct."

Wyatt pinched her nipple again, enjoying the gasp she gave, the dark pools of desire her emerald eyes had become. "That's not my job to worry about someone else's feelings or beliefs. I'm a vampire. I live my life my own way. Now stop talking and kiss me again."

He wouldn't have thought Stella would like to be dominated in bed, given that she was something of a control freak, but that's what his gut told him she wanted. She liked to start it up then turn it over. He was more than happy to oblige.

"Bossy," she said in a flirty voice. "Geez."

"You like it, admit it." Wyatt smacked her ass. It was a good ass. One he'd stared at in the bar many, many times. He'd seen tourists staring at her ass, too, as they drank themselves silly and danced to the music their cover band, The Impalers, pounded out night after night. As far as Wyatt knew though, none of them had ever been allowed to touch Stella's stellar ass. But he was now, and it was small and tight and made him want to slide his dick into her from behind so he could see all her sexy, smooth skin surrounding him.

"Hey!"

It was the most fake indignation he'd ever heard. Especially since her ass actually arched out toward his hand when he pulled it away.

Wyatt popped the button on her jeans, ignoring her obvious request. If he was going to have another crack at her, he wanted no fabric between the palm of his hand and her skin. Her breath caught.

"Did I say you could take my pants off?" she asked.

Little flirt. He was so smacking her ass again. "I thought it was implied." Wyatt yanked the zipper down and flicked his finger on the waistband of her panties. "Once you took off your shirt, you left me with no choice but to get you totally naked and fuck you senseless."

She bit her lip, plump and pink from his kisses. "I suppose you're right. I guess you have to do what you have to do."

"What I'm going to do is you." Wyatt took her jeans and panties down to her thighs, then flipped her onto her stomach so he could work them the rest of the way down her legs.

"This isn't very dignified," she told him. "My face is in the couch pillow."

"If your face was in a pillow I wouldn't be able to hear you bitching about it," he told her, amused. She wanted to play the game obviously, but it was still hard for her to give up that control.

"This makes me feel like a naughty kid."

"There are whole industries based around that feeling, sweetheart." Wyatt lightly hit her now gloriously bare backside. "Are you saying you don't see the appeal?" He gave another soft swat.

"No. Of course not." But her voice and her flesh betrayed her. Goose bumps were on her skin, and she was breathy, excited.

It was the most amazingly sexy thing Wyatt had ever seen and heard. He wasn't sure exactly how they'd gotten here but he fucking loved it.

When he didn't smack her again, he watched the almost imperceptible shift as she raised her ass slightly in offering. Didn't like it, huh? That was such a lie. Determined to tease her, he caressed her flesh instead, skimming his palm over her curves, brushing down to where the curve met her sex. With just his middle finger, he fluttered between those swollen lips, felt her damp welcoming sweetness, and enjoyed her gasp of approval and the way her knees spread apart to give him ease of access.

But he just pulled away and delivered a resounding slap onto her ass.

She wanted to play, he could play.

Stella jumped, clearly startled, turning her head to try and see him. "Wyatt!"

"What?" He slid his hand over the pink stain that had bloomed on her ass cheek, and went lower, planning to repeat the maneuver. "Don't you like this? Should I pull your pants back up? Take you home?"

"Yes. I mean, no. I mean, I shouldn't like this . . ."

She sounded sweetly confused. It sent a rush of blood straight to his cock with the realization that no one else had played with

Stella like this before. He was the first. And she liked it. Which made him really like it.

"I'm glad you do." Wyatt dipped his finger more fully inside her this time, letting his head drop back as he felt how tight and wet she was. Damn, she was just amazing.

"This feels totally dirty or something."

Her words sounded scandalized. Her body told a different story. Her hips had started moving, creating a nice rhythm so that he had to just sit there while she pumped onto his finger. He added another one to the first and was rewarded by a soft moan.

"Nothing that feels this good is dirty." Not between two people who cared about each other. That's what he really wanted to say but he didn't want to risk her freaking out on him again. He wasn't sure why she was so resistant to the idea of them dating. If it was just the timing, or something else entirely.

But he was patient. Hell, he had eternity. Literally.

"Are you sure?"

"Positive." But he didn't want to push her too far out of her comfort zone so Wyatt pulled his hand back. She gave a cluck of disappointment but he just urged her up onto her knees.

"Where am I going?" she asked, eyes glazed with passion, cheeks pink.

Usually vampires got flushed only when they fed, but her arousal had caused a rush of blood to her cheeks and he found that as exciting as anything else. She looked beautiful. Luminous. Stunned at the rush of emotion he suddenly felt, Wyatt leaned forward and gave her a soft kiss. "I want to take my pants off."

"Oh, that's a good idea."

It really was one of the best ideas he'd ever had. Wyatt shucked his jeans and briefs, then brought Stella back to him, one of her legs on either side of his thighs. The soft, dewy warmth of her body teased across the tip of his erection. The carpet definitely matched the drapes in Stella's case, her auburn curls an enticing pop against her pale skin.

He wasn't sure that he had ever experienced a moment with greater anticipation in his life. Torn between wanting to draw out their mutual ache and satisfying it, Wyatt gripped her waist and flicked his tongue across her nipple.

"Please, Wyatt." Stella squirmed in his lap, trying to raise herself up so she could join their bodies.

But he wasn't quite ready. "Bite me again," he demanded. He wasn't sure why, other than he wanted to give her as much pleasure as possible. He wanted to connect them, to feel the pull of her fangs inside him while he was inside her. To be something more.

So maybe he did know why. He was in love with Stella. That was why.

He was trying to bind her to him.

Maybe that wasn't fair. But she never hesitated. Her eyes widened, yet she leaned forward, straight for his neck this time, and licked his flesh before sinking her fangs right into his jugular.

Holy hell. Wyatt groaned at the pleasure her drawing on his blood created inside him. Shifting her hips, he dropped her down onto his cock at the same time he thrust up.

"Oh!" Stella drew back, blood pooling on her lips. "Wyatt!"

Then she went back to sucking him so that every muscle, every ligament, every tendon in his body felt like it was being drawn up on a string by Stella, an erotic tug that pulled him all up and into her. Her mouth was warm, her sex was warm, and he felt like he was floating in a vat of honey, kicking toward an orgasm. He didn't want to get there before her but he couldn't stop himself from pumping hard, taking it deep, enjoying the way she broke contact with his neck to cry out, lips cherry red, back arching. Reaching down between their bodies, Wyatt strummed over her clitoris.

Her eyes widened and she paused before silently exploding. It was the most beautiful thing he'd ever seen. She was the most beautiful thing he'd ever seen. He was overwhelmed with desire and passion and the realization that he did in fact love her and wanted to be with her forever. It was on that thought that he came, hard, holding her tight, his blood on her mouth.

Her gaze caught his and they shared the moment, each riding the wave of their simultaneous orgasm. Stella's emerald eyes darkened and he was surprised how long they stayed locked on his before she let out a sigh and dropped her head back.

Holy hell. Wyatt sucked in a deep breath and let up his death grip on Stella. That was unreal. The way they came together was just sexy beyond belief. He'd never experienced anything like he had with her.

"Baby, that was incredible," he said, knowing it was trite, but not having any other words to describe it. He really wanted to tell her the words that were burning in his heart, but he'd already done that and made an ass out of himself. And he hadn't even meant it then the way he would mean it now.

So he left it at that.

She pushed her hair back off her forehead and gave a soft laugh. "It most definitely was. I could get addicted to this."

Wyatt fought a grin. He liked the sound of that.

But then she frowned and the moment passed. Before he could say another word, she was off him and back in her jeans.

"So we heading to Johnny's?" she asked, pulling on her shirt. Like nothing had happened. Nothing whatsoever.

Wyatt stared at her, naked, his lap sadly empty after smoking-hot sex. He ran his fingers through his hair. Reminded himself he was patient. And that the timing was wrong.

"Whatever you want to do." He wasn't going to push, but he wasn't going to roll over and play dead either.

Standing up, Wyatt strode right up to her and took her in his arms without bothering with his clothes. Then he gave her a slow, leisurely kiss, placing her hands straight onto his bare ass. She tasted delicious. "Next time you can do the spanking."

Her eyes widened. "Oh, yeah? Why, are you going to be bad?"

"If driving you nuts is bad, then yeah. But if you're looking for a bad boy, that's not me. I don't believe in treating women like shit." He kissed the corner of her full mouth. "Just so you know."

Her fingers flexed on his ass cheeks and he knew he'd driven his point home.

Chapter Eight

NOT-SO-FREE BIRD

"OKAY, the only chapel I know that will do quickie weddings is down this way," Cort said, pointing down Burgundy.

Katie looked in that direction, suddenly filled with reluctance again. He started down the street, not seeming to notice that she was lagging behind, at least not until he got to the corner of Burgundy and Dumaine.

"It's just right up here," he said as soon as he realized she'd slowed down. Then he frowned, studying her nervous expression.

"Katie?"

She stopped a few feet away from him, glancing down Burgundy and the place just ahead, which could reveal a part of their night that was darned overwhelming. Would she be relieved if she found out they weren't really married? Or disappointed? She honestly didn't know.

You are just confused in general, she assured herself. *Because of your new state of being.*

After all, a drunken elopement wasn't a big deal when

compared with vampirism. Once she sorted out what to expect from her new . . . existence, the possible marriage would seem a whole lot less troubling.

"Could we try for that drink again?" she asked. "We're near Lafitte's, aren't we?"

Cort looked down the street as if he was debating whether to press her to continue on, but then he nodded. "We are."

He was reluctant to find out, too. Even though he was feeling exactly like she was, his obvious reluctance to go to the chapel as well bothered her.

Babe, you have bigger problems than possibly being married to a man who doesn't want you, she told herself. She ran her tongue over her teeth. Flat, no sharp points. But she knew that wouldn't last.

"Lafitte's?" Cort said, jerking his head in the direction of the bar.

"Yes."

LAFITTE'S BLACKSMITH SHOP was the oldest bar in the United States, and it smelled like it. Katie supposed she'd always been aware that the place was stinky, but this was crazy. She could smell decades of wood smoke and cigarettes and booze. But she could also smell the people. Sweat and soaps and perfumes and, under that, something that wasn't foul in the least. Something she suspected should be foul, but instead made her run her tongue over her teeth expectantly.

Still flat. Thank God, she told herself. If she went spontaneously fangy, she wasn't sure she could handle it. Not at the moment.

"How do you deal with this smell thing?" she asked, trying to distract herself.

She wrinkled her nose as they walked farther into a dark, crowded room. Cort managed to find a small table toward the back of the bar and pulled out the chair for her to sit. It was rickety and uncomfortable, but she didn't care as long as she finally got a drink.

Cort sat to the left of her and the parrot scrambled down his arm to waddle around the perimeter of the table like a beaked sentry.

"Jack and Coke. Jack and Coke."

Cort rolled his eyes, then turned to her.

"I don't even notice smells now, unless I choose to, or I'm—" He paused, clearly changing his mind about sharing that detail. "The longer you are . . . this way, the easier it is to control things like that," he told her, his tone gentle.

She could tell he knew this was very hard, but of course, he would know. He'd been through it, too.

"Did you have a hard time with the . . . transition?"

Cort didn't answer right away. "Well, I wasn't crossed over like you were."

"Not that it's like we know how I was crossed over," she pointed out.

"True, but I had the—the choice. Given that you can't remember, I don't feel like you really did."

She nodded, although she wasn't sure she agreed. As totally strange as this was, something told her this hadn't happened as an attack or totally against her will. How she could somehow know that, and not know how it happened didn't make any sense, but that was how she felt. Deep in her soul.

Wait, did she have a soul anymore? So many questions.

"I know that makes the transition more difficult," he said with a small, sympathetic smile, "but you will be fine."

Would she? How would she ever go back to her normal life? Panic returned.

"What will I tell my parents?" she said suddenly, more thinking out loud than expecting answers. After all, Cort didn't know Janine and George, or the fact that they had a hard enough time with their only daughter being a washboard player on Bourbon Street. They sure as heck weren't going to understand her being undead.

"And how am I going to play with my band?"

They were called "the day band" for a reason. And days were out now, weren't they?

Cort reached across the table and took her hand. "I know this isn't what you wanted, but you will be okay. It isn't bad to be this way. In fact, it's pretty great most of the time."

She looked up from their joined hands, feeling her eyes fill with tears as she met his beautiful gaze and saw kindness. And something else. He almost seemed to be pleading with her, willing her to be okay.

Did he really think he'd done this? What other reason would he have for that look . . . one of almost beseeching guilt?

She swiped at her eyes, feeling silly. She wasn't usually a crier. "I'm fine."

"It really will be okay. I'll be here for you," he told her.

Her eyes welled even more. Damn it, but she managed a watery smile. "My husband."

She forced a smile so he would realize she was making a joke about it. But she couldn't miss that his smile faded a little.

"And the other guys will, too," he added.

He definitely didn't want to be married to her—to the point she couldn't even make light of the situation. That said a lot.

And really, why should that bother her? He'd never shown any interest in her, so of course he didn't want them to be married. She didn't want them to be either, did she?

Of course not.

Let it go, she told herself.

"So how old are you, anyway?" she asked, changing the subject.

"Seventeen," he said automatically. "And I have been for a very long time."

She laughed, even though she knew it still sounded a little snuffly.

"And I suppose you sparkle, too, right?"

He smiled.

"Jack and Coke. Jack and Coke."

Cort looked at the bird. "How did we get saddled with the alcoholic?"

Katie shook her head, staring at the bird. "I don't know, but someone better take our order soon before it gets the d.t.'s."

Cort chuckled. "Yeah, I do not want to see what he does if that happens."

Just then, a woman in her twenties wearing a bar apron and harried expression approached their table, although her expression warmed slightly when she saw Cort.

Did they know each other? Cort smiled at the girl, but Katie didn't see any recognition in his sleepy eyes.

"We have some drink specials," the girl added, clearly talking only to him, her gaze moving appreciatively over his lean, muscular body and handsome face.

Katie supposed that reaction was better than at the last place, she told herself, even as a wave of jealousy washed over her.

But honestly, didn't the hussy even notice their rings? Katie caught herself. Okay, she needed to get a grip. They weren't married. Even if they were, they weren't really.

Katie looked back at the girl, who still acted as if no one but

Cort existed. But this chick didn't know their rings weren't legit. And Katie didn't care if it was irrational, she was still irritated.

"I think we know what we want," Cort said, his expression pleasant, but he didn't seem to even notice the waitress's obvious interest. And he didn't seem to know her.

Wait, what if he knew her from last night? Katie studied the girl closer to see if that could be possible.

"What can I get you?" the girl asked, still not looking at Katie, but not any more familiar with Cort.

"Jack and Coke. Jack and Coke."

The waitress looked a little startled by the bird's request, but then said, "For real?"

"Yes, for the bird," Cort said, his tone exaggeratedly pained. "And we'll both take Grey Goose and tonic. Make them doubles. With extra lime."

Warmth spread through Katie even as she scolded herself for the feeling. So he remembered her drink of choice. And he ordered for her. He'd just heard her order it at the other bar so it was hardly a sign of familiarity and closeness. But Katie still liked it. Especially since the waitress finally seemed to notice her, her moony expression fading slightly.

"I'll be right back with those." The girl left, her harried expression returning.

"I'm pretty old, actually," he said as soon as they were alone again.

"What's pretty old? Over a hundred?"

He nodded.

Weird. "Over two hundred?"

He nodded.

"Over three?"

He made a face. "Really, do I look a day over two hundred and fifty?"

He didn't look a day over thirty. Wow, what a weird concept. Suddenly she realized she was going to look exactly like she did now for all eternity.

"I really wish I was down about five more pounds," she said, looking down at her jeans and her *Abbey Road* T-shirt. Who the heck wanted to go through eternity with muffin top? Not her.

"You look beautiful."

Katie looked up from inspecting herself. Did he mean that? Or was he just trying to be comforting again? She studied him, trying to decide, but all too quickly she could feel herself getting lost in those dark eyes of his. Yet again.

"You are very beautiful," he said, and he leaned in.

He was going to kiss her. He was going to kiss her!

"Jack and Coke. Jack and Coke."

Cort straightened, giving the bird an eye roll.

The parrot's interruption was probably a good thing, she told herself. Kissing Cort would only make an already complicated situation even trickier. She didn't need that.

She glanced at Cort, taking in his mussed waves and painfully handsome face.

Of course, that didn't stop her from wanting it.

SHIT, HAD HE really been about to kiss Katie? Yes, yes, he had.

And he'd been cock-blocked by a damned bird. That had to be a first.

Damn, she looked so pretty and vulnerable and irresistible, and he just wanted to hold her close and protect her. But given the look on her face, which was less than pleased, it was probably a good thing that the stupid parrot was fixated on Tennessee whiskey.

"Here you go." The waitress appeared, placing their drinks on the table, making sure not to get her hand too close to the parrot.

Smart choice, that little ass really hurt when he pecked.

The little ass toddled up to his drink, actually knowing which one was his.

"So freaky," Katie commented, voicing Cort's exact sentiment.

She reached for her drink, but before she could even lift the glass from the table, someone said angrily, "You guys have some serious balls."

Reluctantly, both Cort and Katie turned from their drinks. The bird, of course, kept his little red face in his glass.

Slowly, they both turned to see a tall, muscular young guy in a University of New Orleans T-shirt, who looked like he just wandered out of a fraternity house.

Shit, here we go again, and this guy was slightly more intimidating than the stocky man from the other bar. Not that Cort couldn't kick this guy's ass if he chose to do so. Hell, Katie could kick his ass if she wanted. That particular myth was true—vampires were super strong, but Cort never liked to draw any attention that might be unwanted and raise questions. Plus he'd done enough fighting in his mortal life. The Seven Years' War had really been the pits. Of course, that was how he became a vampire, and how he ended up in Louisiana.

He glanced at Katie. Although he had to admit it would be fun to see her go undead ninja on this brute.

"Why is that exactly?" Cort asked, hoping maybe this time they would at least find out something about what happened last night. Although it didn't sound like it was anything too good. Still, even knowing that, Cort wasn't prepared for what the hulk was going to say.

"Where is my watch?"

"Your watch?"

Why on earth would he have this kid's watch? But then again, why would this guy accuse him if he didn't? And God knows where said watch could be now. Maybe he hocked it to buy the lovely wedding bands both he and Katie wore.

"I'm sorry, I don't remember taking your watch. But I'll be glad to—"

"You didn't take it," the frat boy said, frowning as if he was surprised Cort couldn't remember. As if this kid hadn't had a lost night or two on Bourbon. He'd probably had a few in his own dorm room.

But what did he mean, he didn't take it? Why was he confronting them, if Cort didn't take it? Did that mean . . .

Cort looked to Katie. Her eyes were wide and startled. He imagined he sported the same expression.

Katie had stolen a watch? It was hard to imagine Katie stealing anything, much less from this huge kid.

"No," the frat boy said, watching their exchanged glances. "She didn't steal it. That damned bird of yours did."

They turned to the parrot, which, as it seemed to be its favorite pastime, pecked at the cube of ice that floated in its drink.

"I really don't think this is my bird," Cort said, silently praying that was true.

"It's not mine," Katie stated.

"Well, I don't care whose damned bird it is," the kid said. "It was with you last night and it stole my watch."

"Was it just the two of us here last night?" Cort asked, glancing at the bird again. "Well, I guess three of us."

The guy might be a giant, and might be pissed, but maybe he could give them some insights. If he didn't decide to punch Cort first.

"Damn, you really don't remember?" the man said, looking at them as if they were totally mad.

Cort didn't know about Katie, but he couldn't disagree with the mad assessment.

"Please," Cort said, "last night was a bit of a blur and we could really use your help."

"Bit of a blur" was an understatement, of course.

"Damn it, I just want my watch. Or someone is going to pay," the kid said, crossing his muscular arms across his broad chest. He probably played football, too.

"I understand," Cort said, really hoping this guy wouldn't take a swing. Cort didn't want to fight. After last night, he didn't want a brawl tonight. Hell, he'd probably gotten in a brawl last night, too, for all he knew.

"I'm truly sorry about your watch, but we're in a little bit of a predicament here, because neither of us"—Cort nodded toward Katie—"seem to remember much about last night."

The frat boy frowned and for a moment, Cort didn't think he was going to say anything, then he shook his head. "You don't even remember your own reception?"

Katie shot Cort a wide-eyed look. "Our reception?"

"You told us"—he jerked his head toward a table on the other side of the room surrounded by young guys who looked pretty much like he did—"it was your wedding reception. Even bought the whole bar a round of drinks."

"Oh, right. Right," Cort lied, not sure why he felt the need to save face in front of this kid. Maybe because he *was* a kid and he was a centuries-old vampire. He should be able to hold his drink better than a juicehead college kid.

"I just wasn't sure who was—was still with us," he added.

Out of the corner of his eye, he saw Katie watching him, but she didn't say anything.

"Do you happen to remember?" Cort said, trying to sound casual.

The man sighed, but answered, describing the members of the band. "And there was also some guy with a shaved head and tattoo on his cheek."

Shaved head and tattoo? That sounded like Raven. Why would Raven have been with them?

"And a priest who kept shouting that he'd married you two. He was totally wasted, which didn't seem very . . . religious of him. But then, I guess you were all twisted."

Twisted was a good word. But man, it really did irk Cort that this kid was judging his behavior.

Of course it was hard to defend the classlessness of a wedding where everyone—including the bride, the groom, and the priest—was bombed.

"You bought us all a drink, then your bird stole my watch. And I want it back." The kid held out his hand.

The bird stopped poking its ice cube and looked at the guy, lifting its crest and bobbing its head like it was laughing. The little ass probably was.

"Like I said, the bird isn't mine," Cort repeated.

The frat boy eyed the bird warily, but demanded again, "Where is it?"

Seriously? Cort didn't remember getting married, like he was going to remember where a fowl pilfered timepiece was.

Cort stood and pulled the wallet out of the back pocket of his jeans.

"I couldn't begin to tell you where it is. I'm sorry. But I'm more than happy to pay you for it." He opened his black leather billfold and waited for the man to give him a price.

"The watch was my grandfather's. I can't put a price on that," the frat boy said, crossing his arms over his chest again.

Of course it was a family heirloom. Still, Cort was hoping this guy had a price to go away, because he seemed to be getting more irritated by the moment, if the veins popping in the side of his neck were any indication.

"I just want the watch back."

Katie shifted in her chair, regarding the kid warily, too.

"I'm sorry," Cort repeated, "I realize money can't replace it, but would two hundred help?"

The guy shook his head, the muscle in his cheek bulging as he gritted his teeth.

"How about four?" Cort pulled out several bills.

The man shook his head and took a step closer. Katie shifted again, getting more nervous. Cort moved between her and the large kid. She didn't need to be in the line of fire if there was a fight. She'd been through enough in the last twenty-four hours.

"Listen," Cort said, using all his vampire charm and coercion, "I feel awful about the watch. I really do. And I think you can see I'm not a fan of the bird myself, so I totally understand your irritation, but all I can do is offer you some kind of monetary reimbursement. Just name your price."

The man stared at Cort for a moment, and Cort couldn't tell what he was thinking.

"A thousand," the kid growled.

"A thousand?" Katie said before Cort could reply.

The man nodded. "A thousand and we'll be even."

Cort stared at him for a moment, but then pulled more bills from his wallet. He handed them to the man.

"I don't suppose you'd want a free parrot, too," Cort asked. Behind him the parrot whistled loudly as if it understood.

The man counted the money, then said as he was shoving it into his pocket, "No way in hell. That thing is evil."

The frat boy left then, smiling broadly at his friends.

"I bet that watch wasn't even his grandfather's," Katie muttered, frowning with displeasure. "It was probably a battered old Swatch or something."

Cort wouldn't doubt that either and he sure as hell didn't feel like he got a thousand dollars' worth of information from the kid.

"I think we should go," Katie said, standing up, too. "Who knows what else the bird did here last night."

Cort couldn't argue that, even as he looked longingly at his drink.

Cort took out another couple of bills, his wallet getting seriously depleted, and tossed them on the table to cover their drinks, then he reached for the bird. The damned thing pecked him again, but just like before it then climbed up his sleeve to his shoulder.

"You're an ass," Cort informed the red-feathered beast.

The bird bobbed its head merrily as if laughing again.

"Look at the employees behind the bar," Katie said quietly as if they could hear her from across the loud, crowded bar. "They don't look happy."

Cort covertly glanced in the direction of the bar. Three of the waitstaff were looking their way, talking amongst themselves. And Katie was right, they didn't look happy.

"What else did you do, bird?" Cort muttered.

The bird bounced its head again, quite pleased with itself.

That reaction couldn't mean good things.

"Yeah, we better go."

Chapter Nine

I DO . . . OR DID I?

"So," Katie said as soon as they were outside of the crowded bar. "We had a wedding reception with the marrying priest in attendance. It would appear we are truly married."

Cort nodded, letting himself take a moment to assimilate, as Saxon would say, that information. He had to admit he didn't feel nearly as panicked by the idea as he should. As he always thought he'd feel. Shit, he hadn't handled his last marriage this well. And he'd known Francesca his whole mortal life.

Weird.

He glanced at Katie. She was still painfully pale, partly because of her new state of being, but he suspected some of her wan pallor was also due to this information.

And truthfully, her reaction was far more normal than his own. Sure, they did see each other nearly every day. They did chat and occasionally have a drink together. That was it. And now Katie Lambert was Mrs. Berto Cortez, wife of a Bourbon Street musician and vampire.

"It's pretty weird, isn't it?" he said.

"Yeah. It is. This is all pretty weird." Her blue eyes glittered like sapphires against her wan skin.

It might be weird, but Cort couldn't deny that he was very, very attracted to his new wife. She was beautiful.

Of course, she couldn't remain his wife. That was a ridiculous idea.

"We should probably go to the chapel and see what we can find out about having the marriage annulled," he said, making certain to keep any emotion out of his voice.

She didn't answer for a moment, then straightened, still pale but her eyes glittered even more, this time with what he thought was determination.

"I agree." She didn't wait for him as she started down the uneven sidewalk, weaving through a group of raucous partygoers.

Yeah, this was definitely not a woman who wanted to be married a moment longer than she had to be.

Katie knew it was silly, but she'd actually been hurt when Cort suggested an annulment. It was, of course, the most sensible course of action, but still, it did somehow feel like rejection.

You are being so silly.

How could she even be rejected by this man? She had to have some sort of relationship beyond casual friendship to be rejected.

And again, she told herself, it wasn't like she didn't have enough to worry about what with being a fanged, night dwelling blood drinker and all.

At the thought of blood, her stomach rumbled. She was hungry, but she knew she wouldn't likely want anything she would have normally eaten.

"I'm a vegetarian."

Cort's pace slowed as he shot her a surprised glance. "Really?"

"Well, I do eat fish, but no red meat or poultry or pork in nearly ten years."

Cort didn't say anything for a moment. "Well, you still won't eat any of those things."

Katie hadn't expected that, and she couldn't help from laughing. "But I will live on blood, right?"

She kept her voice low, just in case someone was in hearing range.

"Yes, we do live on blood."

"Human blood?" she whispered.

He gave her a regretful look. "Yes."

"So pop culture has that one right," she said.

He nodded. "There are some who live on human life force, draining energy rather than blood, which might have been more appealing to you. But unfortunately you are a straight-up, run-of-the-mill vampire. And you drink blood."

"Run-of-the-mill vampire," she repeated with a cough of humorless laughter. There was nothing run-of-the-mill to her about this situation.

"Well, like you said, the vampires of pop culture. We can't go out into the sun—I hope you weren't a sun worshipper."

She shook her head. She really wasn't. She just freckled. Still, it was hard to imagine never seeing the sun again.

"You can eat," Cort continued, "but it will make you sick. Some vampires do though, just to keep up normal appearances. And we can drink alcohol—as last night would prove."

"So I will just run around biting people?"

God, that idea was awful, mainly because she didn't find it

awful at all. Just yesterday a hot dog would have made her gag, now she was salivating over the idea of sinking her teeth into human flesh. So much for all those years of ethical eating. And the worst part was, if the tingle rippling her body was an indication, she found the idea . . . thrilling. Hummus certainly never got her so excited, that was for sure.

"Some vampires feed directly from humans," Cort said. "But the band guys and I usually drink bagged blood."

"Bagged blood? Like donated blood?"

Cort nodded. "It's a bit like frozen dinners. Not as good as a home-cooked meal, but definitely easier and more convenient. And definitely less complicated."

"Less complicated?"

"Biting humans can be quite problematic. We can take too much blood, which is dangerous. The human can become addicted to the ecstasy of the vampire's bite, which can lead to weird stalker situations. We can accidentally cross a human over—like what happened to you. It's just safer to go prepackaged."

Katie nodded, trying to take everything in. "Shouldn't I be . . . hungrier? I mean, as a new vampire? In movies, it always seems like newly crossed over vampires are ravenous."

Cort nodded. "Yes, that's another movie portrayal that's totally true. As soon as the crossing over is complete, the new vampire is starving. So I suspect you fed last night and are still satiated. Otherwise we'd know. You'd be toothy and frantic."

Now there was an image.

She stopped walking, realizing exactly what he'd just said. "Do you think I hurt someone?"

Cort stopped, too, turning toward her. He reached for her hands, holding them in his much larger ones. "To be honest, I'm not really sure. Let's face it, we have no idea about anything we did last night. But I'd like to think if I was with you, I wouldn't have let you do that."

Given that he was totally right, that they didn't have any idea what had happened last night, his reassurance shouldn't have made her feel better. But it did.

Or maybe it was his hands, surprisingly warm with strong, long fingers and broad palms, yet so gently cupping hers. She looked down at their joined fingers. Their gold bands glinted in the streetlights.

What would it be like to be married to a man like this for real?

No, not a man, a vampire. And what was the point of even thinking that way? They were about to find out about an annulment. This was not the time to be getting dreamy. Not the time at all.

"We should probably get to the chapel," she said, slowly pulling her hands away from his.

"Right," he agreed, seeming to snap out of his own thoughts. Was he thinking about their crazy marriage, too? Or had he noticed her moony expression and was wondering what the heck was wrong with her?

"Going to the chapel, and I'm going to get married," the parrot crooned in its eerie falsetto as they started walking again.

Not this time, Katie thought. *Not this time.* And she was damned silly for feeling sad about that fact.

"THIS IS IT," Cort said, stopping in front of a brick building with a white awning over the door.

"I never would have known this was a wedding chapel. Have you been here before?" she asked, looking from the building to Cort.

"Aside from possibly last night, you mean?" He offered her a sheepish smile.

"Yeah," she said. She returned his smile with one of her own, although he could see it didn't quite reach her deep blue eyes.

"I actually have. To be a witness for Drake."

"Drake is married?" Katie had never noticed Drake with one particular woman. In fact, most of the time, he seemed to have a new flavor of the week . . . or even day.

"No," Cort said, shaking his head, his smile wry now. "But he did almost marry a stripper."

"What happened?"

"He realized he was about to almost marry a stripper."

"Strippers need love, too," Katie said, smiling. "Besides, you married a washboard girl."

"A very cute washboard girl," he said.

Katie's smile faded, and he immediately regretted the comment. Especially since her smile had been real and she'd looked more like herself in that moment than she had all night.

"At least briefly, right?" he added, hoping she'd be comforted that they could at least rectify this one issue. "Come on, let's go see what happened here."

He hesitated just a second when they reached the door, but then he grabbed the handle and shoved it open. A bell rang announcing their entrance.

He got only the impression of silk flowers and draping white cloth before a woman, who looked like she should be flitting about the room with little wings while strumming a harp, bustled into the room.

"Can I help—" Her cherubic smile faded as soon as she saw them.

Great, someone else who was less than pleased to see them.

"Oh, you two," the lady said, actually looking nervous. She glanced over her shoulder as if searching for reinforcements. When she didn't see anyone coming, she turned back to them, forcing a smile. "You're back."

"We are," Cort said, glancing at Katie, whose pretty lips were pulled downward into a worried frown. She clearly hadn't missed the woman's reaction either.

"Well, it's lovely to see you are . . . feeling so much better," the cherub said, with a sympathetic smile.

Feeling better? Cort wasn't sure about that.

The lady continued, "But as we told you last night, the parrot cannot serve as your witness."

Oh dear God, they'd tried to have the parrot as their witness. Really?

Katie shook her head slightly, but she didn't react any further. Cort supposed, given what they'd discovered thus far, trying to have a parrot as a best man—or maid of honor—wasn't much of a shock.

"We know that," Cort said easily as if he remembered their antics from the night before, even though everything else he was about to say would reveal they had no idea what happened. Period. "We're actually just checking here, because it seems we did get married."

He raised his left hand to show the ring. Katie showed hers, too.

"And it doesn't sound as if we got married here," he added.

"Indeed you did not." A man in a black suit and tie entered the room and stopped beside the cherub.

Yet again, another person who wasn't pleased with them. One

thing was becoming clear. It was probably a good thing they didn't remember their night. They hadn't made any friends, that's for sure.

"Is this the only twenty-four-hour chapel in the Quarter?" Cort asked.

The man nodded. "It is."

"Do you happen to have a priest who works here?"

"This is a nondenominational chapel," the man said, his tone haughty, "and I'm the only reverend."

Cort nodded, instantly uncomfortable with the man's air of superiority. In fact, he really wanted to walk out. After all, they hadn't married here, and that was all they needed to know, right?

Even as he told himself that, Katie asked, "Do you have any idea where we could have been married?"

"I don't," the man said, "but I know if you were still in the same state you were when you arrived here, then whoever he was shouldn't have married you. I certainly could not agree to it."

Again, Cort didn't like his tone. As if this man didn't encounter all sorts of inebriated people in the Crescent City.

"Why wouldn't you marry us?" Katie asked, and Cort shot her a surprised look. Surely she wasn't so naïve as to not realize what the reverend was saying.

"Well, you were very drunk."

Katie had to know that was what he was going to give as his answer.

"And there appeared to be blood on your clothes."

Cort's attention snapped back to the reverend. Now that answer he hadn't expected.

"Blood?"

The reverend and the cherub both nodded.

"Both of us?" Katie asked.

"Just you," the reverend said to her. "I think you can understand my misgivings at the whole situation."

Cort could, but he still didn't like the man's attitude. Definitely not that of Christian concern, but rather holier-than-thou judgment.

So it really irked Cort to have to ask, "Did we tell you what happened?"

"Not exactly," the reverend said. He crossed his arms, looking decidedly unimpressed. "But you did have the strangest reason for needing to marry."

"We did?" Katie asked, her voice reedy like it had been back in his apartment.

The reverend nodded, as did the cherub.

"Yes, you kept saying that you had to marry," the reverend looked at Cort, "because you bit her."

Cort had bitten her. Beside him, Katie swayed slightly on her feet, and he immediately put out an arm to steady her. To his shock, she allowed his touch, even after finding out he'd been the one. The one who crossed her over.

Why? Why?

"You bit me," Katie said, her voice strange, totally dazed. Cort watched her for a moment, then realized the other two were watching both of them, one bewildered, the other suspicious.

The reverend knew something. Something he shouldn't.

"Well, that certainly is an odd reason to insist on marriage," Cort said, trying to sound amused. "Isn't it, sweetheart?"

Katie looked at him, her eyes clouded with a mixture of confusion and disbelief, but she nodded.

Cort gave her an encouraging smile, and she seemed to realize he was trying to get her to calm down. She even managed a slight smile of her own in return.

The reverend nodded, his expression relaxing—but only a little.

"And of course there was your odd choice of witnesses," the reverend added. "The bird, of course. And some long-haired fellow who kept trying to touch my cross."

"He even knocked that one down off the wall." The cherub pointed to a small cross adorning the entryway wall. "It hit him in the head and he carried on like he was dying. He claimed it burned him and he ran out of the chapel."

"Saxon," Cort said softly, shaking his head. Damn, they might as well have walked in and announced they were vampires looking for a late-night wedding deal. Cort got the feeling this man had put the pieces together.

"Our friend can be quite overdramatic when he drinks," Cort said, forcing a laugh. He really didn't want this reverend to continue believing what Cort suspected he did.

All they needed was a wedding chapel officiant turned all Van Helsing after them. And this man looked like he would relish such a position.

"Saxon does like to act ridiculous when he drinks," Katie agreed, surprising Cort with her own little laugh. Man, this woman could rally.

The reverend's gaze was still probing, but he nodded as if he accepted their excuses.

"And then there was the final reason I could not possibly marry you," he finally said.

Oh shit, was this the point where he dramatically announced that he knew they were the cursed undead and he was going to put them permanently back in their graves.

The reverend turned and walked over to an ornate cupboard, bending down to open it.

Beside Cort, Katie must have wondered the same thing, because she shifted closer to him. Cort tightened his hold on her waist, not quite sure what the reverend was going to do either. But if he did come charging toward them with a pointy wooden stake or holy water or a rope of garlic, Cort knew he had a better chance of protecting them than she did.

The reverend reached into the cabinet but Cort couldn't see what he was getting.

"I think you will be wanting this," the reverend said, his back still toward them.

Cort, of course, couldn't feel his heart pounding in his chest, but he knew it would have been, if he were alive.

The reverend turned, and both Cort and Katie just stared.

He walked toward them with a cookie jar in the shape of a bust of Elvis cradled in both hands.

"The final reason I couldn't marry you two," the reverend said, stopping in front of Cort, who still held Katie tight to his side, "you kept demanding I take this as payment for the ceremony. Perhaps this would be accepted as currency in Las Vegas, but here, not so much." The reverend held the cookie jar out to Cort.

"Hunk-a-hunk-a burnin' love," the parrot trilled.

Cort, almost too weak with relief to move, hesitated for a moment before taking the kitschy cookie jar. This had been Johnny's urn. Why had they had it?

"I hate to appear mercenary," the reverend said, "but this chapel is also a business."

"Going to the chapel," the parrot said in his annoying sing-song falsetto.

"Very understandable," Cort said after shooting the bird a look. "We understand your reason for declining to marry us. We also appreciate you being so understanding of our conditions."

The cherub receptionist smiled, and Cort got the feeling she was pleased to see there wasn't going to be any trouble from them, so now she could relax.

The reverend, however, didn't exude any more warmth than he had from the moment he'd arrived in the room.

"Thank you for holding on to this for us." Cort lifted the cookie jar slightly.

"Certainly."

"Well, I think we should be going," Cort said, tucking the jar under one arm like a football. He placed his free hand on the small of Katie's back, ushering her toward the door.

Once outside, Katie stopped on the sidewalk, looking back at the chapel.

"Maybe we should stop trying to find out what happened last night," Katie said. "Things keep getting weirder and weirder."

Chapter Ten

FEELINGS FOR YOUR FRIEND . . . OR YOUR DOM

STELLA wasn't sure where the lump in her throat had come from. Or exactly how her hands had wound up on Wyatt's butt, though that part she liked. The lump she wasn't digging so much. Blame it on being emotional from Johnny's death, but she was perfectly content to stand in Wyatt's arms and have him tell her that he was a nice guy. She knew he was a nice guy. She'd seen it for years.

Yet she appreciated the care he took with her. The intentional and subtle reassurance that he wouldn't dick around with her. It made warm things happen to her insides that weren't just the result of kneading his naked butt beneath her fingers. It was such a nice ass though. Mmm. She gave it one last squeeze.

At the same time, she couldn't stop herself from stepping back. Relying on Wyatt wasn't a good plan. She had always relied on herself and it wasn't fair to him to take advantage of his kindness.

"I'm not looking for a bad boy." She debated adding that she wasn't looking for anything, but that just sounded bitchy. "But I guess right now we need to go looking for the guys and see if they found anything out."

It was not a smooth subject change, but Stella knew if she stayed in the intimacy of Wyatt's apartment she'd end up naked again. Which wasn't a bad thing, obviously, but she was confused about what the hell was happening between them and she wasn't sure it was wise.

Which was stupid, given that ten minutes earlier she'd been sprawled across his lap getting a playful spanking.

She needed medication. She was losing her mind.

"Just call Cort," Wyatt said.

Stella pulled her phone out of her purse. "I can't. My phone is dead." Of course. She had to charge it every three seconds or it didn't work. "Can I borrow yours?"

"Sure." He pulled his phone out of his pocket and handed it to her.

Stella scrolled through his contacts and found Cort, then hit the Call button. She waited impatiently as it rang, feeling an odd sense of urgency to find out what had happened the night before.

"Hello? Hello?"

Caught off guard, Stella paused. That squawking whiny voice didn't exactly sound like Cort. She wasn't sure it even sounded human, actually. "Um, Cort? It's Stella."

There was rustling and then mumbling that she didn't understand. "What did you say? I can't hear you, Cort."

"Can you hear me? Can you hear me now?"

There was no way in hell that was the lead singer. Nor did she think it was Katie, who had left the apartment earlier with Cort. It sounded like . . .

"Is this the parrot?" she asked, suspicious. The weird just kept coming.

"Slap the fat. Ride the wave."

Stella's mouth dropped open. *"What?"* She had no idea what that even meant, but it sounded totally rude. And she didn't like that parrot. He'd been a complete asshole, chasing her when she was in bat form. There was no denying it.

Wyatt was staring at her with his eyebrows raised, clearly wondering what the hell was going on. That was two of them.

"Slap the fat. Ride the wave."

It just sounded so *wrong*. Did this nasty parrot have a fetish? This was getting her nowhere fast and creeping her out. "Put Cort on the phone. Please." She had no idea why she even bothered. Parrots could talk, but they couldn't follow directions. She didn't think.

There was a crash, more rustling, and voices murmuring in the background, but clearly the parrot had decided she wasn't worth his time and had wandered away. "Are you kidding me?" Stella ended the call and handed Wyatt his phone. "That was the parrot. He wasn't much help."

"The parrot answered Cort's phone? Oh my God."

Stella suddenly had the urge to laugh. It was all just too ridiculous. "Polly want a cell phone?"

Wyatt snorted. "Girl, you're losing it."

"Tell me about it."

"I'll try Drake instead." Wyatt touched his phone screen then put it to his ear. "Hey, it's Wyatt. Where are you?"

Stella took the two wineglasses into Wyatt's kitchen and washed them while Wyatt nodded and said, "Uh-huh. Yeah. See you in twenty."

"What's going on?" she asked. Though maybe she didn't really want to know.

"Drake hasn't exactly been on the hunt for information. He

tracked down an emergency dentist and just had a fang implant put in. I'm not sure why that had to happen right this freaking minute, but apparently it did."

A fake fang? Not surprising. Drake was a vain vampire.

"Where is Saxon?" Not that she thought Saxon would be of any help, but because she was worried about him wandering around solo. He wasn't the sharpest tool in the shed and the last thing they needed was him falling off a balcony.

"Saxon said he was coming here to meet us, but since there's no sign of him, we'll just meet up with Drake instead. He's done at the dentist and we're meeting him at Fahy's in twenty minutes."

"Somehow I don't think any of us need a drink. Why are we going to a bar?" The thought of alcohol kind of made Stella want to hurl just a little.

"It's as good a place as any to meet Drake and start asking around about what happened last night. We go there a lot after work so maybe we did last night."

He had a point. Stella felt anxious again and she wasn't sure why. There wasn't any real indication that something super terrible had happened the night before, but she couldn't shake the feeling that they were about to open a big old can of worms.

Stepping outside, Stella almost fell over Saxon sitting on the front stoop. "Ack!" She lost her footing and tumbled down the crumbling brick steps past the keyboardist, who didn't reach out to help stabilize her. He didn't react much at all actually.

Wyatt's arm shot past Saxon and tried to grab her, but by then Stella was down on the sidewalk and had managed to keep herself upright. She turned and glared at Saxon. "What are you doing?"

He glanced up at her, his chin resting on the palm of his hand. His hair was in his eyes and he looked forlorn. "I think I'm starting to have feelings for my dom."

Wyatt let out a startled laugh.

Stella just wanted to slit her wrists. Except she wouldn't die and be prevented from hearing whatever Saxon was about to say, so what would be the point? "You have a dom? Like as in, a dominatrix?" She didn't think there was any other definition of a dom, but she wanted to make sure. She shouldn't even ask, but it was her nature to be compassionate. It was a curse.

"Yeah. It's the woman who owns the crystal shop. She's got it going on and I think that maybe I'm in love with her."

"Well, what's wrong with having feelings for . . . her?" She couldn't bring herself to say "dom" again because she did not want to picture Saxon crawling across the floor with a ball gag in his mouth. Damn. Too late.

His head snapped up and he looked astonished. "I don't know. I guess there's nothing wrong with it, really. Stella-roo, you're brilliant."

That was the end of that? "I'm glad I could help."

Wyatt shook his head. "Well, now that that's solved, can we start walking?"

"Sure." Stella started down Burgundy, moving around a pot-hole in the sidewalk. It was a beautiful night, sixty degrees with lower humidity than normal, and the sounds of the Quarter were ramping up for the night. Her neighborhood uptown was much quieter, but she could see why Wyatt liked the convenience and energy of this location.

Walking next to Wyatt eased her anxiety. He strode with confidence, and he put his hand on the small of her back to guide her around some bags of garbage. She wasn't used to that. She was always the caregiver, not the one being taken care of, and she had no clue how to react.

Fahy's was a bar off Bourbon that had lots of dark wood and

several pool tables. The bartender who worked the night shift was a vampire, and he knew them all by name.

"Hey, Nigel, what's up?" Wyatt said as each of them pulled up a stool and sat.

The bartender was scrawny, a former pickpocket in Industrial Revolution London, who still had traces of his British accent. "I'm surprised to see you tonight. Feel like bollocks, do you? You were seriously pissed last night."

"I've felt better," Stella admitted. But she knew he couldn't have seen her, unless she had somehow managed to morph in and out of bat form. "So . . . you saw us last night?"

Nigel gave a crack of laughter. "Oh, yeah, there was no missing these two. They came in with Drake, drunk out of their minds, and dumped a bunch of money in the jukebox on Barry White songs. I mean, Barry White? I was like, what the fuck."

Stella laughed. Saxon didn't look concerned but Wyatt looked puzzled and more than a little embarrassed.

"Barry's a cool dude," Saxon said with a shrug.

"I'm not drinking with you anymore," Wyatt said. "I can't believe I would agree to that."

"Was anyone else with them?" Stella asked.

"Just the priest. He was right handy with his smartphone. Didn't know men of the cloth took video of their nights out partying." Nigel vigorously shook the martini shaker in his hands and poured it off into three drinks. "I suspect he wasn't really a priest."

Stella sat up straighter. Benny had been with them? "He took pictures and video?"

"Yep."

"Fabulous," Wyatt said. "Now there's proof that I acted like an ass."

"Well, you did try on Trudy's corset. And for the record, red is not your color."

Huh. Stella had a hard time picturing that.

"You're making that up," Wyatt accused.

Stella grinned at him. "You were pretty damn concerned about your hair getting messed up this morning when I was bat-diving you. I didn't realize you were so in touch with your feminine side."

"I'll touch your feminine side," he muttered, taking a sip of the drink Nigel had put in front of him.

"So, Johnny's girl was in here earlier," Nigel said.

The smile fell from Stella's face and she leaned forward so quickly, she almost fell off the cracked black vinyl of the stool. "Johnny's girl? Who is that?" She hadn't been aware that her brother had been seeing anyone.

Nigel looked surprised. "You haven't met Bambi? She and Johnny were in here like two, three times a week."

Bambi? That couldn't be anyone's real name. No mother was that cruel. "I've never heard of her." Which was painful to admit. There was obviously a lot her brother had kept from her, and that was hurtful. Why hadn't he felt like he could trust her? "She never came to see him at work when the band was playing."

"That's odd."

Definitely.

"He never said anything to me either," Wyatt said. "And I never saw anyone at the bar who could have been a girlfriend."

They both looked at Saxon, who shrugged. "Don't look at me. Nobody tells me anything."

Stella couldn't imagine why that would be.

"I guess a man is entitled to his secrets." Nigel moved on down the bar. "But I'm sorry to see Johnny leave us, and Bambi seemed pretty irritated about the whole thing."

Stella didn't give a crap what Bambi felt. She wasn't the one who had spent over a century with Johnny as her constant companion.

"So do you think we should see if Benny has anything relevant on his camera?" Stella asked Wyatt.

"Yeah. And we should try to find this Bambi. Maybe she knows something."

She supposed that was rational, yet she found herself resisting the idea. She didn't want to know that some random woman might have had greater insight into her brother's feelings than she'd had. It took gritting her teeth to manage an, "Okay. Sounds good."

Another chat with Nigel revealed that Bambi was a dancer at a gentlemen's club. Just where Stella wanted to spend her night.

"I guess we can go there first," Wyatt said. "Then on to find Benny. Where does he work again?"

"Bounce." The idea of the band guys in a gay strip club was highly entertaining to Stella. Just imagining their level of discomfort made her smile.

"For Christ's sake." Wyatt shook his head. "We have to go to two strip clubs tonight?"

"I'm down with that," Saxon said.

Stella could think of better ways to spend a night, but they were seeking information, not stimulation, so she could live with it. "Maybe we should split up. I'll go to Bounce, you go to Ecstasy."

Wyatt shook his head. "No way. I don't want you wandering around alone until we know what's going on. We'll go together, but man, I hate those places. There's a sad quality to them that I don't like. Mortals wasting their short lives."

That made Stella like Wyatt even more. It was exactly how

she'd always felt about the many strip clubs on Bourbon Street. "We'll make quick work out of it. You guys aren't going to embarrass me in Bounce, are you?"

"Why would we do that? And I'm secure enough in my sexuality that it's not a big deal to me."

"I'm not," Saxon said. "Maybe I should stay here."

Stella smacked his leg. "You're just saying that because you don't want to walk five blocks."

"Bingo."

"Tough tamales, you're going with us." If they left Saxon at Fahy's, they might never find him again, the way things were going.

The door opened and Drake walked in. "Wassup?" he said, slurring his words as he saluted with one hand.

If Drake was drunk, Stella was going to hogtie him to a chair. "Have you been drinking?"

"No, my mouwth ith numb from da dentist."

Excellent. Wyatt paid their tab and they set out for the club.

Stella had very little hope that this wasn't going to result in total disaster.

WYATT GAVE A polite smile and refused the girl in the doorway who offered him a lap dance the minute he walked into the gentlemen's club. It smelled like sweat and desperation in this particular place, and the dim lighting didn't completely mask the grimness of the setting or the boredom of the girls dancing. He reached back for Stella's hand, feeling the need to make it obvious they were together. Even if they weren't together exactly. They would be. He hoped.

Though he wasn't sure who he was trying to protect—Stella or himself. The predatory look on some of these dancers' faces was a little scary. He had faced down thieves and guns and other vampires, yet women looking to make a buck off him were not who he wanted to deal with tonight. So he just cut to the chase. "Is Bambi here?"

The girl who had been smiling so suggestively a second ago made a face and dropped her arm from her hip to lie limply. "We don't take personal requests."

"I just want to talk to her."

"She don't work tonight. She'll be here tomorrow." The girl messed with the strings of her bikini bottoms and Wyatt got a flash of flesh he would have preferred not to see.

"Okay, thanks." Dragging Stella, he got out of there. Hopefully Saxon and Drake were following them.

"You're about to break my hand, Wyatt."

He glanced down at Stella, whose face was pinched. "Sorry." He loosened his grip on her, not really sure what his problem was. "We're just getting more questions than answers, aren't we? This is frustrating."

They paused on the sidewalk a few feet down the uneven cobblestones from the doorway. Saxon was staring into the window of a T-shirt shop and fiddling with his bangs with one hand, applying a layer of ChapStick with the other. He must have the smoothest lips of any vampire in Louisiana. Drake looked distracted, poking his cheek with his finger and working his jaw.

"The last forty-eight hours have been nothing but frustrating," Stella said, her hands going into her front pockets.

Wyatt's eyes were drawn to the ribbon of skin that was exposed above her waistline from the action. He wanted to lick her flesh. To really have the opportunity to lay her down and kiss her from head to toe. That was frustrating. "You've had some satisfying moments in the last forty-eight hours, too." He leaned forward and whispered, "You liked it when you came, didn't you?"

He felt, rather than saw, her shiver. "That goes without saying."

Wyatt took her hand in his and stroked the inside of her palm with his thumb. "We're going to figure this out as quickly as possible so we can put all this behind us and get back to the bedroom."

"You make it sound so simple." She licked her lips in what was probably a nervous gesture, but it served to turn him on.

"It can be simple." Now he found he wasn't talking about just sex. But he also was a quick learner. He knew it was time to back off. He took a step back and gave her space. "Okay, so where is this place? Benny better have some information, that's all I'm saying."

"It's in the eight hundred block of Bourbon. Let's go before Saxon hurts himself."

If Wyatt wanted to be responsible for a loyal and not-so-bright living creature, he'd get a dog. But he sighed and called to Saxon and Drake. "Yo, come on!"

Normally Drake was a little swifter, but the numbing medication seemed to have gotten to him. He was wandering as aimlessly behind them as Saxon was. Wyatt walked beside Stella and steeled himself to be annoyed by Benny all over again.

Nonetheless, he wasn't quite prepared for the sight of Benny dancing on a bar in his infamous orange underwear, gyrating suggestively. Nor was he prepared to pay a five-dollar cover charge at the door.

"What the hell?" he said to Stella. "I'm annoyed on behalf of gay men. Why do they have to pay a cover charge when no other bar on Bourbon charges one? That sucks. It might even be discrimination."

"Maybe it's because there's entertainment."

"Um, what are we? We're not on that stage every night because we wandered up there by accident."

Stella made a face. "You're right. I don't know. I guess they figure if they can get money they'll charge it."

"If someone hits on me, you have to pretend to be my girl-friend," Drake said to Stella, his slur improved dramatically.

"No one is going to hit on any of you. Trust me."

Should they be insulted? "And why is that, exactly?"

Wyatt crossed his arms over his chest and stood on the edge of the dance floor. The music wasn't really that loud, because it wasn't meant to be danced to. It was just setting a beat for the dancers on the bar and on the elevated stage while allowing customers to still talk. Benny had spotted Stella and had enthusiastically waved, but other than that they didn't seem to be attracting any attention. Whenever a guy glanced their way, he quickly dismissed them.

Well. Apparently none of them were attractive to men. Wyatt was a little insulted.

"This is a sweeping generalization, but scruffy musicians seem to be something only women find hot," Stella said.

"Scruffy? You think I'm scruffy?" Yeah. Insulted.

She rolled her eyes. "I mean longer hair."

That didn't soothe his feelings in any way. "Alright. Whatever. I see how it is."

"I refuse to deal with any of your wounded egos tonight." Stella moved away from him with a fair amount of attitude and sway in her hips.

Bewildered, he turned to Drake. "What the hell did I do?"

"You spoke. That's what you did. Hey, uh, what's going on with you and Stella?"

"Something's going on with you and Stella?" Saxon asked. "Dude."

"I don't really know what's going on with us. Maybe something. Maybe nothing." Brooding, he stood with his legs apart, arms crossed, and watched Benny bend over and talk to Stella. Neither of them seemed concerned that they were interrupting his work, such as it was.

"What's the deal with the guy? She have a thing for the priest?"

Wyatt glared at Drake. "No." And he didn't really appreciate having his secret fear pointed out—that she would find another man more to her liking.

Stella felt a sense of responsibility toward Benny, that's all. She wasn't attracted to him. But was she attracted to Wyatt? None of these guys here were. Maybe he wasn't attractive.

And maybe he was a moron.

Her conversation with Benny was taking way longer than it should. Wyatt strode over to them.

"Hey, what's going on?" He nodded to Benny.

Benny's smile disappeared when he saw Wyatt. "Oh. Hey."

"Everything taken care of?" he asked Stella.

"Yes. Benny said he'll go get his phone for us to look at after this dance. He said he hasn't looked at the pictures so he doesn't know what, if anything, is on there."

"Okay, cool. Thanks, man."

"Anything for my Dark Angel."

Oh, please.

Benny stood back up and went back to throwing his hips around. *Dancing* was a bit of an exaggeration in Wyatt's opinion. Leaning against the bar, he studied Stella. "So what was all that conversation about, Dark Angel?"

It wasn't the right thing to say. He knew it the second the

words were out of his mouth. Her expression confirmed this. She looked like she wanted to hit him with her purse again.

"The jealousy thing? Not cool. Knock it off."

He wanted to protest but he wasn't sure there was much point. "Sorry. Do you want a drink?"

"I'd love a diet soda."

Wyatt tried to flag the bartender down, but the guy ignored him. He wasn't used to that. He knew half the bartenders in the Quarter and he always got good service. Being ignored yet again was not what he wanted when he was trying to be cool and smooth things over with Stella. Looking around, he realized most of the men in the bar were well-dressed and aloof. It seemed to be a theme. Maybe Wyatt needed to wave a twenty to the bartender and act pretentious to get service.

Saxon seemed to be having the same problem with the bartender. He made choking motions and said, "Dying. Of. Thirst."

Which was, of course, ridiculous. Vampires weren't going to die of anything and definitely not of human thirst. They didn't need to drink liquids besides blood at all. Most of them did it as a habit more than anything else or used it as a mixer for blood.

Wyatt didn't need to feed more than once a night, or sometimes even for several nights, given his age. But Saxon was a young vampire. He probably was struggling with true hunger, and Wyatt knew that if you were craving blood, a bar was as torturous as it was for an alcoholic. All those sweaty, aroused bodies dancing and flirting and moving. Their blood scent hung over the room like a London fog, surrounding them with its enticing sweetness.

Saxon was hard to take seriously because he was such a goof, but he was a vampire and he did struggle with the same urges they all did. Wyatt had the feeling he needed to take Saxon seriously right now. "Hey, you okay? You want to go home and get a bag?"

"That might not be a bad idea."

Saxon lived on Decatur above a souvenir shop, and if he cut down Dumaine they weren't that far. "We're only five minutes from your place so you might as well. Meet us back here, okay?" Not that he wanted to hang around indefinitely but he still thought it wasn't a bad idea to stick together.

"Why does he get to wander off when you nixed me coming here alone?" Stella looked put out.

Which seemed to be her look of the evening except for when she had been riding him.

"Because I'm not sleeping with Saxon," he told her. No point in putting any other spin on it.

Drake, who had been playing with his phone, glanced up. "You two are sleeping with each other?"

Though he didn't sound particularly surprised or concerned about the idea. Which really made Wyatt wish he'd kept his mouth shut. Drake, that is. Wyatt was glad he had said something. Stella needed to know he wasn't playing around here—he could be patient but he did want a relationship with her.

"No," Stella sputtered. "Well, yes, actually. But only twice. Why do you care?"

"Can't say that I do," Drake said, going back to his phone. "I figured you'd get around to banging each other sooner or later."

Wyatt watched Stella for her reaction to Drake's nonchalance. Maybe Stella was the only one who hadn't noticed Wyatt's lengthy crush on her.

"Don't be crude," was her scathing, prudish response.

"What, banging each other isn't what you're doing? Is Wyatt making love to you, Stella?" Drake teased her.

She looked embarrassed. Wyatt felt embarrassed. If Drake started calling him her lover he was going to have a real problem with it.

"You know, just mind your own business." Stella looked relieved when Benny hopped down off the bar and came over, his cell phone in his hand. "Thanks, Benny, we'll just take a peek and get it right back to you."

"Whatever you need, goddess." Benny used a stool to leap back up onto the bar, earning him a few catcalls from patrons.

"You sleeping with him, too?" Drake asked.

"No. How's your fake fang?" Stella paused in navigating Benny's phone to glance up and wrinkle her nose at Drake.

"Ouch." Drake laughed. "It's actually pretty damn sore, but I'll be fine. And I get the message. You want me to back off. But how often do I get to give you a hard time? Indulge me."

She started to speak, then her eyes went wide as she looked at the phone. "Oh my God. Wyatt, you really are wearing a corset."

Chapter Eleven

THERE'S SOMETHING ABOUT BETTY

KATIE wasn't totally kidding. She wasn't sure she wanted to know anything else. It already seemed pretty apparent that Cort had been the one to bite her. And they legitimately seemed to be married, too. Okay, not by the Lurch of a minister back there, but by someone. Probably the priest in the bathtub. Which somehow seemed apropos.

And they had found out what happened to Saxon's forehead.

She glanced at the cookie jar cradled in Cort's arm. And now they had an Elvis cookie jar. That was probably enough for tonight.

But she didn't say that. Instead, heaven help her, she did exactly what she'd just told herself she didn't want to do. She asked another question.

"Do you think the blood on me was mine? Or someone else's?"

Cort shook his head. "Honestly, I have no idea."

Katie wasn't sure which option disturbed her more. But it did explain why she was now wearing a T-shirt and jeans. They'd gotten her a change of clothing at some point, obviously.

They walked a bit, silent. Katie considered asking where they were going, but instead addressed the other issue at the forefront of her mind.

"Do you think the reverend knew?"

"Knew what?"

"That we're vampires," Katie said.

Cort was quiet for a moment. "I had the same thought, but I guess it doesn't matter. He didn't seem like he was going to do anything about it."

They were silent again, heading down Burgundy back toward the center of the Quarter.

Katie supposed he was right. But it did make her wonder, if the reverend suspected something about them being vampires, couldn't others, too?

"What if he isn't the only one who knows?" she asked. "Couldn't that be dangerous?"

Cort glanced at her, then shrugged, the parrot ruffling its feathers at the movement. "Maybe, but again, I don't think we should worry unless we find out something concrete. We have enough to worry about tonight, don't you think?"

Katie suspected he was just playing down his own concern, but she nodded anyway. She'd found the reverend very unnerving, and she found the idea of other humans knowing their secret worrisome, too. What if they saw them as monsters? Cort himself said that some vampires did survive by sucking human blood. What if a human who knew about them was behind what happened last night?

"Listen," Cort said, obviously noticing her worry. "I really don't think we have anything to worry about. I mean, if the reverend had wanted to do something to us, he'd had a perfect opportunity last night. We were totally out of it."

Katie nodded, but decided to share her thoughts anyway. "But didn't you say that it's very strange for a vampire to black out, especially from drinking?"

"Yeah."

"So what if someone did something to you all intentionally."

Cort stopped and turned to Katie. The bird ruffled again.

"Like drugged us or something?"

"I don't know. It's just a thought."

Cort didn't speak, but he didn't start walking again either.

"It is strange that everyone in the band blacked out," he finally said.

She nodded.

"But you blacked out, too."

"Maybe I was just collateral damage. Maybe I wasn't meant to get whatever you got."

"That is an interesting thought," he admitted, realizing Katie might have a valid point. It was strange they all blacked out. At Johnny's wake. And Johnny's actual death was the strangest part of all. "We all found Johnny's sudden suicide damned odd. He wasn't upset or depressed or acting unusual in any way. At least not that I saw."

"I realize I didn't know him that well, but I was surprised, too. Johnny always struck me as the type of guy who didn't sweat the small stuff."

He didn't. Johnny loved being a vampire. He loved being a drummer. He loved living in New Orleans and living the constant party. His suicide definitely didn't make sense, so the more Cort thought about it, the more Katie's idea that someone wanted to hurt them made sense.

But who?

"I know we didn't need another potential mystery." Katie offered him a weak smile.

No, they didn't. Although in his mind, he sort of felt like they basically knew the truth about their personal mysteries. Whether they liked it or not.

And he felt oddly accepting of both. He'd bitten Katie and married her. Two things he'd vowed never to do again. And he'd broken his promises to himself with a woman he didn't know all that well. But even looking at her now, he felt like he knew her.

Like he was *supposed* to be with her.

But he returned his attention to this theory of hers. It really might have merit, but where did they start to find out about this new mystery?

"Maybe we should just head back to my place and see if we can talk to the priest. Maybe he can at least give us a little more info about what happened."

Katie deserved to know why she was a vampire. He did think it was at his hands—or rather fangs, but why? And did they simply marry because he drunkenly felt obligated to take care of the new vampire he'd created?

He looked at Katie. She worried her lower lip again, although stopped when she noticed his gaze falling to her lips.

Yes, he would have married her for that reason. He would, even coherent and sober, he realized. He needed to protect and care for her. He didn't know why, but he did know that. Period.

"Yes, I guess talking to the priest would be the next best step." She sounded less than excited about that idea.

Of course, the fact that he'd felt marrying her was the right thing to do didn't mean she felt the same way. In fact, the dread in her voice was an indication she didn't feel even remotely the same way. And why would she? Again, he suspected none of this had been her choice.

Still, he felt a little hurt by her obvious reluctance to talk to the priest. But there was no way in hell he was going to show her that. He'd just stay focused on finding out the facts and then handling the annulment or whatever they needed to do to set her free. She'd probably already been made a vampire against her will. He wasn't going to try to push marriage on her because of his own sense of responsibility.

"Well, let's go," Cort said, keeping his tone impassive, businesslike. "Hopefully the priest is still there, and we can wake him and find out what he knows."

"Do you really think he married us?" she asked.

"It seems like the most likely conclusion," he said, deciding he wasn't going to sugarcoat it. She probably wanted to be reassured that maybe they weren't married, but like it or not, he suspected the passed-out priest, or whatever denomination he was, had done the deed and they were hitched.

She nodded.

"So let's head there, and maybe we can find out how to get this situation rectified."

She nodded again and started down Burgundy in the direction of his apartment. Neither spoke the several blocks before they reached Toulouse, the street he lived on. But just as they were about to turn the corner, someone called out to them.

"Yoo-hoo, newlyweds! Cort and Katie!"

They both turned to see an older couple waving to them from the other side of the street.

"Do you have any idea who they are?" Cort murmured out of the corner of his mouth.

"Not a clue," Katie said even as she waved at them. The older couple beamed back, waited for a car to pass, then dashed across the street.

"How are our favorite newlyweds tonight?" the woman asked, giving both of them a brief hug, which neither Cort nor Katie returned with the same enthusiasm.

The man grinned, then hugged Katie, too. He offered Cort his hand, much to Cort's relief.

"I can't believe you two are headed back to Bourbon," the woman said. "I figured you would both need at least a day or two to recuperate. Ah, to be young again. Isn't that right, Ed?"

Ed nodded.

Cort got the feeling that's what Ed did. Agree.

"Well, we are a little . . ." Cort didn't know what to call it exactly.

"Hungover," Katie said, clearly deciding to go with the truth.

"You know what they say," the woman said and patted Katie's arm, "hair of the dog. Hair of that dog."

"We've tried," Katie told her.

"Well, come with us," the woman said, hooking her arm through Katie's. "We're headed to Johnny White's."

Katie looked down as if she were being held by a tentacle rather than an older woman's arm clad in a crocheted sweater.

"We were actually headed—to my—headed home," Cort corrected himself. After all, they did think they were happy newlyweds. It might seem odd if he referred to *his* apartment. Then again, he couldn't exactly say why it mattered what total strangers thought of their living situation.

"Oh, just a quick drink with your matron of honor," the woman insisted.

"Matron. Of. Honor?" Katie said, not keeping the shock off of her face.

Betty's eyes widened. "Don't tell me you forgot. We had such a good time."

"No—I—I didn't forget. The night is just a little bit of a blur."

Betty smiled, seemingly pleased with that answer. Cort supposed being sort of forgotten was better than totally forgotten.

"So now you see, you have to come have a drink with us," Betty stated. "Ed, tell them to join us."

Again, obedient Ed did as he was told. "Yes, join us."

Cort wondered if obedient Ed had been his best man.

"Just one drink," Betty said, tugging Katie's arm.

Katie grimaced, clearly wanting to rip her arm out of the woman's grasp, but she was too polite. Cort definitely knew that about his wife. She was always so kind and sweet.

"Jack and Coke. Jack and Coke," the parrot suddenly decided to pipe up. The damned drunk.

Both Betty and Ed laughed. "See, even your bird needs a little hair of the dog. Plus, I want to show you all the pictures I took at your party. I couldn't take any of the wedding, of course, because I was in it, and you know Ed, useless with technology."

Of course, Cort thought. *Silly Ed.*

Still, there were pictures of the wedding party? Cort looked at Katie, her expression stating that she'd rather be anywhere else right now, but when their eyes met, she nodded.

She wanted to look at the pictures, too.

What couple didn't want to look at photos of their forgotten wedding? Or, in this case, wedding party.

Katie smiled at the woman. "I guess one drink would be fine."

The couple looked tickled. Okay, Betty looked tickled. Ed looked relieved that his wife was getting her way. And Katie still smiled. Only Cort would know that smile wasn't her real one. Her real smile lit up her whole face and made her deep blue eyes shimmer with true joy. That smile was beautiful enough to fill him with awe.

His body reacted just thinking about it. Kind of sad, given he knew she was feeling anything but joyous at the moment.

Betty continued to hold Katie's arm as they started down Toulouse toward Bourbon.

"Elvis fan, huh?"

Cort started, surprised that Ed had spoken before being told to do so. Ed pointed to the cookie jar.

"Oh yeah, but this belongs to a friend of ours."

Ed nodded as if it was perfectly reasonable that Cort was wandering around Bourbon Street carrying a cookie jar. An Elvis cookie jar at that.

Cort supposed there was something to be said for Ed's long-suffering ways. He just didn't question.

Maybe that's what they all should be doing.

But when he looked at Katie, listening to Betty's story with that fake smile plastered to her face, he knew he had to ask questions and get the answers. For her, at least.

Johnny White's was several blocks back in the direction they'd come from, and if Cort had been thinking clearly and not fixating on Katie and her lackluster feelings toward their marriage, he'd have suggested they go back to Burgundy, then cut back down to Bourbon.

It was longer to go that way, but it wasn't as if ole Ed was going to question his reasoning. And Betty was too busy chattering Katie's ear off to notice anyway. And that would have kept them off Bourbon for a majority of the walk.

He studied Katie. She was doing a good job holding it together, but he could see that Bourbon Street was overwhelming her. Crowds and lights and noise were extreme sensory overload for a new vampire. It was like bringing a newborn to a rock concert. Not pleasant and not well-tolerated.

At his age, he barely registered the glaring lights, blaring music, and masses of revelers. But for Katie, the whole experience had to be downright torture. He'd seen that even Lafitte's had been difficult, and this was like Lafitte's times a thousand.

Betty still had her arm looped through Katie's and she continued to babble away, but Cort could see his wife wasn't truly paying attention.

She couldn't. Too many other stimuli bombarded her. And he could tell by the way her blue eyes darted from one thing to another, not really focusing, and the deathly paleness of her skin, she wanted to bolt. To just escape.

"Betty," he said, stepping up on the other side of Katie, "I hate to be so greedy, but I'm already missing my bride. Do you mind if I steal her away?"

Betty instantly released Katie's arm, grinning. "Of course not."

Cort shifted the cookie jar to the same side as the parrot. Katie didn't need that damned thing squawking, or pecking at her. Or singing. Man, he was so sick of the singing already.

He reached for Katie, tucking her against his side with his free arm. Again she surprised him with her willingness to lean against him. He knew she had to resent him. After all, she was feeling this way thanks to him.

Betty moved over to take Ed's hand, apparently moved by new romance.

Cort leaned his head toward Katie's, his mouth near her ear. "You're okay," he murmured softly. Soothingly. "Just focus on my voice."

She nodded, not speaking, and he suspected she couldn't. It was all too much.

"Just listen to me, focus on me." He rubbed a hand up and down her arm, in slow, reassuring strokes. "Listen to the sound of my voice and my touch."

KATIE WANTED TO groan with relief, which was still all she could do even though the sights and sounds of Bourbon Street no longer assaulted her. And *assault* was the absolute right word. She'd felt like the sounds of loud music, shouting people, and raucous laughter were attacking her ears. Her eyes ached and watered from the harsh flashing lights and the smells . . . In some ways, that one was the hardest for her to deal with. The foul scents of sweat and stale liquor. The rancid scent of old vomit and urine. And the harsh chemical overlay of the bleach they used every morning to wash down the street. But the smell that battered her, distracted her, filled her with a raging desire she had to use every bit of her willpower to control. She didn't even fully understand what the sweet, luring scent called her to do, she just knew with every fiber of her being she wanted to do it. And it scared her. But then Cort pulled her to his side, his arm strong, reassuring, and suddenly she felt better. Not perfect. Not normal. But she wouldn't have believed anything could have distracted her from the wild party that surrounded them. She was wrong.

Cort's nearness, his scent, the friction of his hand on her arm and strength of his body close beside her, all of him, seemed to center her and shield her from everything else.

Oh, she was still filled with longing. But the kind of longing she understood. His hand moved on her arm, skin stroking over skin and she ached to be in his arms, without the barrier of clothing, his body rubbing completely against hers. Another part of him deep inside her.

She wasn't sure if she could blush. But she suspected she could, because her cheeks burned. Of course the rest of her burned, too.

"That's it," he murmured, his voice husky and rich. "Just focus on me."

As if she could do anything else.

"We're almost there," he said, his breath brushing against her cheek and ruffling her hair.

She shivered.

"I know this is hard," he said, misunderstanding her shudder. "But it will get easier."

No, this feeling would never get easier, or less intense. Her attraction to Cort had a life of its own. Oh, sure, he didn't see that, but she did. She always had. A part of her wanted to simply turn her head and kiss him. His lips were right there. She could do it. Before he even realized what she intended.

But she didn't. Apparently being a vampire hadn't made her any braver, any more audacious. Damn it.

"Just a little farther."

Yes, just a little farther to his lips. She should kiss him, right? After all, they were newlyweds. Betty and Ed expected it.

She debated making her move. Just a quick turn of her head. That would most certainly block out anything else, but before she could muster the courage, Cort steered her up a couple of cracked and chipped concrete steps and into Johnny White's.

The sudden quiet startled Katie. The small, alleylike bar was open to Bourbon and contained several patrons, but it seemed like a warm cocoon compared to the craziness outside.

Still, she didn't move away. She couldn't. He felt too good. Like an anchor keeping her safe from being set adrift. A hunky, great-smelling anchor with an amazing body, killer smile, and those sexy, sleepy eyes.

Okay, maybe she was still losing it.

He led her to a barstool at the end of the bar, obviously trying to put as much space between her and the chaos outside. If he only knew what he was doing to her insides right now.

"Situations like this will get easier for you," he said.

Why'd he keep saying that? He was so wrong.

"You'll learn to block the lights and sounds and smells," he assured her.

Lights, sounds, smells. Right. That's what he was talking about. *Pull yourself together, girl.*

"Jack and Coke. Jack and Coke."

"Well, your bird certainly knows what it wants," Betty said, sliding onto the stool beside Katie. "He was making the same demands last night."

"Damn, this bird went everywhere with us. He probably knows exactly what we did last night," Cort murmured in Katie's ear.

"Can't you mind-meld with it or something?"

"Yeah, no. Not one of our abilities." He grinned, and more desire shot through her, electrical, powerful.

"Your bird was the life of the party." Betty laughed.

Katie glanced at the parrot, which bobbed its head as if to say, "Oh yeah. Oh yeah."

"That bird is so freaking eerie," she whispered to Cort, who nodded.

The bartender, an older woman with obviously dyed black hair, weary eyes, and a stern set to her jaw approached. Katie wasn't sure, but she suspected Cort was just as prepared as she was for the woman to tell them they had to go or owed money or did something so embarrassing it was better off forgotten.

But instead she simply asked in a tired voice, "What can I get you all?"

"Jack and Coke. Jack and Coke," the bird demanded, as always. Katie could have sworn his words were a little slurred. Of course, the bird was the only one who'd managed to get a drink so far.

Maybe their luck was changing.

Although as soon as the bartender left with all their orders, Cort murmured, "Let's see if we actually get to drink these," voicing Katie's own thoughts exactly.

"Don't jinx it."

Cort smiled again and her breath caught. God, he was so gorgeous.

"Let me show you the pictures," Betty said, managing to draw both of their attentions to her. She dug around in her purse, pulling out a small digital camera.

She turned it on, then began pushing a button in rapid succession.

"Now where are they?" the older woman said more to herself than them.

"Do we even show up in pictures?" Katie whispered to Cort, who chuckled.

"Yeah, that one is a myth, too. Vampires are too damned vain to not have reflections or show up in photos. After all, who doesn't want to admire their eternal youth?"

"Boy, we sure took a lot of pictures of the swamp tour today, didn't we, Ed?" Betty still pressed the little button, peering at the small screen on the back of the camera.

Ed nodded, although Katie already knew he hadn't taken a single picture today, nor, she suspected, had he paid any attention to how many his wife took either.

"Eureka," Betty cried as if she'd just discovered gold rather than photos of last night's drunken revelry. "Here they are."

She held the camera out to Katie. "Just press this button here to see the next one."

Katie accepted the camera and squinted down at the small screen, trying to make out what she was looking at. A picture of Cort and Drake mugging for the camera. Definitely a drunken picture, but not very revealing.

Cort leaned closer, and again Katie was distracted by his nearness and scent. Her body stirred, hungry, alive. Her fangs reacted, too, lengthening just a little, but the sensation startled her and they retracted.

"That one doesn't tell very much," Cort said, yet again voicing her thoughts. Eerie.

She gathered herself. "No, it doesn't."

She pressed the button. This one showed Wyatt, Cort, Saxon and . . .

"Is that Raven?" Cort said, disgust clear in his voice.

"Yes."

"Oh, that was your best man's name," Betty said. "I'd forgotten."

"Raven was my best man?" Cort said, now stunned as well as disgusted.

"Yes. Such a nice young man."

Katie looked at Cort and shrugged. She was pretty sure no one had ever described Raven that way before, but last night had apparently been an alternate universe. So he probably was nice last night.

In the photo, all of them were grinning widely, arms around each other. And from the background Katie could tell they were at the Old Opera House, the bar where both Katie and Cort worked.

In the background, Jacob the bartender, was giving Cort and Raven bunny ears. It was a pretty classic picture actually.

She pressed the button again. This time it was a picture of her and Cort. Cort held her in his arms, and she gazed up at him with utter adoration.

And he . . . he gazed at her with the same tender expression.

"I love that one," Betty said, and both Katie and Cort started. Katie brushed her hair away from her face, the action nervous, and a little self-conscious. Cort fidgeted with the sleeve of his shirt.

"You can just see how in love you two are." Betty sighed.

"Yes," Katie managed after a moment, her voice an odd croak as if her throat was swollen. She stared at the picture a moment longer, not daring to look at Cort, although she could tell out of the corner of her eye, he stared at it, too.

She pressed the button.

"Actually I was wrong," Betty said, leaning in on the other side of Katie. "That one is my favorite."

This time the picture actually sent chills through Katie. She looked at herself, held in Cort's strong arms, kissing. And not just a peck, but a deep, passionate kiss. His hands on her back and tangled in her hair. Her hands held his face. Anyone looking at this would see a couple sharing an intimate moment, a truly romantic kiss.

Katie stared at those people, unable to correlate that she was looking at herself and Cort. They might look like them, but those people had to be someone else.

And in truth, she felt jealous of them. She wanted that for herself. She wanted those feelings. She wanted that connection. That touch.

She couldn't look at him, and the total truth was, she wanted them with Cort.

"I was just telling Ed today that I can tell a couple who will last. And you two, well, I can just tell you two are going to last an eternity," Betty said, although her voice sounded far away like Katie was hearing it in a dream.

Katie continued to stare at that couple kissing. She and Cort kissing. She'd wanted to kiss him from the moment she'd met him. And apparently she had, but she didn't remember. Nothing.

"Here you go," the bartender said, placing glasses in front of both Katie and Cort.

At the same time, they reached for the tall glasses, and in unison, they both downed half of it.

Chapter Twelve

867-5309

(Who Can I Turn To?)

BESIDE him, Katie pulled in a deep breath while Cort took another long swallow of his drink, nearly polishing it off.

Clearly they were both shaken.

Her finger stayed on the button, as she clearly debated if she wanted to see more. Cort understood. Looking at these pictures was hard. It was hard to believe these things happened without them even knowing it.

But to her credit, she did press the button again. A picture of Betty and Ed with them lit up on the small screen. There was also one of Cort and Raven giving each other bunny ears. Now that was total weirdness. A picture of Drake and Wyatt doing shots. That was normal. Another of Saxon doing the hang-loose sign to the camera. Equally normal—if anyone could describe Saxon as normal. One of Katie sitting on Cort's lap, both of them laughing, but he could still see that expression on both their faces. It had been there in all the pictures of just the two of them.

Love. They really did look in love. Totally and genuinely in love.

Katie's hand shook as she lifted her glass to her lips, nearly finishing off her drink.

She pressed the button again to see a photo of a man who seemed to be covered in a layer of dirt and sweat, his filthy gray shirt that might very well have been white at one point clung to his tall, skinny frame. His equally dirty shorts threatened to slip off his narrow hips as his pose revealed he was dancing madly.

"Oh, that's some vagrant who came in to dance while we were listening to a band at Cajun Cabin right before we met up with you," Betty said with a chuckle, taking the camera. "That guy could really dance. Couldn't he, Ed?"

Ed nodded.

"What time was that?" Cort asked.

Betty pursed her lips in thought. "Oh let's see. That must have been around eleven or so, because your wedding happened around midnight. Isn't that right, Ed?"

Ed nodded.

Cort knew Ed wasn't exactly a bastion of accuracy, given that he'd agree to anything his wife said, but if Betty was right, they must have been off the riverboat fairly quickly after they all blacked out. Cort knew that Stella had reserved the riverboat until 2 A.M. Why hadn't they stayed on the boat and partied? Had something happened? Was Katie crossed over on the boat or afterward? Or had they married before the actual bite?

More mysteries. Damn.

"I guess that's all I have, although I could have sworn I took more," Betty said as she took the camera back. The older woman began browsing through the pictures, talking to Ed about this one and that.

Katie signaled to the bartender for another drink. Cort could see her hand still trembled.

"Are you okay?" he asked even though he knew the answer.

She nodded, then she shook her head. "Is it possible to feel embarrassed, ashamed, disappointed—and excited all at once?"

The bartender arrived, giving him a moment to think about her question. A question he didn't really like. Or rather he didn't like the implications of it. He could understand embarrassed. He was, too. And excited—well, he was assuming she was referring to having another clue about what happened last night. But ashamed and disappointed. Wow, now that didn't sound good at all.

Real or sham marriage, no man wanted a woman to be ashamed and disappointed about it. Okay, maybe he couldn't speak for all men in this position—if any other man had ever been in this position—all he knew was he wasn't pleased with her feeling these things about their nuptials.

He certainly hated the fact that he'd looked at those photos and felt excitement, too. Excitement at seeing himself touching her. Kissing her. Doing all the things he'd imagined doing to her.

And he had—and he couldn't remember a bit of it. Oh, cruel irony.

The bartender returned, and again Katie downed her drink. Another sure sign she was very agitated. In the time he'd known her, she'd never been a major drinker. He'd noted that, not only because he noted most things about this beautiful woman, but because the fact that she wasn't an overdrinker or major partier stood out in a town like New Orleans.

She was very upset. And that upset him.

"Well," she said once her drink was gone and she'd pulled herself up, stick straight, "those didn't reveal too much."

Cort nodded, even though he was in total disagreement. Those pictures revealed a whole damned lot to him. For example, how much he was into Katie. His desire for her might as well have been written on his face in marker.

I'm crazy about Katie Lambert.

He wondered if she saw it, too. Was that part of why she felt the way she did?

"Well," he said, willing himself to sound as calm as she did, "we know we were at the Old Opera House at some point. And Raven was with us. And that, again, it would seem that we are married."

"Yes," she agreed, her tone actually sounding almost sad.

Wasn't it bad enough she didn't want to be married to him, did she have to be depressed about it, too?

"I wonder how Raven ended up being your best man?" she said, reaching for her drink, only to realize it was empty. She dropped her hand back to her lap.

"Another?" he asked, and she shook her head.

"I don't know. That is a mystery," he said. "I personally can't stand the guy."

"I'm not a fan either," Katie said, and her admission pleased him.

Now there was his worst nightmare—Katie dating Raven after their annulment.

"I'm glad to hear that," he said. "I'd have to deny you an annulment if you told me you had a thing for him."

Sure, he'd said that to be funny, but he wasn't sure it was totally untrue.

And apparently it hadn't sounded like a joke to her either, because she turned slightly on her barstool to study him.

Shit, he shouldn't have said that.

But to his relief, she managed a small laugh. "You really must dislike the guy."

Cort disliked the idea of him anywhere near Katie. And if he was going to be really honest, at least with himself, Raven's obvious interest in Katie was probably the primary reason he didn't like the man.

He smiled, then used her words. "I'm not a fan."

She smiled back and he got lost for a moment. He loved her smile. It was light, sunshine, warm and cheery. He'd been drawn to that from the first moment he saw her.

"Maybe I took some pictures on my phone, too," she said suddenly, looking around her. "Oh wait, I don't have my purse. Oh no. I hope it's at your place."

"It probably is," Cort reassured her, although who knew, with the night they had? He patted his own pocket, remembering his phone was in his jeans.

He dug it out and pressed the sequence of buttons to get him to his camera.

"I don't have any," he said, not surprised. He didn't use his phone for much but phone calls and the occasional text. He noticed he didn't have any of those either. He wondered what the other guys had found out. Probably as little as they had.

He set the phone on the bar as he reached for his drink again.

"We really had a great time with you all last night," Betty said, her attention no longer on her camera. She shifted so she was smiling at both of them. "You two are just the cutest couple. Ed and I can't wait to see your bands play."

How weird to know that these people, these strangers, didn't see them as strangers. And why should they? Betty and Ed had been a part of their wedding. That was bonding.

Cort wanted to ask where they'd been married but couldn't bring himself to admit he had no idea. Especially since this woman seemed to consider them the romance of the century. William and Kate had nothing on Cort and Katie and their forgotten wedding.

"And your story is just so romantic," Betty said with a sigh, backing up his theory. The older woman took a sip of her drink, her expression dreamy.

What story?

Cort glanced at Katie.

"It is romantic," Katie said. "But what especially about our story did you find romantic?"

Betty made a face like it should be obvious, which for people without complete memory loss, it probably would be.

"Well, that Cort saved your life," Betty said, shaking her head.

"Oh right," Katie said. Cort could tell that comment didn't trigger any memories. Nor for him.

But Cort couldn't help find the comment rather ironic, since he knew he was still the prime candidate for actually taking her life. Sure, he gave her a new, immortal existence, but still, to cross her over, Cort had to have drained her mortal life.

Katie glanced at him, but then refocused on Betty. "It is so romantic. Do you mind telling us the story?"

When Betty made a confused face, Katie added, "Both Cort and I actually love hearing it, too."

Katie smiled then so radiant and so sincere, that Cort almost believed her. They did love hearing the story.

"Well, I have to admit that when you shared it with me, I might have been a little tipsy," Betty said, a little embarrassed, which she hardly needed to be with them, "but you did tell us that Katie had a terrible accident and Cort saved her. You even gave her your own blood to rescue her."

Gave her his own blood. Cort would have had to give her

his own blood to transform her into a vampire. Another indication he was the biter—which he'd suspected right from the start anyway.

But Katie had had a terrible accident?

"A terrible accident," Katie said, her tone pondering, their thoughts synched.

Then Katie seemed to realize how she sounded, because she nodded, and said definitely, "Yes, it was a terrible accident."

"It sounded horrific," Betty said, reaching out to pat Katie's hand, although she looked almost as puzzled as they did. "Although, you didn't really tell us exactly what happened. Aside from Cort being your hero."

Cort could tell Betty wanted more details.

Oh, if only we knew, Betty.

"I don't actually like to talk about that part," Katie said, offering Betty a sad smile. "It's—it's difficult, you know, to remember that part."

Very difficult. Damned near impossible.

"I can only imagine," Betty said, sympathetically patting Katie's hand again. "But thankfully Cort was there."

"Yes. Thankfully."

Katie couldn't be feeling nearly as grateful as she managed to sound. How could she be pleased about being a vampire against her will? And at his hands—or rather his fangs? It was a wonder she didn't hate him.

Hell, maybe she did. Cort suspected it would be hard to tell if the sweet, sunny Katie hated anyone. Not a comforting thought at this moment.

Beside him the bird shuffled around, and he thought he heard the awful creature say something about slapping some fat. Or maybe riding a wave. He wasn't really sure. He was too busy watching Katie, trying to read her expression. The real one beyond her fake smile.

She must have sensed his intent look, because she turned to him, regarding him back. Looking directly into her eyes, he could see all those emotions still there.

He opened his mouth to say they should leave, when he heard a loud clatter next to him. He looked around, trying to figure out what caused the noise.

"Your phone," Katie said, pointing to the floor beside his stool.

The bird stood on the edge of the bar, bobbing its head and looking quite pleased with itself.

Cort rose from his stool, then bent down to pick up the phone. He shoved it in his pocket, suddenly feeling too frustrated to deal with any of this. All they were doing was going around in circles. For everything they did find out about last night, there was just another question.

And he was sick of it.

He couldn't fix Katie being a vampire. But he could fix the marriage situation. And as far as whatever else happened, he didn't give a shit. They'd go find the damned priest, find out about an annulment, and things would go back to normal as much as they could.

"Okay, we have to go," he stated, his tone so gruff that even Betty didn't argue this time. And of course, if Betty didn't argue, Ed wouldn't think of it.

Katie, however, looked surprised by his sudden change of mood. Her brow creased slightly, and now she studied him. Even the bird stopped its pleased head bobbing and spread its wings and cawed loudly, as if to share opposition to the idea. Adding to that, it tottered back to its drink.

"Screw that, buddy," he muttered to the bird. "You are done, too."

He reached for the feathered bastard, which pecked him, yet again. Cort snatched his hand away, shaking out the sharp pain.

"Then stay here, you asshole," he growled lowly to the beast, and he reached for the Elvis cookie jar instead.

Remembering they had drinks to pay for, he shoved his free, non-injured hand into his pocket.

"We've got the drinks."

Cort's attention shot back to the older couple, startled. It had been Ed who offered to pay. Maybe he did make decisions in the relationship after all.

"Thank you," Cort said, giving the man a genuine nod of appreciation.

"Are you ready?" Cort said to Katie.

She nodded, still looking confused by his sudden need to leave. Betty insisted on hugging them both again. Finally, Cort gestured for Katie to go ahead of him, then they both started toward the door.

"Oh, your bird," Betty called.

Cort turned to tell them that bird wasn't his and he could stay right where he was, but the bird took that moment to decide he, too, was leaving after all.

The parrot flapped its wings and swooped off the bar, navigating the narrow room without incident to land right on Cort's shoulder.

The few patrons in the bar applauded as if the bird had done some amazing feat of acrobatics.

Cort nodded in a very feeble attempt to be gracious, then he stepped out onto Bourbon Street.

"Next time you peck me, buddy, you are going straight to the pound," he muttered to the winged beast.

The parrot bobbed its head in antagonistic response.

Chapter Thirteen

TAKE THE MONEY AND RUN

"**W**HAT?**"** Wyatt grabbed the phone from Stella, mortified. He winced when he saw the image of himself, grinning the smile of the very drunk, his hair looking insane. He had taken off his T-shirt and put on Trudy the bartender's corset. His chest was shoved up and spilling out the top. It was horrifying. "Nigel is right. Red is not my color."

"And you look fat," Drake commented with a crack of laughter.

"Why would I do that?" It just didn't seem like his brand of fun, but if the guys had egged him on, it was possible. He just wished he could remember because it did look like they'd been having fun. Vampires cutting loose.

"I have no idea. Nor do I understand why Saxon is riding the mechanical bull." Stella turned the phone and showed them Saxon holding on to the bull for dear life, Drake crouched down on the mat in front of it like he was spurring the fake animal on.

Wyatt laughed. "What the hell? Is that the Bourbon Cowboy? We never go to that place."

"Am I the bullfighter?" Drake shook his head. "Why do I have the feeling the bull won?"

"Oh, he did." Stella swiped her finger on the screen and they watched the progression of Saxon losing control and flying into the air while Drake raised his fist, mouth open on a yell. Then Saxon hit Drake as he fell, knocking him forward into the horns. In the next picture, he was holding his bloody mouth and they were both laughing. "You didn't exactly take the bull by the horns."

"I think we have an explanation for how you lost your tooth." Wyatt shook his head. "Man, we're idiots. Is there any video, Stella?"

Drake rubbed his jaw. "Seriously? I lost my fang on a mechanical bull? That's not a good story. That's lame."

"It's not like you fell and chipped it on your toilet," Stella told him. "That would be lame."

"No, that would be gross."

"Here's a video." Stella held the phone out again so they could all see the screen. "What magical moment are we about to witness now?"

The camera was bouncing around, whoever held it not exactly steady, as the clip played. The back of Saxon's head was in view, and not much else. The music of the street faded in and out as the cameraman walked, though Wyatt couldn't pinpoint where exactly they were.

"Well, this is stupid," Drake remarked.

"Seriously. Who taped this? I'm assuming Benny, right?"

"I guess," Stella said. "It's his phone. But then again, you all weren't exactly behaving the way you normally do. How did Benny even end up hanging out with you guys in the first place?"

"I have no idea." That was the real mystery, in Wyatt's opinion. He couldn't imagine any of them just dragging Benny into their group to hang out for the night. Especially dressed in a priest's robe.

"Congratulations! Whooo!" a random female voice screamed out.

Saxon's head moved slightly out of the way and they saw Katie, the mortal Cort had apparently turned the night before, smiling and waving. "Thanks!" she yelled back. When she turned, they all saw the JUST MARRIED pageant sash she was wearing. And heard Benny's bodyless voice call out, "I married them!"

Well, that explained a thing or two. Wyatt glanced over at Stella. "I guess we should call Cort and tell him he's not really married. I don't think Benny is a minister of anything."

Stella gave a small laugh. "Minister of muscles, maybe."

Why did Benny's muscles have to come up? Wyatt shook his head. "Still doesn't explain why Katie is now a vampire and why Benny was even with us in the first place."

"I'm guessing the answers to those questions are as stupid as the answers we've already gotten," Drake said. "I think I'm going home. This is our last night off for four days and my tooth hurts like a motherfucker. It figures that even undead, going to the dentist sucks."

"Alright. Feel better, man." Wyatt clamped Drake on the shoulder and watched him head out the door. "We could probably give Benny his phone back and head out." Wyatt wanted to take Stella back to his place and have a repeat performance of her on his lap.

"No, wait." Stella was sitting on a barstool and she tapped Benny's phone again. "There's another video."

Wonderful. What stupidity would they get to view now? "Am I wearing a dress this time?"

"No dress. Look." Stella held it out for him to see. "It looks like *The Blair Witch Project.*"

It did. Benny was obviously running at full speed. They could hear his heavy breathing and he yelled, "Come on! Come on! Run!" The camera turned and they caught a bouncing shot of Saxon's panicked face.

"Go, go!" Saxon said. He looked behind him, clearly scared.

The phone dropped to the ground, the voices no longer clear. Benny obviously picked the phone back up, but the video stopped there.

"What was that?" Wyatt asked. "They both look terrified."

"I have no idea." Stella rubbed her forehead. "What's terrifying is that all of this happened and none of us remember it. Not that I was there for this, but where was I? It's so damn frustrating and unnerving."

"Agreed." Seeing yourself moving on camera when you had no memory of it was a truly bizarre experience. "And where is Saxon, by the way? He should have been back here by now."

"Do you think he's in danger?"

"I don't know what to think," Wyatt said truthfully. "It feels like nothing out of the ordinary has happened in ten years and now all of a sudden everything is crazy."

"I know exactly what you mean."

The bartender tapped Wyatt on the shoulder. "Are you ordering a drink or not? Because about nine thousand people would like this stool."

Wyatt glared back. He knew bartenders worked off of tips. He did, too. But the guy didn't have to be a dick about it. And hadn't he tried to get drinks ten minutes ago and been ignored? "We're leaving."

"Wonderful."

"Let's head toward Saxon's. If he's walking back, we'll pass him on the street."

"Okay. Let me give Benny his phone back." Stella walked over to the other bar and passed the phone to Benny. She got a kiss on the cheek for her efforts. Wyatt refrained from rolling his eyes. After all, he could totally understand digging Stella. He suffered from the same problem himself.

"Let's go." Stella gripped the strap of her purse and tossed her red hair back.

"I'm going to have Cher stuck in my head for the rest of the night." Wyatt stepped out into the fresh night air. Or as fresh as Bourbon Street got. He wasn't the least bit sorry to leave Bounce behind.

"Don't be hating on Cher. She's awesome."

"I'm not hating. I just said it's going to be stuck in my head all night. That's not the same thing. Though I have to say no one was at all friendly in that place."

"I know. It's like they were drinking Hater-ade."

Wyatt laughed. He put his arm around Stella. "I'm glad to see you haven't lost your sense of humor even if it is goofy."

She made a sound of irritation and elbowed him in the side. "I'm not goofy."

"No. You're gorgeous."

She stopped walking.

Wyatt looked down at her, curious to why she'd stopped in the middle of the street. What he saw made his eyes go wide. She was looking at him like she cared about him. Like she wanted nothing more than to be in his arms, kissing him. Her lips were parted, her eyes were dark and glassy with desire, and her body leaned toward him.

It was a look filled with more than lust. There was a raw emotion there as well, an intimate longing, and Wyatt didn't have a choice. He had to kiss her right here, on the street.

Not that it would be the first or last time someone had shown affection on Bourbon, but it was a first for him. Using one hand, Wyatt cupped her chin and tilted her head up toward him. Then he bent down and kissed her gently, wanting his lips to convey how much he admired and respected her. How much he loved her.

Because he loved her.

He could admit it.

Hell, he'd already admitted it.

She had run then.

But she wasn't running now.

She was kissing him back, with more tenderness than passion, and Wyatt felt his heart swell. She was giving in, he could feel it.

"Wyatt . . ."

"Yeah?" She was going to say something important, he was sure. Something that would change the course of his immortal life.

"Ack!"

That wasn't it.

Stella stumbled as someone plowed into her, and Wyatt grabbed her arm to keep her upright.

He was ready to give attitude if whoever bumped her didn't apologize, but when he focused on the intruder, he swore. It was Saxon.

"What the hell are you doing?" he asked indignantly. He and Stella had been having a moment, damn it. Trust Saxon to ruin it.

"Sorry, Stella." Saxon put his hands on her shoulders to stabilize her but then took off running down the street.

"What are you doing?" Wyatt called after him.

"Gotta go. Trouble."

Looking around, Wyatt didn't see any obvious reason why Saxon was running. There was no one after him and no one else on the street looked concerned. He was about to ask Stella if they should follow Saxon when she took off.

"Well, that answers that question." Wyatt starting jogging after both of them.

Saxon was running full steam, yelling, "Ahhhh," the whole time.

Wyatt wanted to laugh. It was just too ridiculous.

"Saxon! Stop!" Stella shouted, her arms pumping as she ran to keep up with him.

Saxon was dodging and weaving like a Dickens pickpocket, even going sideways to slide through a pack of women in skirts and heels. Stella veered around the women entirely and lost a few feet on Saxon. Wyatt was torn between wanting to hang back and see how this absurdity played out, and just tackling Saxon's sorry ass to the ground. His foot landed in a puddle of God only knew what, splashing up onto his jeans, and he nixed the tackling-to-the-ground idea. He didn't want to touch anything on the street with any part of his body other than the bottom of his shoes.

So he went with plan B. With a burst of vampiric speed, he passed Stella and fell in line with Saxon. When there was a break in the crowd he slammed into his friend, shoving him to the left until he had him pinned on the wall. "What the hell is going on?"

"Let me go! Raven is after me. He's going to chop my head off and drain my blood. And then I'll be dead. Like for real dead."

Saxon's eyes were darting wildly around Wyatt and he looked genuinely afraid.

"Raven?" Wyatt eased up on Saxon and also looked around. Stella had drawn up next to him and he moved closer to her, his protective instincts kicking in. He still didn't see anything. No sign of the telltale shaved head. "Why would Raven want to kill you?"

"He says I owe him money."

"Do you?"

"Not that I'm aware of. But I'm not always aware of a lot."

That was the God's honest truth. Wyatt dusted off the front of Saxon's T-shirt. "Did he say why?"

"No, just that he was going to kill me if I didn't give him the money. I told him I didn't have it and he hit me. So I ran."

"He hit you? What an ass." Wyatt frowned at Stella. She looked worried.

"Did he say anything else?"

"Something about shooting Bambi. I thought it was Bambi's mother who got shot. I'm so confused."

"Where the hell is he then?" Wyatt wanted to have a word or two with him about roughing up Saxon. That was kind of like kicking a dog who was happy to see you. It wasn't right, and Wyatt wanted to rectify the situation. He had some money and he'd pay Raven off if he had to.

The wording Raven had used earlier in the night came back to him. *"Watch your back."* Wyatt could say the same to Raven.

"Bambi? Didn't Nigel say that was the name of Johnny's girlfriend?" Stella bit her lip in worry.

"Yeah." That just added yet another piece to a very confusing puzzle. "Raven was working tonight. I'm going to take you two back to my place then I'm going to have a word with Raven. He must be about done with his break and I can head him off at the door."

Stella shook her head. "We're going with you."

It figured. She was stubborn, no doubt about it. "Stella, no. This may be a bit of an argument."

"Which is why you shouldn't be alone."

Yeah, that was stubborn. "I'll be at Famous Door. There will be fifty people there, easily. And you know Sanford is the bouncer at the door. He'll have my back."

"Johnny was my brother. If he was in trouble, I have the right to know."

Wyatt sighed. They could stand there all night arguing about it, or he could just give Stella what she wanted. "Fine." He had a feeling he'd just caught a glimpse of his future. Funny how he wasn't anything other than thrilled by that thought. He loved Stella as she was and he wanted to make her happy. Being with her made him happy. It was win-win, as far as he was concerned.

Saxon was slinking away. Wyatt shot an arm out and grabbed him. "You're going, too, then."

"Why? Do you have a death wish for me?"

"No one is going to kill you. Raven's riff on 'Crazy Train' might damage your eardrums but nothing is going to kill you. Buck up, bro."

"Fine," Saxon grumbled. "Though I have to say I'd rather go home."

"We all would, trust me." Wyatt didn't mean that he would like to go home. He was agreeing with Saxon literally. He would definitely like Saxon to go home and not encounter him for about a week, but that wasn't going to happen. "But you live in the opposite direction and I'm not walking you back."

Wyatt was getting sick of tromping up and down the street. If one more tourist threw beads down onto him from a balcony, he was going to jump up there and bite them. Hard.

Raven wasn't at work and after a few inquiries Wyatt confirmed he was on break. They stood by the beer tub, prepared to wait. The cart was cold on the back of his legs as he glanced around the bar. Nothing looked out of the ordinary. Couple of women with big hair and short denim skirts tearing up the dance floor. Older guy alone creeping on a trio of thirtysomethings. Shot girls wandering around in hot pants and tank tops, trying to fob off watered-down Jell-O shots on horny men. The usual.

"I'm going to step outside and call Cort," he yelled into Stella's ear. The deejay had the bass pumping and it was too loud to really communicate in the bar. He wanted to tell Cort what they'd seen on the video.

She nodded.

"Wait right here. Don't go anywhere."

She rolled her eyes.

Hey, a guy couldn't be too careful.

Waving to the doorman, Wyatt stepped outside and took a few steps down Conti to the relative quiet. He dialed Cort. "Hey, man, what's up?"

"I don't know. We haven't found out jack."

"Well, we've figured out the priest with us last night who supposedly married you is really a stripper. I don't think that's legal and binding."

"For real?"

"Yeah, so you're off the hook." Not that Katie the washboard player wasn't a cute girl, because she was, but marriage was a big step. Or so he'd been told. Wyatt had never taken the plunge himself.

"Yeah, I guess so."

Cort didn't sound nearly as thrilled as Wyatt would have expected him to. But he had more important things to worry about. "Hey, you ever hear anything about Johnny or Saxon owing Raven money?"

"No. Why?"

"Saxon got roughed up by Raven, who said Saxon owes him some cash. Did you know Johnny was seeing a girl?"

"Johnny was always seeing a girl."

Good point. "This one's name was Bambi. Ring any bells?"

"Uh, no. That one I would remember. Look, I gotta go. The parrot keeps trying to peck my balls. I swear, I'm going to kill this thing."

Wyatt fought the urge to cross his legs. Yikes. He valued his testicles highly himself. "Alright, I'll talk to you later."

Putting his phone back in his pocket, he went back into the bar.

Only to discover that Stella and Saxon were not there.

They were gone.

Chapter Fourteen

THE CALL OF THE RAVEN

STELLA played Rock, Paper, Scissors with Saxon and wondered when this night was going to end. She wanted to go back to bed and sleep for two days. She wanted to wake up next to Wyatt, tucked in warm and cozy under his arm.

That thought made her push up off the beer tub and stand up straight. She did?

"One, two, three." Saxon threw out paper.

She did rock.

"Ha-ha!" he said.

But she was barely paying attention. She was wondering if her feelings for Wyatt were confused by Johnny's death. Maybe she just wanted comfort, companionship. It wouldn't be fair to Wyatt to lead him on if that was the case. But how was she supposed to know for sure? It wasn't like she had any real experience with relationships. She'd never been in love. She'd been in lust. She'd had crushes. But true, deep, soul mate kind of love, that she'd never experienced. Which was kind of pathetic, now that she thought about it. How had she gotten to be more than a hundred years old and never fallen in love? Or had a man fall in love with her?

Stella suddenly felt like she was going to cry. She swiped at her face. "Saxon, I have something in my eye."

"Yeah, your finger."

Oh, geez. She glared at him. "I'm going to the restroom to flush it out." To cry in private in a stall. "I'll be right back."

She never made it to the restroom. When she got to the entrance, arms around her waist yanked her up the stairs and into the back room.

"What the hell?" Stella kicked and elbowed whoever had grabbed her. It had to be a vampire because he didn't let go. A mortal would have been doubled over from the impact and would have dropped her.

"Calm down."

She whirled around and found herself face-to-face with Raven. "What are you doing?" Shoving at him, she said, "Get your hands off of me."

He did let her go, but he blocked her entrance back into the bar. "Just give me a minute. I don't want to hurt you, Stella."

"You punched Saxon," she said dryly, arms loose and at her sides. She hadn't been in a lot of altercations but she did know how to defend herself if necessary.

"He owes me money."

"Hitting Saxon is like kicking a kitten."

"He borrowed five hundred bucks last night and blew it at the casino. When I asked him when he could pay me back he told me money is the root of all evil. It got worse from there. Having a conversation with him is like talking to a stoned twelve-year-old."

Well, Raven did have a point. "Five hundred bucks is a lot of money," she said begrudgingly. "And I'll talk to him about paying you back. But please refrain from punching those less mentally fortunate than yourself."

"Okay, sorry. He just irritated me."

Stella sighed. Saxon was irritating, she couldn't deny it. "Was there something else you wanted?" Raven didn't look like he was quite done with the conversation, but frankly, she was. She wanted to find Wyatt and go home. With Wyatt. There, she'd admitted it.

She wanted to cuddle with him. Feel his strong arms around her supporting her while she relaxed and slept off the remnants of this wicked hangover.

"I wanted to ask you out."

"What?" Stella just stared at him. She'd known Raven for at least twenty years and he'd never once expressed any interest in her. Not that she had noticed. Why did that always happen? You went years without any male interest and then suddenly they were crawling out of the woodwork. It was like they could smell competition and it roused them into action.

"You know, with Johnny's death and everything, it just made me think that this isn't forever, you know? That we need to live each night to the fullest."

She'd never thought of Raven as a deep guy and he looked uncomfortable with the words coming out of his own mouth. She wasn't sure what to make of the whole thing. Raven was a hedonist. Having him interested in her was just hard to believe. "I can definitely appreciate what you're saying. But now isn't a good time."

"It's Axelrod, isn't it? You're seeing him."

"I wouldn't say that precisely." She wasn't sure what she and Wyatt were doing.

"Shit, I knew it. I guess I shouldn't have dragged my feet. Same with the washboard player. I'm striking out all over the place."

Raven had been eyeing Katie, too? That was flattering to think that she was just one of a number of women on his list. Charming guy, that Raven. "Sorry. Hey, do you know Bambi, the girl my brother was dating?" It seemed likely that Raven would know a stripper and Saxon had mentioned something about Raven shooting Bambi.

"Sure."

"Do you know where she is tonight?"

"She was at Erin Rose fifteen minutes ago." Raven glanced back into the bar. "I have to go back onstage."

Stella nodded. "You ever want to shoot her?"

Raven started. "What? Why the hell would I do that? Are you okay, Stella?"

Not really.

She couldn't decide if Raven was the type to drug them or not. He certainly wasn't acting sinister, just more like a douche bag. She decided to see if she could get a reaction from him. "Johnny's blood vial is missing. Have you seen it?"

Raven gave her a long look. "No. I would hunt that down if I were you. Not a good thing to lose track of."

Stella wasn't sure what that meant but before she could question him further Raven was gone, taking the steps two at a time onto the stage and picking up his guitar.

Had he seriously just cornered her in the storage room because he wanted to ask her out? It seemed suspect. But she didn't really have any choice but to take him at face value.

She figured she could stop at the local bar across the street and see if she could find Bambi and ask her some questions. What, she wasn't exactly sure. Pausing on the edge of the dance floor, she glanced around. No Wyatt. No Saxon. Seriously?

She went out the front door. Still no sign of either of them.

Wyatt was the one who had told her so pointedly not to go anywhere and then he disappeared. Typical man. Couldn't make up his mind.

If he thought she was going to stand around looking abandoned, he was crazy. A woman alone in a bar was a target for more stupidity than she was prepared to deal with tonight. Or any *more* stupidity than she was prepared to deal with.

Erin Rose was a hole in the wall. It always smelled like fried food and something else that she'd never quite been able to identify. The counters were sticky and the air stale, but the bartenders were awesome and it was a quiet place for locals who worked the street to sneak away from the raucous tourist places. Stella hadn't been there in a while, but she waved to the bartender in the back. "Hey, what's up, Peter?"

"Not much. How you been? Sorry to hear about Johnny." The bartender was tall with dark hair and a slew of tattoos racing up and down his arms. He wiped the counter down with a rag as he gave her a look of sympathy.

"Thanks. I appreciate it." Would this tightness in her chest ever go away?

She glanced around the bar. There was only one other woman in the room and a couple of guys. Taking a drink from Peter, who remembered that she preferred red wine, she changed stools, aligning herself next to the blonde, who glanced at her and gave a sharp smile.

"Hey, I know you," she said. "You're Johnny's sister."

"Yes, I am. Are you Bambi?"

That was greeted with a snort. "No, I am not that tramp. I'm Karen. I bartend at the Door. Day shift."

That would explain why Stella didn't know her. But how did she know Stella? "I guess you knew my brother?"

Karen waved her hand, an unlit cigarette between two fingers. "Just casually. He was a big flirt. Happy guy though. Never thought he would kill himself. That's really sucky."

"Tell me about it."

"I'm sorry."

"Thanks." Stella shifted on her stool, studying the vibrant blue eyeliner Karen had penciled in uneven lines above each of her eyes. "So Bambi is a tramp?"

"Totally. I kinda had a thing for Johnny but then I realized that he wasn't my type because he always went for chicks like Bambi. Double-D disasters. Not my scene, you know?"

Oh, yeah. She wasn't into that scene. As her less than buxom chest proved. She puffed it out to show Karen. "I prefer the natural look myself. Even if there isn't much to look at."

Karen laughed. "Me, too, girl." Twisting in her chair, she shoved her chest to Stella. "A cup."

Stella smiled, in harmony. Then almost fell off her stool as she focused on the necklace dangling just above Karen's breasts.

It was Johnny's blood vial.

What the hell.

"Where did you get that?" she asked shrilly, pointing to the necklace. Maybe she should proceed with caution, but she was too emotional to hold back.

"Huh? Get what?" Karen looked startled, and eased back on her stool away from Stella.

"That necklace." Stella supposed it was technically possible that more than one person could have a skull pendant wrapping around a vial containing red liquid. Blood. It was possible. But not very freaking likely.

"Oh. Wyatt Axelrod gave it to me last night. Do you know him? He plays bass with Cort."

Did she know him? Oh, she knew him. She knew every sorry inch of him. The scum-sucking, sexy, lying rat-bastard asshole. "That's my brother's necklace," she told Karen, well aware that her voice sounded tight and venomous.

The other woman got a little defensive, which was probably natural under the circumstances. "Well, why would Wyatt have it? And why would he give it to me?"

That was the million-flipping-dollar question. "I want it back." She held her hand out, all pretense of politeness gone. She was a vampire on the edge.

How could Wyatt play her like that? Pretending to be so concerned? Why had he lied about the necklace when he knew how much it meant to her? What did he really know about Johnny's death and last night, and how could she possibly trust him?

"No way, you crazy bitch." Karen picked up her bottle of beer and moved three stools over.

Stella followed her, anger driving blood into her face and making her temple pulse. She knew she needed to calm down, that Karen was an innocent bystander, mortal to boot, but she couldn't seem to stop herself. "How do you know Wyatt? Have you had sex with him?"

She couldn't even believe she'd just said that. Never in her entire long life had she uttered such confrontational and irrational words. If Wyatt had slept with Karen what business was it really of hers?

Peter had moved over to them. "Stella. You need to take it down a notch."

Now she was being reprimanded by the bartender, which only served to piss her off further. "I'll take it down when she answers the question. Actually, when she gives me Johnny's necklace back."

"I know your brother just died, but calm down, sweetie. Maybe you shouldn't be out drinking tonight. You want me to call you a cab?"

Peter was being sweet and rational but Stella didn't want to be rational. The world had ceased to be rational the second Johnny had purposely thrown open his curtains and barbequed himself. "No, I do not want a cab. I want that necklace."

"It was given to me, fair and square. I'm not giving it back."

"Bitch," Stella accused. If someone wanted their dead brother's necklace back, you should give it to them. It was just the decent thing to do.

"You're the bitch. How do I know you're even telling the truth?"

"Here's the truth—I'm taking it." Stella had spent her entire life being polite, doing the right thing, taking care of others. Being in control. She lost her control in one fell swoop when she reached over and yanked at the necklace, breaking the chain. Gripping it in her fist, she pulled it away from Karen, even as the woman screamed and grabbed for it.

"Stella, you need to leave," Peter told her. "Or I'm calling the cops."

"Fine. I'm leaving." Now that she had the necklace. She pushed back off her stool and stuffed the necklace in the front pocket of her jeans.

What she didn't anticipate was that not every woman spent her life restraining herself. Not every woman overthought things the way Stella did. Some women just reacted.

Like Karen.

Who jumped on Stella's back and knocked her to the floor.

Chapter Fifteen

DO NOT DISTURB

SHE shouldn't have said what she had, Katie thought as she followed Cort down the first side street and away from Bourbon.

She was willing to bet her admissions about how she'd felt about those pictures had freaked him out. As soon as she'd said it, she'd wanted to take the words back. Especially admitting she was disappointed and excited. He had to have realized what that meant. And even though she was embarrassed at admitting those feelings, the feelings were still there.

Even thinking about those pictures, she was excited by them. By being in his arms. By having kissed him. And she was bitterly disappointed she didn't remember it. And of course she felt embarrassed and ashamed that she'd been that drunk or whatever had happened to them, period. But at least she wasn't alone in her overindulgence.

Of course, that wasn't making her feel any better.

Especially the way Cort was striding down the street like he couldn't wait to get away from her.

She doubled her steps to catch up with him. He glanced at her and slowed his pace.

"I'm—I'm sorry," she said, "if I said anything back there to make you . . . I—I guess I should have kept my feelings to myself."

Cort's gaze stayed focused ahead of him. "You can't help the way you feel."

Katie nodded, even though she knew Cort wouldn't see it, but she couldn't speak. She didn't expect him to return her attraction. After all, he'd never shown any sign of interest before, but she also didn't expect this reaction. He seemed almost—angry.

Talk about rejection. Her desire for him pissed him off. Wow. That was pretty harsh.

Neither spoke even as they stepped into Cort's silent apartment. Cort immediately went to the bathroom, not even putting down the cookie jar or the bird.

He returned seconds later. "The priest is gone."

"Oh." Katie wasn't sure what else to say. She knew Cort was disappointed. He wanted answers. But more important, he wanted to find out about the annulment. "You didn't really expect him to still be there, did you?"

He gave her a long look, and for a second, she wondered if he knew more than he was telling her. But then he just crossed over to the kitchen counter and put down the cookie jar with more force than necessary. The bird cawed loudly at the sound.

"Get the fuck off me," Cort yelled, shaking his arm. The bird cawed again, but flew away to perch on top of the refrigerator.

For some reason that was the last straw for Katie.

"You don't have to take out your frustrations on the stupid bird," she shouted. "I know you are angry with me. I know you are upset that I'm a vampire, because you feel responsible for me and you don't want to. And I certainly know you are even more upset that we're married. But most of all, I know you just want to be rid of me."

Cort turned away from the counter, his usually sleepy eyes wide.

"Well, don't you worry about it," Katie continued, "I'm sure I can go to the courthouse or something and file the annulment. As far as being a vampire, there seems to be plenty of them in this city to get tips from, I won't bother you. And right now, I'll help you out with your last problem, too. I'm leaving, and you can forget any of this ever happened."

She turned to leave, but before she could even take a step, Cort had grabbed her wrist.

"Is that what you think?" he said.

"Well, duh," she responded, her unusual anger apparently making her childish, too. But she didn't care. She was hurt and upset and scared.

And very, very mad at herself, because even in this state she was still altogether too aware of Cort's hand on her skin.

"Katie, I'm not angry with you. Hell, none of this is your fault. I feel guilty that in one night, I turned your whole world upside down. But I don't blame any of that on you."

Katie stared up into his beautiful dark brown eyes, lost in his sorrowful expression.

"And I don't blame you," she said.

"I will admit I was hurt that you're ashamed and disappointed to be married to me."

Katie started to speak, but Cort raised a hand to stop her.

"I realize you can hardly be thrilled about finding yourself married to someone who is little more than a casual friend, but

I will admit, hearing you use those words," he shrugged, "they hurt. No one wants a person to be ashamed and embarrassed and disappointed about their marriage. Even an accidental one."

Katie found herself smiling slightly at that description, even as she tried to absorb what he was saying.

He was hurt. She'd been hurt.

"I didn't mean those words that way."

He frowned. "How did you mean them?"

Katie wanted to groan. She supposed it was her surprise at his candidness that made her answer without measuring her words.

But he had been candid. Maybe it was time she was, too. Hadn't she always said she wanted to be wilder, more rebellious?

Just tell him what you meant.

"I—I said I was embarrassed and ashamed, because I couldn't remember anything about those pictures. That's not me."

Cort nodded. "I get that. It's not me either. But why were you disappointed? Because the pictures didn't give us more answers?"

Katie could have just said yes, that was why. But she wasn't going to. Maybe it was time to admit her feelings for Cort. It had been three years of hiding her feelings. She was at the start of a new existence. Maybe it was time to tell him. He might reject her, he probably would, but given everything else that had happened, this seemed like as good a time as any.

"I was disappointed because I didn't remember anything in those pictures."

Cort didn't speak for a moment, then he said, "You mean the partying?"

She shook her head. "No, I was disappointed—I am disappointed, because I can't remember being held in your arms or kissing you."

Cort was quiet again, and regret and panic spread through her chest, tight and painful. She shouldn't have said anything. She wasn't ready for rejection after all.

But just when she would have told him to forget what she said, he tugged the wrist he still held.

"Well that's one thing we can fix right now."

He pulled her against him, and his lips found hers as if they had a dozen times before.

And maybe they had, although that thought was quickly lost as she became overwhelmed by the masculine feel of him now, in this very moment. This was real. This was what she'd imagined for so long and now that he was touching her, kissing her, it was so much better than the pictures or even her imagination.

His lips explored hers, strong and soft at the same time. His hands moved up her arms, sending delicious chills throughout her body.

She whimpered, overcome, weak with her desire. Her fingers dug into the muscles of his shoulders, feeling his strength.

She moaned again as he deepened the kiss, his tongue finding hers. She could taste the lime from his drink, the tang of the fruit and him making her shiver. He was utterly delicious. They stood, bodies pressed together, lips moving hungrily over each other's.

God, he was so much more amazing than she could have ever dreamed up in her overactive imagination.

"My darling I, can't get enough of your love, babe."

Okay, that wasn't a part of her imagination. She'd never heard Barry White, ever, while kissing a man.

Had Cort heard that, too?

He lifted his head and shot a puzzled look around the room.

"Did you hear that?"

She nodded.

"Can't get enough of your love, babe."

They both looked up at the parrot, who was still perched on top of the fridge. It bobbed its head as soon as it saw them looking at it.

"I've thought about this so many times. Although we were never being serenaded by a klepto bird with a drinking problem, I must say."

Katie looked up at him, stunned. He'd thought about this before.

"You don't have to look so surprised," he said, giving her a crooked smile. "I don't think many men would think of seducing you with a bird present."

"You thought of seducing me?"

His gaze held hers, dark and burning with his own desire. "Many, many times."

His words thrilled her, as did the smooth, sexy cadence of his voice. She also noticed his words held more of an accent now. He had a slight, barely noticeable accent normally, but now it was thicker, becoming more pronounced with his desire.

That thrilled her, too. Longing swirled through her body even stronger. Everything about this man was so sexy.

Sinfully sexy. And she felt wicked in his arms.

And she liked it. It made her feel more daring, more brazen, and sexier herself.

"I have, too," she told him. "I thought of this from the very first time I met you."

She hesitated, her good-girl side resurfacing despite her goal to keep it under wraps, at least for tonight. But would he see that as rather stalker-ish. Or pathetic?

Instead he kissed her again, and all her concerns fled. Soon she was swept up again in her desire, her hands moving more frantically over his shoulders and arms and back.

"You're the first, you're the last, you're my everything."

Again Katie wasn't sure if she was really hearing those words outside of her head. If not, she couldn't deny that she could feel that way about Cort. He could easily be her everything.

She moaned as he lifted his head, not ready for his lips to leave hers again. He smiled sympathetically at her forlorn expression as he laced his fingers through hers and led her down the hallway.

Her lust-hazed brain realized he was taking her to his bedroom.

"I'm not making love to you for the first time in my kitchen," Cort said with a lopsided smile. "I'm certainly not opposed to making love on the kitchen table. In fact, I'd love that. Just not for the first time. And not with that damned bird singing Barry White throughout the whole thing."

She nodded, feeling tingly and dazed. She did agree the cawed Barry White was a little distracting. And she didn't want anything diverting her attention from his man.

Her mind, fuzzy with desire and excitement and nervousness, still managed to lock onto something else. He said "first time." She wasn't sure if that implied there'd be more than one time, but then she decided not to analyze that now. Right now, she was going to thoroughly enjoy that she was getting a first time.

Then another thought occurred to her. "Maybe this isn't our first time."

He paused inside the doorway. He turned and looked at her, those sleepy eyes fringed by dark lashes that any woman would kill for. He released her hand and touched her cheek, brushing a lock of hair away from her cheek.

"I don't know what we did last night. But I know I'm treating this like it's the first time."

She nodded. He was right.

He kissed her again, this time the kiss as sweet as it was sensual.

Vaguely Katie heard a noise behind her, but she didn't connect what it was until another Barry White lyric filled the hallway behind them.

They parted again to find the parrot perched on the hall light that swung lopsidedly under its weight.

"Come on." Cort ushered her into his room and quickly shut the door before the bird could follow them.

"I'm starting to feel like I'm in an Alfred Hitchcock film," Cort muttered, and she had to laugh.

"Let's be happy there's only one bird."

"True."

They stood there smiling at each other for a moment, but quickly the atmosphere changed, sparking again with their awareness of each other.

Cort walked back over to her, again touching her cheek. "You are so beautiful."

Katie had never considered herself beautiful. She was the average girl next door with her plain old blue eyes, hair that lingered somewhere between blonde and light brown and the smattering of freckles over the nose. She had an average figure, her breasts not too big, her hips maybe a little too wide, her weight average. But the way Cort looked at her now, she felt absolutely beautiful.

"You are beautiful, too," she said, reaching out to touch his cheek. She loved the chiseled strength of his jawline, the slight rasp of stubble under her fingertips.

He smiled at her words, then captured her hand and pressed a kiss into her palm.

Katie could feel that kiss throughout her whole body. Every nerve ending tingled and sang at the sensation.

"I'm so aroused," she whispered, stunned a simple, sweet kiss like that could stimulate her so much.

"That's part of your change, too. We feel everything more, because of our state."

She believed him, but she also knew it was him. Period. Maybe the vampirism heightened her senses, but she knew she'd have reacted to him just as readily as a mortal.

"Come here," he said, pulling her over to his bed. He eased her down onto the tangle of bedding. Had they created this knot of sheets and blankets? Maybe.

But they definitely were going to do so now. Cort followed her down onto the bed, his mouth finding hers again. They kissed, their hands exploring again, this time slipping under their clothing, hands running over bare flesh.

She gasped at the rasp of his fingers over the lace of her bra, over the sensitive hardness of her nipple. But he didn't rush, his hand sliding back down her belly, to the top of her jeans, then back up her belly.

She didn't feel as capable of being patient. Her own hands stroked the smooth skin of his back, over his sinewy sides to his stomach and up his muscular chest. The skin there was smooth, too, except for the tiny poke of his nipples.

As hard as hers, she thought with satisfaction, as she swirled a thumb around one of them.

He released a shuddering breath, revealing he liked her touch.

She liked it, too, but she was greedy for more of him. All of him.

Her hand slipped down his chest to discover a light dusting of hair that swirled around his navel and then narrowed downward into his jeans.

She followed the trail, her fingers moving to work at his belt. But his hand came down to cover hers.

"Not yet."

She looked at him quizzically. He was going to make her wait? She'd waited three years already.

But then his hands moved to the button of her jeans. He deftly popped the metal fastener open then slowly slid down the zipper.

Katie gasped before he even touched her. Just the knowledge that he would had her painfully aroused. She ached between her legs, a feeling painful and wonderful all at once.

Then he actually lifted her, his arm sliding underneath her and raising her off the bed. With his free hand, he worked her jeans down over the curves of her hips. Definitely a vampire trick.

He settled her back amidst the bedding, bare from the waist down. She was glad she'd gone for a waxing just the day before—especially if that trait about being a vampire was like it was in Anne Rice's version. She could just picture a scene like the one where Claudia hacked off all her thick, curly locks only to have them reappear exactly the same. Claudia had been utterly freaked out by that. Imagine if the thick, curly hair was on another part of your body.

That would be highly embarrassing as well as a nuisance.

Okay, she must be slightly delirious about what was happening, if she could think of something like that at a moment like this, she thought, gazing up at Cort, who studied her with a hot, intense gaze under hooded eyes.

Her body reacted to the look, burning for him.

He reached for her hands, pulling her into a sitting position. Then as slowly and sensually as he'd removed her pants, he peeled off her T-shirt. He tossed the garment to the floor. Then her pink lace bra joined the rest of her clothes.

Her first inclination was to cover herself, but she fought the feeling. She'd waited so long for this. She wanted it so badly, she wasn't going to shy away from Cort in any way.

And again, when she looked at his expression, all she saw was desire that seemed to match her own.

"God, I want to touch you everywhere," he murmured. He grazed his fingertips lightly over her breast. Her nipple tightened to the touch.

She groaned, the slight, fleeting caress enough to make her nearly explode. Dear God, what would it be like to have him fondle her more or press his lips to her or, she shivered with need, to have him deep inside her.

Then he leaned forward and caught her painfully sensitive nipple between his lips, and she couldn't stop herself. She cried out as the most intense orgasm of her life shook her whole body.

Chapter Sixteen

THE TAO OF SAXON

WYATT had seen a lot in his lifetime. What he never would have expected to see was Stella rolling around on the floor of a bar in the throes of a full-blown girl fight.

He stopped in the doorway of the bar, so astonished that he couldn't even react. "What . . ."

Peter the bartender was coming out from behind the bar, cursing. "God, I hate this shit. I hate drunks. I hate women. I hate my job."

This was so unlike Stella, that Wyatt still stood there, wondering if Stella had a doppelganger. She tossed the woman off of her with a fair amount of restraint for a vampire, but with way more anger and intensity than he would expect from Stella. Stella was calm. Stella took care of everyone else. Stella did not fight with anyone. Except maybe with him. But that was only in the last few days.

Stella was half up off the floor when the woman launched herself at Stella again with a growl. There was a lot of hair flying, screaming, and fistfuls of T-shirt as they slammed back onto the ground.

Peter pulled the blonde off Stella, who hissed and kicked like a cat.

Wyatt finally got his head out of his ass and moved forward to help Stella up. Only she kicked out at him. "Get away from me, you lying sack of shit!"

Uh. Now what? Wyatt stared down at her, speechless. Where was the woman who had kissed him so tenderly on the street an hour ago?

"What are you doing?" he asked her. "I told you to stay at Famous Door. I was worried about you."

"Worried you were going to get caught in your lies." Stella sprang up off the floor, swiping her hair off her face, and adjusting her purse. After patting her pocket to reassure herself something was there, she glared at him. "How could you?"

"If I knew what I supposedly did, maybe I could answer that a little better."

Her reply was a snort of disgust. Wyatt didn't know if she would have expanded on that or not because the other woman suddenly darted around him and took a swipe at Stella.

"She's loose! Grab her!" Peter said. "I'm calling the cops. I'm not paid to deal with women fighting over a dude."

They were fighting over a dude? Wyatt caught the blonde as she hurtled past him and lifted her up so that her feet dangled uselessly.

"Put me down!"

"Can someone explain to me what the hell is going on?" Wyatt said, exasperated. Fortunately, his vampire strength allowed him to hold the woman with ease, but she was still getting a kick in on his shins every other second and he was not enjoying it. He turned her to the side a little so he could see Stella better.

"She was wearing Johnny's necklace. She says you gave it to her."

Wyatt stared at her blankly. She looked spitting mad. He had no idea what she was talking about. "I never had Johnny's necklace. I left it on the counter of his apartment."

"That's what you said. But why did she have it then?" Stella pulled the necklace out of her front pocket and held it up in front of him.

It was definitely Johnny's necklace. There couldn't be two of them. What the hell?

"I had it because Wyatt gave it to me!" This was from the dangling woman.

Wyatt dropped her to the ground so he could take a good look at her face. He knew her vaguely. "Karen?"

"Yes, Karen, you asshole. Don't even stand here and try to tell me you don't remember last night."

Actually, he did not remember last night at all. A sick, horrible feeling started to twist in his gut. He wouldn't have. He couldn't have. Not even drunk or drugged or whatever the hell he had been last night. He wouldn't have cheated on Stella. Because in his mind that's what it would have been, even if they didn't have any real understanding of what was going on between them. He wanted to be with Stella. He wouldn't have been with Karen.

He was almost 100 percent sure of it. Ninety-nine, at the very least.

Oh, God.

"Maybe we should go discuss this somewhere else."

"Yes, please, do." Peter rolled his eyes.

"No. There is nothing to discuss. You suck and I want you to die." Stella turned to Peter. "What's my tab?" she said with great dignity.

"Don't worry about it," Peter told her.

But she still dug in her purse and threw a ten down on the bar. Then shifting her shoulder so she wouldn't touch Wyatt or Karen, she stomped past with her chin up, tugging the bottom of her T-shirt down.

"Stella . . ." Wyatt pleaded, but she ignored him.

"The necklace," Karen sputtered.

"Let it go," Wyatt said in a low voice. "It really does belong to her."

The words gave Stella pause, but Saxon appeared in the doorway. She went to him, took his hand like he was her eight-year-old son, and said, "Come on, let's go."

Saxon frowned, but he went with her.

Wyatt was left to face his mistakes, whatever those might be. "Sorry about that," he told Karen. "Can I buy you a drink?"

"Sure." She sat down on a stool and smoothed her hair. "The skinny bitch is stronger than she looks."

Karen had no idea how strong Stella could be. Wyatt was grateful she was enough in control of herself to not hurt Karen, but other than that, he wasn't grateful for much. "She's grieving, you know. It's only been a couple of days since she lost Johnny."

"I get that. But if that necklace wasn't yours to give away, why did you?"

Hell if he knew. Wyatt sighed, putting his feet on the rungs of the stool he was sitting on. "The thing is, Karen, I got loaded at Johnny's wake last night. I don't remember much after we left the boat. So I can't really say as to why I would do that."

"You don't remember last night? Seriously? Well, that's a little insulting."

The sick sensation in his gut started to crawl up his throat. "Did we, uh, do anything that I should know about?"

Karen blinked at him. "Like what?"

She was going to make him spell it out. "Did we have sex?"

Now she looked aghast. "What kind of a slut do you take me for? Good Lord, we just hung out and had a couple of drinks. You at least need to buy me dinner if you want in my pants."

Relief coursed through him. He hadn't thought he would, but then again, he had never blacked out before either. "I wasn't saying, I mean definitely I would buy you dinner, not that I would ever hit on you. I mean . . ." Wyatt clamped his mouth shut and regrouped his thoughts. "I'm glad to hear I wasn't a total jackass, unlike right now."

"You don't remember anything, huh? I didn't think you were that drunk, but then again, what do I know? Some people hide it well and I haven't spent a lot of time with you."

Now that the air was cleared on that potential disaster, his thoughts were wandering back to the matter at hand—Stella was pissed at him. Rightly so. Why had he had Johnny's necklace? It hadn't been in his apartment, he was sure of it. "In what context did I give you that necklace? And by the way, I'm sorry for dragging you into anything with Stella. It's totally my fault and I can't explain what I thought I was doing since I don't even remember it." That was definitely frustrating.

"It wasn't that big of a deal. You were wearing it and I complimented it. Said it was cool. And then you asked me if I wanted it."

That was just stupid. Wyatt shook his head. "Again, I'm sorry. I had no right to give that necklace away. Seems my head was really up my ass last night."

Now he needed to go and explain to Stella. Beg for forgiveness. Wyatt sighed.

"It's okay. Happens to the best of us." Karen lit her cigarette and took a hefty drag. "Can't say I won't hold that against Stella for a while though, grieving or not. She went batshit crazy on me."

"Speaking of Stella, I really should go check up on her. Apologize. Make sure she's okay."

"Yeah, no problem." Karen waved. "Good luck. You're going to need it."

"Ain't that the truth." Wyatt stood up and paid for Karen's drink. He left Peter a large tip to compensate for the disturbance. "Have a good night, Karen."

"Always do."

Wyatt went off in search of absolution.

And flowers. Women liked flowers.

But he had a feeling it was going to take a hell of a lot more than a crappy bunch of hot pink carnations from Rouses Market to fix this mess.

So he got daisies, too.

"LYING, JERKFACE, SHITHEAD, asshole, cocksucking loser," Stella ranted as she tromped down Conti, dragging Saxon behind her. "I cannot believe he gave that person my brother's necklace. I wonder if it was before or after he fucked her." The thought of which made her want to pick up a car and hurl it all the way to the river.

It was safe to say she had never been this furious in her entire life. Or hurt, damn it.

Even when the Chicago banker had thrown her over for the heiress it hadn't felt like this—a searing stabbing sensation in her heart. A punch to the gut. A kick to the knees. A blow to the lungs, driving all breath out of her and replacing it with shock and agony.

"I mean, *we* had sex two nights ago, then tonight. How could he have sex with her last night, in between when we had sex? That makes her the meat of his sexual sandwich. I was just the bun, the dry, unpalatable bun. No one really wants the bread. It just holds everything else all together." Stella paused at the corner, not really sure where she was going. She was just going.

"You're hurting my hand."

"I am not," she snapped at Saxon. She stared at the keyboardist, her chest heaving, tears in her eyes. "Why would he do that?"

Saxon shook his head. "Maybe he's building a mystery."

"What?"

"I don't know. I don't even know what you're talking about."

"Wyatt had sex with Karen."

"Who's Karen?"

"The woman in there. She works at Famous Door. He had sex with her."

"Why would he do that? Anybody can see that he's crazy about you."

That was a little balm to her ego. "Well, obviously not that crazy about me if he could have sex with someone else in between having sex with me." The tears were going for real this time. Stella's voice started to crack. "I forced him to have sex with me, didn't I? I was a pity fuck because I threw myself at him and my brother had just died so he felt sorry for me."

A couple of girls walking by stared at her and whispered behind their hands. Great. She'd become one of those people who dissolve into drama on the street.

"Come here. Let's go somewhere and sit down. Somewhere with waffles." Saxon turned around and retraced their steps.

Stella dug her heels in. "No! We can't go back that way. Wyatt will see me."

"Okay, we'll go around the block. But we're going to Déjà Vu and we're going to have waffles with blood syrup. The waitress there makes it for me all the time."

That sounded like vomit on a plate to her, but Stella allowed herself to be led. It was better than crying in front of every man, woman, and vagrant on the street. "What is blood syrup?"

"It's just blood. The waitress there is a vampire. She tells people it's boysenberry so the mortals don't freak."

"Oh." Stella shuffled along behind Saxon, feeling like complete and utter shit. "I want to go home. I want to cry in my pillow."

"The last thing you need is to be alone, and I want waffles. I know you old folks don't understand why I dig eating food still, but it's comforting. Like eating makes me feel that nothing changes, man. You know what I mean?"

She nodded. She did. Vampires hung on to odd remnants of their mortal lives. Stella had hung on to her brother. Now he was gone. She was alone. Just like she had told Wyatt.

Saxon walked in long, loping steps. He reminded her of Shaggy from *Scooby-Doo*. Though he didn't wear bell bottoms. Her short legs struggled to keep up with his lanky strides. "Slow down, I'm petite."

"You're a runt," he told her good-naturedly.

"Thanks." Was this helping her? Was this him cheering her up, or making her want to stab herself repeatedly? "I think I'm going to get a cab and go home." Her anger seemed to have deflated and in its place, she felt exhausted. Weepy. Bruised.

"No. I forbid it."

Stella was so stunned, she paused outside the diner. "You forbid it? Is that something you picked up from your dom?"

"Hey, don't bring her into this. That's of a delicate and private nature, you know."

She didn't know anything. "Are you really like a genius who just has us all fooled or are you actually this random?"

"I'm guessing the second one." He pulled open the door and hit his shoe with it.

Yeah, she was, too. "Why can't I go home?" she whined. And why was she staying? It wasn't like he could really stop her. But for some reason, she went in with him.

Maybe she didn't really want to face the emptiness of her apartment just yet. Maybe she didn't want to feel the loneliness that was bound to wash over her like a tsunami. Eternity was a long time, people. She didn't want to go through it solo. Let it start tomorrow night. Tonight she was going to sit across the table from Saxon and pretend the last forty-eight hours hadn't happened.

Saxon placed his order with the dark-haired vampire waitress. She offered Stella a glass of juice with a wink when she declined the waffles. "Sure, thanks."

The seat was sticky. The floor was sticky. The air was sticky. Saxon's thumbs drummed on the tabletop.

"So you and Wyatt finally did the dirty, huh?"

"Yes. Yes, we did." Stella pictured riding him, the way he had penetrated her deep and thoroughly. This wasn't helping her forget the last few days. "But never again, because apparently he just felt sorry for me and he much prefers Karen."

Saxon's hand came out. He held up his left hand. "Okay, like this is the information you have. And like this is where you're going with it." He jerked his arm way to the right. "There's all this space in between, man. You got to fill in the gaps before you send him packing."

She got what he was trying to say, but her battered ego and shattered heart protested. If she went digging for answers, she might hear even more things she didn't want to. "Here is the one indisputable fact we have. He gave Karen my brother's necklace. After lying to me and telling me he didn't have it. That is seriously not cool."

"Weird shit went down last night. Who knows? Maybe he didn't know he had it. Maybe he didn't have it."

"Now you're just reaching." Stella played with a pack of sugar that was on the table, flicking it back and forth. "Why was he with Karen?"

"Look, I don't mean to be like rude or whatever, but you said you had sex with Wyatt. So did you tell him you care about him? Did you guys say you were like in a relationship or whatever?"

A flush creeped up her neck. "No, not exactly." She had mostly run away.

"Cuz he's been digging on you for a long time and it's like a vulnerable thing for a dude to go there with his fantasy chick. If he didn't say anything about you dating or whatever it's probably because he was waiting for you to say something."

"Well . . ." She bit her lip, squirming in the plastic booth. "He did suggest that maybe we could date. And that he loved me."

Saxon shot her his hang-loose sign. "Cool. What did you say?"

"I think I just ran away. Then the next night I yelled at him and told him there was no 'us.'" A strange pit had lodged itself in her throat. "It's my fault, isn't it? I sent him into the arms of another woman."

"Maybe," Saxon agreed. "But don't leap to the clouds just yet."

"What?" She assumed he meant conclusions.

Saxon continued without pause. "And that doesn't mean you can't work it out."

"But the necklace . . ." she protested weakly, starting to realize that Saxon was actually making sense.

Making a *pfft* sound with his lips, Saxon shook his head. "We were all drunk as skunks last night. Wyatt put on a corset. I rode a bull. We probably would have given away a baby if we'd had one. You can't put any stock in what happened last night."

She was starting to doubt herself. But one thing she didn't doubt. "Being drunk does not make cheating okay."

"But you told him you weren't in a relationship, so that is not cheating. And come on, what does every man do when the woman he loves tells him to buzz off? He gets drunk and fucks somebody else. It's a fact."

"That's a grim fact." The scary thing was, she knew he was right. It didn't make it any less wrong or any less difficult to swallow, but Saxon had a point. She had screwed up first by not telling Wyatt her own feelings. She hadn't even asked him for time, for them to take it slow. She'd just freaked out.

"So's murder."

"What?" Stella frowned.

"Murder is a grim fact."

"What does murder have to do with sex?"

"Sex, lies, and murder."

He'd lost her, but fortunately she was spared from having to respond by the waitress setting down Wyatt's waffle and her glass of blood. She was thirsty. That hangover had a wicked hold on her. She sipped while Saxon chewed, as she mulled over everything that had happened. She sifted through the facts and speculation, worrying her bottom lip. There seemed to be very little they knew 100 percent other than what Saxon had said—he'd ridden a bull and Wyatt had worn a corset. There was one other fact that just occurred to her though.

"How are you going to pay for this?" she asked him. "You told me you were broke."

Saxon gave her a sheepish grin. "I was kinda hoping you'd treat me. You know, for being your shoulder to cry on."

That so did not surprise her. "What if I don't have any money on me? How could you be so sure?"

He shrugged. "Because you're you. You're organized. There is no way you're out for the night without cash and a credit card in your wallet."

Saxon knew her well. She liked to be prepared. "Fine, I'll pay. And thanks for the advice." Frankly, he had talked her out of violence. She could buy him a waffle for that.

"No problem. You going to find Wyatt and talk to him? 'Cause that's like the mature thing to do, you know."

Saxon throwing maturity in her face was quite a cruel irony, but she couldn't argue with him. "Yes, I'm going to talk to him. Now stop chewing with your mouth full and get your elbows off the table."

"Yes, Mom."

That felt better. More normal. She sipped her drink and tried to think of what to say to Wyatt.

"Bite me" might be a good place to start.

Chapter Seventeen

SAY IT WITH FLOWERS

(But Not to Saxon)

WYATT walked down the street with his flowers and called Stella. He seriously doubted she would answer and he wasn't sure then what his plan would be. Maybe she would go to Johnny's. Or home. He didn't think she would still be with Saxon, and she wasn't the type to defiantly stay out all night making the bar rounds by herself.

Of course she didn't answer. It went straight to voicemail. He paused on the corner, undecided. If he went home, he wasn't going to be able to sleep. His body was weary, but his mind was still racing around the track. For all the bouncing around his thoughts were doing, he felt like he couldn't think.

His phone rang in his hand. It was Stella. His heart started to thump heavily in his chest. Hitting Answer he said, "Hello?"

"Hey. It's me."

She didn't sound like she wanted to rip his testicles off. That was a good sign. "Hey. Where are you? Are you okay?" Maybe she was calling for bail money. She'd left the bar mad enough to do vandalism.

"I'm okay. I'm at Déjà Vu. Can we talk?"

Fear crept along his spine. She was going to dump him again, more calmly and permanently. "Sure. I'm right around the corner. I'll be there in five."

"Okay. Thanks."

What the hell was she thanking him for? Wyatt knew it had to be bad then.

When he got to the block where the restaurant was, she was already outside with Saxon. She was touching Saxon. Tenderly, it seemed. Jealousy coiled in his gut. He really needed to get a grip on that, but he didn't think he was going to until she was his— which she wasn't going to be, clearly. So he was facing an eternity of feeling like someone was driving nails into his nuts every time Stella smiled at a man. It didn't sound like a fun future.

Swallowing hard, determined not to make matters worse, he approached them and forced a casual, "Hey, guys."

Stella glanced at him and gave him a shy smile. "Hey. I'm just putting some ointment on Saxon's cross burn. I think it will help it heal. This stuff works wonders on mortals, so it will definitely work on a vampire."

Her fingers were massaging something into Saxon's forehead while he stood there patiently. Just Stella being maternal as usual. Nothing untoward. Wyatt relaxed, feeling like even more of a jackass, his damp fist curled tightly around the flowers dangling by his side.

"You don't want to keep the scar?" Wyatt said, injecting levity into his voice. "I thought chicks dig scars."

"This one's just creepy," Saxon said. "No one is going to want to have sex with me if they see the cross staring down at them."

Well, there was that. "Good point."

"Are those flowers for me?" Saxon asked, brown eyes homing in on the blooms Wyatt was clutching nervously.

"No. They're for Stella."

Her head snapped toward him, her fingers drifting down from Saxon's forehead. "They are?" Her gaze met his, warm and nervous, before dropping down to the flowers.

"Yes." He lifted them up in offering. "I'm sorry for giving away Johnny's necklace. I had no right to do that, and while I can't even begin to explain why I would do something so awful and I don't remember it at all, being shitfaced doesn't excuse it. I'm really sorry," he repeated.

Her mouth fell open, her tongue slipping out to wet her pink lower lip. "Thank you for apologizing." She took the flowers from him and nuzzled them to her nose. "They're beautiful."

They really weren't. They were cheap grocery store flowers in a cellophane sleeve, but he was pleased she understood he was sincere. "And for the record, I had a drink with Karen. That's it. There is no other woman I want but you."

"Are you sure?" Saxon asked. "Because no one would blame you if you slept with Karen. I'm just saying. And honesty is always the best policy."

Wyatt turned to his friend and struggled to not snap his head off his shoulders and toss it down the street like a bowling ball. "One: Mind your own business. Two: I am being honest. I did not sleep with Karen. Three: Go away."

Saxon's eyes went wide. "Fine. I can take a hint." He rolled his eyes and looked at Stella. He mouthed "crazy" to her and pointed to Wyatt behind his palm. Stella let out a laugh.

Wyatt told him, "It wasn't really a hint. I want to be alone with Stella. We'll see you tomorrow night back at work."

"All right. Night." Saxon waved. "Thanks for the waffles, Stella-roo." His hand shot out and he snapped the head off of a carnation and tucked it behind his ear. "Catch you all on the flip side."

Wyatt watched him walk away. "That is one odd duck."

"I wonder what he was like as a kid."

"He still is a kid." But Wyatt didn't want to talk about Saxon. As the keyboardist crossed the street, he turned back to Stella. "I swear to you, I have no idea how I got that necklace."

Her lips pursed, but she nodded. "I believe you. Last night was insane. I'm not sure we'll ever really know what happened."

"I guess if this is the worst of it, we're lucky."

She nodded in agreement. "Though I'm not sure how lucky Katie is feeling. Have you talked to Cort? How is she doing?"

Wyatt was embarrassed to realize he'd been so wrapped up in his own concerns, he hadn't actually asked how Katie was doing. Waking up a vampire was kind of a big deal. "He didn't really say. But he didn't sound as excited as I thought he would about not being married."

"He likes her. He has for a while. I've seen him watch her."

Wyatt went for it. Staring down at her, he said tellingly, "Like I watch you?"

Stella sucked in a small breath, the flowers bouncing below her chin as her hand shook. "Do you watch me?"

He nodded, slowly. "So much that I can't believe you haven't noticed."

"Maybe I was afraid to notice."

"Do I scare you? Do you want me to back off?" He would if she asked him to. He wouldn't like it, but he respected Stella too much to push her.

A car drove past them, the bass pounding. Stella stared at it, contemplative. "I don't understand why you like me."

Relief allowed him to stop clenching his fists. If that was all she was worried about, he could work with that. He moved a step closer to her. "Are you kidding me? What's not to like? You're smart, compassionate, beautiful. You care so deeply about the people in your life. I think you're amazing."

"I don't feel amazing. I feel uptight."

"It's because you weren't getting any," he teased. "I know it wasn't doing good things for me either."

She gave a short laugh. "Maybe. But I've never been into casual sex."

"Me either." He'd thought the "I love you" had made that pretty obvious. "I can show you again how not casual I am about it if you'd like."

"Saxon told me I should have told you what I was feeling. That it wasn't fair of me to run away like that. He's right."

Nerves drew taut again. This could work in his favor or it could go horribly wrong. She had yet to really define her feelings for him. And she hadn't answered his suggestion to get it on again. This wasn't a big deal. Just the rest of his eternal life.

Total torture.

"You did what you needed to do." He wasn't going to criticize her emotions. It had been bad timing. "Johnny's death may have opened the door for us to do what we did, but it also made it just about impossible for you to deal with it. I get that."

"You are probably the most solid, stable, kind man I've ever known."

That was something. A little like what you'd say about a pet, but at least it was positive. The street was quiet, oddly so, no one coming in or out of the diner. The cobblestones were dark and damp from having been recently hosed down, and hanging plants twirled lazily to his left from a balcony. He didn't respond.

wanting more than that. Wanting not just compliments, but her heart.

"I've used my brother as a crutch to hold on to the past, you know. Saxon reminded me of that—that no matter how it's been, we cling to pieces of our mortal selves. Johnny's death reminded me that you can't fight change, and sometimes you shouldn't." She gave him a smile. "Being afraid of love is just stupid. Why would I deny myself the chance to be in a relationship with someone as wonderful as you?"

She thought he was wonderful. She had said "love." Wyatt felt pleasure build up inside him, warming his limbs, his heart. This was good.

"You tell me," he told her, brushing her hair back off her cheeks. He would never get tired of the sensation of her skin beneath his fingertips, of staring into her deep green eyes, luminous pools of desire.

"I wouldn't. Because while I may be a lot of things, I'm not stupid, and I'm not usually illogical. And being with you is actually very logical."

Wyatt drew his finger across her lip, teasing the flesh, before pressing the pad of his thumb into her fang. "You're going to have to give me a little more than that, Stella. I don't want to be your logical choice. I want to be the choice you can't resist."

Maybe it was stupid to push. Maybe he should just take what he could get. But he would be miserable that way, when he wanted everything. He would be insecure and jealous and would ruin it before it could ever grow into something permanent. He knew that. So he asked for everything and held his breath waiting for her response.

She leaned into his touch, her eyes half-closed, her lips parted deliciously. With her fang, she pricked his thumb and sucked his blood gently. "Oh, I can't resist you. I love you."

That was more than he could have ever hoped for and he figured he could pretty much die a happy vampire now. "Stella, I love you, too."

He drew his finger back and replaced the probing touch with his mouth, his lips a soft press onto her while he processed his emotions. His. She was his. It was almost impossible to comprehend. But he could hear it in her sigh. Taste it on her tongue that quested for entrance before he could even get his bearings. He could feel it in the grip of her fingers in his shoulder. He could smell her arousal. For him.

Their kiss turned from gentle and appreciative to carnal in a heartbeat.

Before, he had held back just a little, unsure of her reception. Now there was no dissembling on either of their parts. They wanted each other and they wanted each other now. Her hot little fingers threaded into his hair and her tongue tangled with his as he crushed her against his chest. The floral packaging crinkled in protest, but he didn't care. He wanted to feel her, every inch of her, and he pulled her hips in tight against his throbbing erection.

Then he remembered that they were still standing on the street corner. "Will you come home with me?" he asked. "We can put your flowers in water and you in my bed."

"Having sex in a bed this time would be nice," she said.

Wyatt laughed. "Taking all our clothes off might be cool, too."

Stella took his hand with a grin and they walked down the street.

He was ridiculously happy.

With a silent vow, he promised Johnny to always take care of Stella, as long as she would let him hang around her.

Then he twined her fingers in his and ate up the sidewalk, full of pride and anticipation.

This night was going to end on a high note after all.

Chapter Eighteen

GET IT WHILE THE GETTING'S GOOD

BEING a vampire made a person more sensitive. More aware. Cort certainly knew this after centuries of existence, but never had he experienced a female as responsive as Katie. Maybe it was because she was newly crossed, but he didn't think that was the sole reason.

He suspected Katie Lambert was always very sensitive, and now her natural sensual nature was just heightened. But as she shook with her release, he also realized no woman had ever made him feel this aroused either.

She'd come for him just from his licking and teasing her nipple. How much would she come from his tongue between her thighs or his hard cock thrusting in and out of her wet heat?

He nearly came himself just imagining her reaction. God, she was so amazing. So beautiful and sweet and giving in her arousal as she was in every other part of her life.

He shouldn't be surprised. And maybe he was actually more surprised at his own desire for her. His body throbbed, pulsed, desperate to be inside her gorgeous, supple body, but he also wanted to take this slow.

Maybe this wasn't the first time they'd made love. But it would be the first time she remembered, and he wanted it to be perfect. A moment she remembered forever.

He moved his lips to her other breast, swirling his tongue around her other tight, pert nipple. She tasted like raspberries and sunshine, and his cock strained against his jeans.

He pressed kisses down her belly wanting to taste more of her. She moaned and wiggled her hips as he inched closer and closer to the place he wanted to be. Where they both wanted him to be.

He nipped her hipbone, smiling against her smooth skin as she writhed again, demanding without words that he give her what she wanted.

He did, parting her creamy white thighs and positioning himself between them. Her warm, musky scent filled his nose, reminding him of a dewy morning with the sun warming the green grass.

"You have no idea what you do to me," he whispered.

She gazed down at him with her sapphire-blue eyes, her honey hair tangled around her heart-shaped face. She was truly his idea of a perfect woman, and he was finally going to make love to her.

Last night was the best night of his life, as far as he was concerned.

Sorry, Johnny—no disrespect to you.

But last night's events brought him to this moment, and he couldn't regret that.

He lowered his head, running a tongue up the sweet slit between her thighs. She gasped, raising her hips off the bed, demanding more. He delved his tongue deeper, swirling the little bud, the place that begged for his attention.

He licked and nipped and teased her until he could taste her release on his tongue, sweet and tangy and completely Katie.

Only once she was mindless with her ecstasy, her head thrown back, broken cries escaping her parted lips, only then did he pause to undress.

She watched him with hungry eyes that spurred him to hurry, to return to her and make her his completely. And he intended to do just that. Possessiveness mingled with his desire, ramping up his need for her to a level that should have shocked him, maybe even frightened him a little. But it didn't. In fact, it felt perfectly natural.

Just like it felt perfectly natural to move back over her and feel her soft, supple body underneath his. He gazed at her for a moment before lowering his head and kissing her again.

"I think we must have made love last night," he murmured against her lips.

"Why?" Her voice was husky and breathless and seemed to stroke over his skin just like her small hands rubbing down over his back. He suppressed a pleased moan.

"Because," he said, refocusing on his thoughts, "this feels so natural, so right."

She smiled and nodded. "It does, doesn't it?"

He smiled back, then kissed her. She returned the kiss, wrapping her arms and legs around him. Her body felt so wonderful encircling him, he had to know how it felt to be deep inside her.

Positioning his hips, he pushed gently, parting her, entering her just a little.

She gasped, and their eyes locked.

He pushed a little deeper. Her lips parted, shiny in the lamplight.

He tilted his hips, just allowing a bit more of his rock hard length into her wet heat.

She cried out, lifting her hips, wanting more of him. He wanted that, too. To bury himself deep inside her, as deep as he could go. But he also wanted to savor this moment.

"You feel so good," she whispered.

Damn, she felt beyond good. But he kept his pace slow, savoring every gasp and moan Katie made, every movement, every sensation.

Once he was inside her to the hilt, he couldn't take it slow any longer. He had to move and Katie was urging him to with each grind and swivel of her hips.

"Please," she begged, urging her hips upward again, and he gave in to his need, pulling out and thrusting in deeply.

She cried out, and her fingers dug into his shoulders.

"God, yes."

He wasn't sure who said that, all he knew was that he agreed fully. Her tight heat and the feeling of her writhing underneath him, reacting fully to each of his movements was pure heaven. The abandon on her face was pure beauty. The pleasure radiating throughout his body was pure ecstasy. He'd never experienced anything so perfect.

Underneath him, she shuddered, her muscles tensing, her body pulsing around him, and he almost followed her into an orgasm. But he focused, not an easy task with her so warm and giving and utterly lovely against him.

But he wanted her to come again. As many times as she could before he found his own release.

And she did orgasm several more times, until she was limp

and satisfied, small, pleased whimpers replacing her wild cries. Only then did he allow himself to come. Deep inside her.

For a moment, she stiffened when she realized what he'd done. Years of being conscientious about birth control, he suspected. But then she relaxed again.

And while he fully enjoyed his own climax, her reaction had him thinking about the consequences of what had happened last night. Katie was a young, caring woman. She'd probably wanted to have children one day, and that was no longer a possibility.

He was reminded of another time, when losing options like that had ruined his relationship with a woman he truly loved.

He looked down at Katie, who lay with her eyes closed, and her honey-colored hair tangled around her on the mattress. A slight smile curved her pretty pink lips.

She didn't look upset. In fact, she looked quite content but that was probably because the reality of her situation and all the changes that would cause in her life hadn't sunk in yet.

He hated the idea that bitterness and regret might overshadow her cheerful nature. But he didn't see how it couldn't. Becoming a vampire hadn't been her choice. That would anger her eventually. He'd seen it happen. It had destroyed his first wife. And in the process, it had destroyed him. He'd vowed then to never let something like this happen again. But now it had.

"What's got you looking so serious?"

Cort realized he was still staring down at Katie, although in the moment, he hadn't been seeing her.

Katie smiled up at him, then caressed his cheek. Her gentle, affectionate touch thrilled him, but it also stirred more feelings of guilt inside him as well.

"I'm just blown away by how amazing that was," he told her, which wasn't a lie. Not in the least. It was the best sex he'd ever had. And for someone who had lived as long as he had, that was saying a whole lot. He'd even believed at one time he'd once been married to his soul mate, but the crazy events of last night had him questioning that, too.

He was starting to believe Katie Lambert—wait, she was Katie Cortez now—was his soul mate.

Oh yeah, totally crazy. Totally crazy. Sure he'd known her a long time, but really? Could the events of one night really prove this woman was his destiny?

And let's not forget that he didn't even remember the events. Yeah, he couldn't make an assumption like that.

But with their bodies still touching, his cock still nestled between her thighs. Her hands stroking him so sweetly . . .

He looked down into her eyes, so blue he felt as if he could drown in them. And drowning in those beautiful eyes, there was no doubt in his mind that she was supposed to be with him.

He knew that, but did she? Did Katie feel the same way? Because he'd believed once before the woman he wanted to spend eternity with felt the same way. But he'd been wrong. Deadly wrong.

He couldn't risk that kind of assumption again. And he couldn't try to force his feelings on this woman. She seemed to be taking her vampirism amazingly well, but he was pretty sure that was because it hadn't fully sunk in. How could it?

"Are you sure you are okay?" she asked again, her fingers twining through the unruly waves of his hair.

He nodded, then lowered his head to kiss her lingeringly.

"I'm better than okay," he murmured against her lips.

He felt her smile, and joy—joy he knew he probably didn't deserve—warmed his chest, making him feel almost human again.

He realized in kissing this woman that he was in love with her, and had been from afar for a long time. Which explained so many things that he hadn't been willing to look at before now.

Like the fact he hadn't really dated since he'd met her. Three years without dating. Okay, three years to a vampire wasn't even a blip on the radar, but it was also unusual for a male vampire to abstain—or any male, really. And since he didn't bite to feed, and he hadn't gotten laid on a regular basis for years, he was sort of the king of self-denial.

But he hadn't been interested in sex with anyone but Katie. And now that he thought about it, the only time he had found any contentment was when he was around her. And he'd found reasons to go into work early, just to catch her playing. He also found reasons to convince her to stay to watch them. Which, now that he thought about it, he never really had to twist her arm to convince her.

So what the hell had stopped him from making this move long ago?

He looked back down at her, mussed and sated. She was beautiful, as always, but her beauty was slightly different now. Her skin glowed paler, almost pearlescent, and her full lips were a deeper pink, rosy and ripe. Her looks were changing, even this soon. Vampirism enhanced the vampires' looks, making them more alluring, more appealing. Cort supposed it was nature's way of making them more effective hunters, another way of drawing their prey to them like some lovely and very deadly flower.

He knew the changes would happen, and he was just as susceptible to her increased beauty, but those changes upset him, too. They reminded him that she truly never would be the same Katie she'd been yesterday. And he'd changed her.

Would she really be alright? Would she eventually resent him?

He met her eyes, noticing under her content, lowered lashes, they looked different, too. More pupil than iris, more black than cheerful blue.

Katie raised her head then, and kissed him. Her movements were hungry and aggressive, and his body instantly reacted, his cock, still nestled between her thighs, stirred and quickly hardened. Now that was one definite upside to being a vampire—little to no recovery time.

"I want you again," she murmured against his lips, her hands roaming over him, as demanding as her lips.

He could tell, and he wanted her, too. Desperately.

For a moment, his concerns were overshadowed by desire. He couldn't think of anything but her body writhing underneath him, her fingers digging into the flesh and muscle of his back.

Her lips strayed from his mouth to kiss the length of his jawline and sensitive underside, moving downward toward his neck.

He found himself angling his head, finding her open-mouthed kisses as exciting and sensual as everything else about her.

Damn, everything she did drove him wild. He ground his hips against her, his cock prodding the entrance of her sex. She parted her legs more, inviting him inside. Back inside her, where he belonged.

Just as he positioned himself, the head of his penis just sliding inside her, he felt it.

Pure ecstasy. He gasped, then groaned, the sound broken and breathy.

She'd bitten him. Her fangs punctured his skin in that perfect place along his neck, just above his collarbone.

Oh. Dear. God. This had to be what heaven was like.

His eyes drifted shut, and he submitted to her, and just when he would have orgasmed from the sheer ecstasy of her bite, a moment of reality hit him.

She was a fledgling. She wouldn't know when to stop. She could literally suck him dry. And for another brief moment, he wondered if he even cared. It simply felt too wonderful right this moment.

"No." He managed to struggle away from her, stopping her, stopping himself.

Katie blinked up at him, dazed and confused. Desire still glazed her eyes, making them glassy and unfocused. His blood glistened on her lips, glossy and deep red.

She touched the back of her hand to her lips as if to stifle a whimper of frustration, but as she moved her hand away from her mouth, she saw the blood, and her eyes widened. All hazy hunger and lust gone, replaced by dismay and disgust.

"I—I bit you," she said, her voice reedy.

"I'm fine," he assured her, knowing that the reality of what she could do, that she could bite and drink another's blood, was horrifying her. As if to prove his thoughts, she gaped at the blood smeared across the back of her hand.

And this would be the start of her resentment of him. The beginning of her anger at what she'd become. What he'd made her.

"I'm sorry," she murmured, not looking at him but at his blood on her.

"There is no reason to apologize," he told her, shifting out from between her still spread thighs. She became aware of her position and quickly closed her legs and reached for the sheet, pulling it up around her with her non-bloody hand.

He didn't want her to feel ashamed at either her hunger or at her desire. Both were normal. But he was afraid the moment was already marred.

"I should have realized you needed to feed," he told her, moving to sit on the edge of the bed, still facing her. "Since you are new to this, I'm sure you didn't even realize you were hungry."

He should have realized that as soon as he'd seen her eyes were so dilated. But he'd been too distracted by his own physical need for her.

"I—I didn't," she admitted, the new blood in her system allowing her to blush. "I thought I was just—aroused again."

"Well, those two feelings can be very similar. And one can actually trigger the other."

She stared at him for a moment. "Was—was that how you were feeling, too?"

"No." Cort shook his head. "I was definitely feeling very, very turned on. Not hungry."

Her body seemed to relax slightly against the mattress.

"But I will admit, your bite was also very, very enjoyable," he said.

She stared at him, her eyes more blue than black now, although they were still a little dilated.

"You—you liked it?"

He nodded, smiling slightly. "It was pretty awesome."

Her body relaxed even more, and she was silent for a moment, then she asked, "So why did you stop me?"

"Because, like I mentioned before, when you are new to this, it's easy to take too much. Even from another vampire."

"So I could have killed you?"

Cort shook his head. "Probably not, but definitely incapacitated me."

She nibbled her bottom lip, looking worried again.

"It's really no big deal," he assured her. He leaned down to snag his jeans from the floor. He rose and tugged them on.

"Where are you going?" She still looked worried.

He smiled reassuringly. "I'm just going to get us a drink. I think we both can use it."

"I don't think I need any more liquor."

His smile broadened. "Not liquor."

"Oh. Right."

"Just relax here. I'll be right back."

She nodded, pulling the sheet up around her more. She was so damned pretty, even looking confused and vulnerable and worried.

"Really," he said, reaching out to brush a lock of her honey-blonde hair away from her cheek. "You didn't do anything wrong, and you definitely did not hurt me. Quite the opposite."

She nodded. "Okay."

He smiled again, then left the room.

She was so sweet. He didn't usually think of vampiresses as sweet. He thought of them as tough and determined and savvy, much like male vampires. He really only hung around one vampiress these days. Stella, their sound woman and self-appointed manager. And that's how he thought of Stella. Very together and strong. Even during this awful time, what with her brother's suicide and everything.

But he didn't think that description would ever fit Katie.

As he walked to the kitchen, he realized it was a good thing he and Katie were married. She needed him. And he'd push for them to keep the marriage intact. She might not agree. At first. But he thought he could convince her.

If her reaction to their sex was any sign, she was very attracted to him. They could build from there, couldn't they?

And he could help and protect her.

Yes, that was it. He'd make their marriage work. Decision made.

He opened the fridge and started to reach for a blood bag, fat with deep red blood. B negative, his favorite. But before he could pick it up, his phone rang.

He pulled the ringing, vibrating rectangle from his pocket.

Wyatt.

He pressed Answer.

"Hey, Wyatt. What's up?"

Chapter Nineteen

POSSIBLY KATIE OVERREACTS

KATIE had bitten Cort and liked it.

She looked down at the back of her hand. His blood was now dried to her pale skin. She stared at it, then looked away disgusted, not only at her actions, but at the fact, even now, she was tempted to lick the stain.

"This can't be right," she said to herself. It couldn't be normal to want to . . . eat a person you loved.

She froze for a moment, realizing exactly what she'd just thought to herself.

A person she loved? Did she—she remained totally still—really feel that way?

She sat up, looking around her as if someone or something could give her that answer. But nothing external could or needed to do that. She knew the answer deep inside herself.

She did love Cort, and had for a long time—as fanciful and schoolgirlish as that sounded.

She looked down at her hand again. And she needed him, too.

She wasn't sure she knew how to be a vampire—or at least control all of these new desires.

The blood on her hand had dried, but she still felt the urge to lick it. That couldn't be normal. Although maybe, in vampire terms, it was a bit like eating dried fruit or something.

"Yeah, I don't think so," she muttered to herself and threw back the covers. She slipped out of bed and gathered up her T-shirt and her panties. She pulled them on, then headed across the hall to the bathroom, but she stopped just inside the bathroom door. She could hear Cort talking.

"For real?" There was a pause. "Yeah, I guess so."

His tone sounded strange, but Katie couldn't tell what he was talking about. Or to who.

She went into the bathroom and quickly washed her hands in the sink, then wiped them on a dubiously clean towel hanging on a rack by the shower.

She stepped back into the hallway to hear Cort say something about the parrot always trying to peck his balls. The bird was darned annoying and did like to peck, but she didn't think it had attempted that particular area before. It sounded to her like he just wanted to get off the phone.

He sounded strange. Maybe a little upset, or disappointed. She wasn't really sure. Who had he been talking to?

Just as she started toward the kitchen, she heard the apartment door open.

"Yo." She heard Drake's gravelly voice.

"Hey." Cort sounded distracted.

She hurried back to Cort's bedroom door, not wanting to be caught in just her panties and a tee. But she left the door open partway and listened.

"I have good news for you, my man," Drake said. Or at least

that's what Katie thought he said. His words were a little slurred and thick like he had cotton in his mouth.

"Oh yeah, what's that?" Cort still sounded like he was only half listening.

"That priest—" Drake said in a leading way as if he expected Cort to respond.

Cort obviously didn't.

"You know, that one from the bathtub," Drake prompted.

"Yes, I know who you are talking about. It's not like I know many damned priests."

Wow, Cort sounded downright testy.

"Well, excusth me," Drake slurred. "Well, it turns out, he's a—"

"A stripper," Cort finished for him. "Yeah, I know. I just got off the phone with Wyatt."

"Oh," Drake said, clearly disappointed that he hadn't gotten to share the news first. "Well, shit, man, you don't exactly sound as pleased as I thought you would."

Cort didn't answer for a second, then he said, "No, it's definitely a good thing. I mean, married. That would have been totally crazy."

"Totally crazy," Drake agreed, his tone decisive even through the slurring. But Katie wasn't concerned with Drake's feelings about her and Cort's marriage. She only cared about how Cort felt.

"I didn't think it could be real," Drake said. "Marriage is not your thing, my man. We all know that."

"No," Cort agreed. "I'm not about that. Not at all."

Katie's stomach sank—no, more than sank. She actually felt sick to her stomach. Here she'd been thinking about the fact that she loved him, had loved him for some time, and needed him to show her how to adapt to her new life. Or death. Or whatever.

Damn, she could feel tears welling up in her eyes. She was a vampire, for crap's sake, didn't that mean she shouldn't be able to cry or something?

She sure as heck didn't want Cort to find her all blotchy and red-eyed. She turned and hurried to find her jeans and flip-flops.

She threw them on then paused at the door. She also didn't want to greet Drake looking all tousled, smelling like sex, which she knew firsthand he would smell with no problem, and bleary eyes. She'd suffered enough embarrassment for one day, but she had to get out of here.

She crept back to the door and listened again. The two men's voices still emanated from the kitchen, which meant she couldn't leave yet, since the apartment door was off from the room where they were.

She looked around her, glancing at the window. That was a no-go, since the jump from the window had to be more than twenty feet down. But she walked over to look anyway.

Easing up the window, she winced and glanced over her shoulder as the noise from Bourbon Street filled Cort's room. Had they noticed? She didn't hear anything, so she stuck her head out the window, trying to judge how far away the ground was. Could she make that jump?

Oh hell no.

But wait, she was a vampire now. She might be able to make it. She looked back down at the dirty, cracked pavement below.

Nah, she'd wait to find out about that ability. Not to mention, even as rowdy and drunk as the partiers on Bourbon Street were, they'd definitely notice a woman jumping out of a building.

She debated other possibilities. She could turn into a bat, couldn't she? That was a potential option. But how did she go about it?

Try focusing, she told herself, visualizing herself as a small black creature with large ears, beady black eyes, and flapping wings.

That was kind of disturbing, actually. Maybe she would be a cuter bat, more like a Disney movie sort of bat. She liked that image better.

She refocused, imagining her new bat self as well as adding a little of the Peter Pan version of how to take flight—happy thoughts, minus the pixie dust, of course. She scrunched up her face, squeezing her eyes closed, and began to talk quietly to herself.

"Warm puppies, strawberry smoothies, rainstorms, warm breezes, pedicures, hot fudge sundaes, good music, laughing, riding a bike without hands, Christmas morning . . . believe, believe."

After a moment, she opened one eye, then the other, and looked down at herself.

Nothing. No wings or ears, cute or otherwise. Nothing had changed, except several tourists had stopped on the sidewalk below to peer up at her. She backed away from the open window, realizing she probably did look rather crazy.

Okay, so the window was definitely not an escape option.

She tiptoed back to the door, just in time to hear footfalls coming down the hall. She slipped behind the door, hoping they passed.

They did.

"You still got the bird, huh?" Drake said.

"Yeah. No one would take that damned thing even if you paid them."

Katie had to agree with that.

Drake chuckled.

"The new tooth looks good," Cort said, their voices becoming more muffled as they walked into the living room.

"Thankth, man. Although thith Novocain otuff othuck."

Well that explained Drake's sudden and strange lisp.

"What happened to Katie, anyway?" Drake asked.

"She's resting," Cort said, and Katie noticed he didn't add that she was resting in his room. Was he ashamed of what they'd done as well as being relieved that he wasn't saddled with her as a wife, for even a brief time?

Well, that was fine. Right now, she just needed to get out of here and think. She listened. They were definitely in the living room. Now was the time to make her break.

She slowly pushed open the door, glad the hinges didn't creak. She poked her head out and looked toward the living room, praying neither man was in a place where they could see her.

They weren't, so she crept into the hallway, moving as quickly and quietly as she could. When she reached the kitchen, she actually allowed herself a moment to pull in a deep, calming breath.

She'd just finally made love with the man she'd fantasized about for years, and it had surpassed every one of those fantasies. And now she was sneaking away, hoping to not see him again for a good, long while. That definitely was not how their lovemaking had ended in her fantasies.

She glanced over her shoulder, struggling with another wave of tears. She swiped at her eyes, irritated that she was being such a damned girl. She forced herself to stand tall, and suppress any more crying.

Go, she told herself. *Just go.*

The apartment door also cooperated, making no sound as she eased it open. She stepped through the door into the dingy, narrow stairwell, and was about to pull the door shut, when a loud *caw* echoed throughout the kitchen.

Startled, she looked around to see the parrot still perched on top of the refrigerator. The annoying creature cocked its head to the side as it watched her, its beady little eyes regarding her as if it realized she was trying to escape without notice. And it wasn't going to let that happen.

"She's gone, she's gone," the bird warbled in that eerie sing-song way.

Katie glared at the animal. The darned thing was narcing on her. Was it really possible that a bird could be that smart? And that conniving?

"She's gone, she's gone," it repeated, louder this time.

Katie put a finger to her lips to shush the bird, then realized what she was doing. Smart or not, she was still trying to reason with a darned parrot.

Okay, the bird might want to stay perched in the kitchen, but it was time for her to take flight. With a little more force than she intended, she pulled the door closed and turned to rush down the narrow wooden staircase.

Her heart pounded in her chest as she reached the street, or maybe it didn't. Probably not, now that she came to think about it, since she was now undead. But she did feel panicked, which seemed silly, since she was pretty certain Cort wouldn't follow her anyway.

Why would he? He'd made it pretty clear in his conversation with Drake that he didn't want to be married to her. Sure, Cort was a nice guy and would have made the best of the situation, but he didn't want her. And here she'd been so willing to fall into bed with him. And stay married, too, if she was being honest.

Talk about being pathetic. It was probably childish to run, but she was too embarrassed to face him, still wanting him, still being crazy about him.

So she wouldn't face him. She looked toward Bourbon but immediately dismissed heading in that direction. It would be the easiest place to get lost, amongst the crowds, but it was too much of a sensory overload nightmare. She headed right instead, with no destination in mind. She just had to get as far away from Cort as she could.

"WHAT THE HELL ith that?" Drake said, then wiped his mouth. Clearly he wasn't used to the new fang yet. Or Novocain really affected vampires. Cort didn't know the answer to that, since he had his original fangs.

"That stupid parrot."

Drake made a face. "It's really off-key."

"It's a bird," Cort pointed out, moving away from the window, looking down the hallway.

"I thought birds could sing."

Cort shrugged, really not concerned with birds' abilities to carry a tune. "Did you hear the door, too?"

"I don't know."

Cort frowned back at Drake, who had now gone from fiddling with his missing tooth to fiddling with his fixed one.

Cort shook his head and walked down the hall. Obviously Drake had spent too much time with Saxon.

When Cort entered the kitchen, the only one he found there was the parrot, which flapped down from the fridge and landed on his favorite perching spot, Cort's left shoulder.

"She's gone, she's gone."

Cort winced slightly at the loud, irritating sound of the bird so close to his ear, but then the parrot's awfully sung words sank in.

Katie had left.

He spun and hurried to his bedroom. Sure enough, the room was empty and Katie's clothes were gone.

Shit! Why would she leave? Had she heard they weren't married and she figured she didn't need to hang around any longer? Or had she regretted the fact that they'd made love? Was she ashamed and embarrassed of that, too?

No, he believed her reaction to him was real. She had been genuinely attracted and responsive. He believed that. He had to believe that. He couldn't deal with the possibility that she hadn't felt anything when he'd felt so much. So damned much. Enough that he'd wanted their marriage to be real.

Even now, he knew he had to find her and try to convince her they had to give being a couple a shot, marriage or no marriage.

Wow, that sounded weird, but oh well. He was determined to be with this woman. Forever.

"Drake, get off your ass," he yelled. "We need to go find Katie."

Drake appeared in the doorway of the living room. "You lost Katie?"

Cort sighed. Yeah, Drake had definitely spent too much time with Saxon, but at least his dentist-induced lisp was lessening. He hoped.

"Come on."

Drake fell into step behind him. "Where are we going?"

Cort had no idea, but he had to find her. Not only because he needed to talk to her and see what she was thinking, but also because she was a new vampire, and that could be dangerous for herself and others if she got into a situation that she didn't know how to handle.

"Just come on."

AS KATIE MADE her escape, it didn't take her long to realize something very important. It probably would have made a lot more sense to have spent the time alone in Cort's bedroom looking for her purse rather than attempting to turn into a bat flying on the wings of happy thoughts.

She stopped on the corner of Dumaine and St. Peter, looking around, debating what to do. Her options were sort of limited since she didn't have a wallet, or a phone, or the keys to her apartment. And it was way too late to wake up her curmudgeon of a neighbor, who'd had her spare key from when she'd watered Katie's plants the last time she'd gone home to visit her parents. Katie was pretty sure her neighbor wouldn't answer even if she knocked.

Yeah, this was definitely an unfortunate situation she was in.

She looked around her again. The streets were quieter down this way, nearly empty at this time of night. Even a little bit eerie, because they were so empty.

Although she quickly realized she wasn't totally alone. Across the street and down a little ways, standing in a doorway, was a dark figure. Tall, almost unnaturally thin. She got the feeling it was male, and definitely creepy.

Katie decided she'd better head back toward Bourbon, at least close enough to have other people milling around. She started down St. Peter, her gait swift, although she tried not to appear unnerved in any way.

From behind her, she sensed rather than heard, or maybe she did hear—either way, she knew the dark figure had left the doorway and followed her.

She doubled her steps.

"Hey!" a voice called from a few feet behind her, male and gravelly.

She didn't stop to look behind her.

"Hey," he shouted again, and Katie could tell the guy was getting closer. In fact, she sensed that he was going to touch her, even before a hand clamped down on her shoulder. She didn't need to see the hand to know she was being touched by a large palm and long, bony fingers.

Alarmed, she spun and swung at the creepy figure. Her poorly fisted hand connected with the side of his head, and to her amazement, the man reeled under the force of her hit, literally lifting off the ground and slamming against the wooden shutters of the building beside them. The tall figure crumpled to the ground like a flung-aside rag doll.

Katie knew this was her chance to flee, but she couldn't move, too amazed at what she'd just done. Was she really that strong now? Or had that been a lucky punch?

Really? Was now the time to wonder about her preternatural abilities? This was her opportunity to get away from this weirdo; she could debate her possible superhuman strength somewhere else.

She turned to rush away, only to stop again when she heard his pained, mumbled words. "I just wanted my parrot."

Slowly, she spun back to the man, who still lay slumped against the wall, holding a large hand with long, thin fingers to the side of his head. His face was hidden by shadows, and she was reminded of a skeleton. But as she stared at his prone body, she realized he reminded her of more than a skeleton—something about his dirty shorts and tank was actually familiar.

Katie crept closer, although she made sure not to get close enough that he could suddenly reach out and grab her. She'd seen enough horror movies to know how these situations could go.

But then again, she would probably be considered the monster in this scenario. Totally weird.

"Your parrot?" she said to the man.

"Winston."

Katie thought about the red bird back at Cort's apartment. She would have gone with Satan, herself. Maybe Beelzebub. But she supposed Winston could work, too.

That was, if they were talking about the same parrot. She caught herself. Really? What were the chances of a stranger chasing her to get a parrot back if he wasn't looking for the parrot they had? New Orleans was a strange place, but not that strange.

Of course, this was a newly created vampire thinking this. Maybe it was that weird, but she still doubted it.

"You didn't lose Winston, did you?" The man tried to struggle upright, but groaned, pressing a hand back to the place where she'd hit him.

Guilt filled her, and she tossed her better judgment to the wind and stepped forward to help him. She immediately regretted her moment of sympathy as his overwhelming stench assaulted her nostrils. She suppressed a gag, and continued to hold his arm until he struggled to his feet.

He swayed slightly, but as soon as he seemed to have his balance, she released him and backed away. She was sorry she couldn't be more helpful, especially when she'd been the one to hurt him, but that smell. It was like the man just rolled out of bed from cuddling with a skunk and then bathed in a hot, decomposing landfill.

"Did you lose him?" He sounded so heartbroken, that for a moment Katie forgot the stench.

He stepped forward, his face coming fully into the light of the streetlamp for the first time. Again, Katie got the feeling she'd seen this man before. Well, obviously she had, but she actually recognized him. Maybe she was actually remembering something from last night. She searched her brain, but nothing definitive came to her.

"Did you lose Winston?" he asked again.

Katie shook her head, studying him closer, trying to remember where and when they'd met last night, and maybe, just maybe, the events that surrounded the meeting.

"Does your husband still have him?"

Husband? Well, he must have been a part of her sham wedding celebration, and didn't know that she and Cort weren't really married.

That silly feeling of disappointment weighed on her chest again.

"Yes, Winston is still with Cort," she managed to say past that heavy tightness.

The man smiled, but only briefly as his large hand returned to the side of his head and he grimaced.

"You pack a hell of a wallop for such a tiny thing."

"I'm—I'm sorry," she said sincerely. She supposed that was part of now being a vampire that she'd have to be aware of. She was very strong. And fast.

Even though she wasn't pleased that she'd actually hurt this man, she had to admit, it was kind of thrilling to be able to protect herself in a way she wouldn't have been able to before. It certainly didn't make her the typical girl next door that she'd always considered herself.

"Could we go get him?" the dirty man said, still rubbing his head.

Katie would love nothing more than to give this man back his bird. She was certain Cort would love nothing more, too, but there was no way she was going back to Cort's place. Not yet. She couldn't face Cort yet. She felt too confused and fragile.

"I'm sorry," she said again, "but I can't."

The man frowned through his layers of filth. "Why not? I

mean, I know it's not proper to ask for a wedding gift back, but I was so hyped up from dancing and whatnot, and I didn't think through giving you Winston."

The parrot had been a wedding gift. Of course. Why else would they have the bird? Right . . . just more weirdness.

It was already strange enough that this . . . well, he appeared to be a vagrant . . . would have a talking parrot.

"He's my best friend," the man added.

A talking parrot as a best friend. It all made perfect sense. Totally.

The vagrant stepped closer and again, Katie backed away.

"I wouldn't hurt you," he said, and she believed he was sincere. The problem was, his scent just might.

"Please don't worry. I'm sure Cort—" When the man frowned, Katie clarified by saying, "My husband will gladly give you back Winston. We'd never expect you to part with something so dear to you."

The vagrant smiled then, revealing what might have once been quite a charming grin, before the yellowed and missing teeth.

Suddenly Katie knew where she recognized him from, and it wasn't from her own memories of last night, it was from that couple Betty and Ed's photographs.

This was the vagrant dancer that they'd mentioned. But why hadn't they also mentioned him as being a part of the wedding party along with them?

"Where did we meet last night?"

"After your wedding ceremony. You were married by one of my dear friends, Annalese Bonvieux."

Katie frowned. She was pretty sure the priest in the bathtub would not have that name.

"Could you bring me to . . . her?" Katie guessed he must be referring to a woman.

"Of course I can," the man agreed with another wide smile. "And you will get me back Winston?"

"Absolutely."

The man gestured for her to follow him and they headed toward Bourbon, which again made her feel a little more secure going with the homeless man. Of course, she did know she could defend herself, but old cautions died hard. Harder than she had, apparently.

As they walked, the vagrant chattered on about things and places that he seemed to think she should know about. Some tarot card reader in Jackson Square who could tell the future as sure as if she were reading a book. Katie wasn't even sure what that meant. And about a band he loved over at Boney's, a bar Katie had never heard of. The man talked like they were old friends, and for all she knew they might have talked about all these things last night. But tonight, she had no idea what he was talking about.

In fact, from his erratic rambling and changing of subjects, Katie wondered if she should even trust that this man really did know who had supposedly performed her and Cort's wedding.

He was a vagrant after all. He was probably no more of a reliable source of information than his bird had been.

But at this point, what did one more wild-goose chase really matter?

"Oh, hear that?" the man said suddenly, grinning wildly. Katie frowned, since getting closer to Bourbon she could hear dozens of things. Bands, people, laughter, fights, even faintly under all of that, the beating of their hearts. So given all of those sounds to choose from, she couldn't begin to guess which sound he referred to.

"I love this band," he said, suddenly beginning to jig right there in the street.

Katie found herself smiling as she watched the man's utter abandonment to the music and his dance. And in truth, he was actually rather good.

"I have to go listen for a while," he said, heading to a bar on the corner.

"Wait," Katie said, but the man disappeared into the crowded mass of partiers.

She debated following him, but knew she couldn't handle being bombarded by all the sounds and smells. Never mind the jostling of the crowd, bodies close to her, body heat, and the sweet scent that seemed to cling to every mortal like a sugary coating. Even now, keeping her distance, that smell called to her.

She distanced herself a little more from the hopping bar and waited. And waited.

After standing there for more than fifteen minutes, she decided maybe she should just go. Following the man in the first place had probably been a fool's errand, and the longer she stood out here, with people wandering everywhere, the more she could feel that underlying hunger building deep inside her.

But where could she go? She had a name, Annalese Bonvieux. She could try to find this woman on her own. But she didn't even know where to start.

Darn, she really just wanted to go back to her apartment. She wanted peace and quiet.

She wanted the bag of blood in Cort's fridge, she realized with mild disgust. Sadly, *very* mild disgust.

She guessed she'd have to settle for somewhere here in the Quarter. But what place would be even vaguely quiet.

Fahy's, she decided, risking cutting across Bourbon and down one of the side streets. Fahy's could be busy at times, but she thought it was probably late enough to be safe. Plus, Katie knew the bartender well, and he'd probably let her order a drink and just give him the money tomorrow night once she figured out how to get her purse back from Cort. If it was even there.

When she reached Fahy's green front door, she knew she'd made the right choice. The place looked quiet tonight. Thank God.

She opened the door and stepped into the calming dimness. The dark wood of the bar also seemed to ease her tension, as well as the soft rock coming from the jukebox. Who would have thought Air Supply could soothe the savage beast?

"Nigel," she greeted the bartender with a smile, glad to be somewhere that felt normal and familiar, but the normalcy, at least, was short-lived.

"Katie-Katie, my girl," Nigel said in his wonderful British accent. "I'm surprised to see you out and about tonight. I would have thought last night would have been more than enough excitement for a while."

Katie forced herself to return his smile.

Nigel reached for a mug hanging on a rack above his head, then he placed it under the spigot of her favorite beer. Once it was filled, he set the full mug in front of her and leaned on the bar.

"After all, it isn't every day a young bird like you meets her maker," he said, shaking his head.

"Meet my maker?"

"Aye," he said, then regarded her closely. "Don't tell me you don't remember a thing about last night either."

"Either?" She was starting to feel a bit like Winston, repeating everything Nigel said. Not that Winston seemed to be the type of parrot that did that. He had plenty to say without mimicking.

"Yeah, some of the others were in here earlier," Nigel said. "Wyatt, Stella, that confused kid with the long blonde hair."

"Saxon," Katie said automatically.

"Yeah, him. They were here and seemed a little confused by the events of last night. Of course, they didn't have nearly the reason you do to be confused."

Well, Nigel was right, she was confused. Very confused. "They don't?"

Nigel shook his head, giving her a sympathetic look. "You don't remember a thing about what happened on the riverboat, do you?"

She shook her head. She hadn't even realized Nigel had been there, although it made sense he would be. Katie knew Nigel was friends with the band guys, and Johnny had come here often after he was done playing. Of course, Nigel would go to the memorial to pay his respects.

"Probably a good thing you don't remember," Nigel said and reached out to pat one of Katie's hands in an almost fatherly way. "All I can say is thank Mary and Joseph that Cort was there. If he hadn't done what he did, well, you wouldn't be sitting here with a pint, I can tell you that."

"What did he do?"

"Why, saved your life, of course," Nigel said frankly, then he leaned forward. "Well, you know, our version of life anyway."

Katie stared at Nigel. He was a vampire, too? Holy crap, was everyone she knew a vampire?

"What happened to me?" she asked, the question as surreal as finding out all the people she'd known for years were undead.

"Well, you cracked your head open, dear."

Chapter Twenty

FIND A BEER OR YOUR TRUE LOVE,
WHICHEVER COMES FIRST

"**Y**ou did lose Katie, didn't you?" Drake said after he and Cort entered and exited yet another bar. This one on Conti.

Cort shot Drake an irritated look. Did he have to keep using the word *lose*? Lose. It made it sound like he'd lost his chance with her. But what if he had?

He didn't know what had made her leave like that, and it was killing him. He had to find her and talk to her.

"I didn't lose her," Cort stated, not for the first time.

"She's gone. She's gone," sang the bird, also not for the first time.

Drake gave the parrot and Cort a pointed look. "I think the bird knows something you don't."

Cort glared at his bandmate again. Drake fell silent, at least for a few seconds.

"Seriously," he said, as they strolled back toward Bourbon, "why are we scouring the Quarter for her?"

"She's a new vampire. She shouldn't be wandering around

alone. She could get into real trouble, not understanding her powers, her limitations. She needs looking after for a while anyway."

"I didn't have anyone to look after me."

Cort gave his friend an incredulous look. "You were made a vampire by the captain of a ship and then kept on board for weeks, with other vampires. You were pretty much on the *School at Sea* version of vampirism."

Drake smiled, clearly remembering those days fondly. "Did I mention the whole crew was women dressed as male pirates?"

"Several times."

Drake shrugged, but continued to smile. Finally he snapped out of his affectionate memories to say, "It's true that she probably shouldn't be on her own, but why do I get the feeling you aren't just worried about that?"

"No idea."

Drake raised an eyebrow, but remained silent, but not for long enough. "Let's try Bourbon Cowboy. We were there last night. Maybe she remembered something and ended up there, too."

Cort nodded. "Why not?"

At this point it was like looking for a needle in a haystack anyway. And just like any good haystack, the Bourbon Cowboy revealed nothing more than any of the other places had. Just tourists drinking too much and cheering each other on as they fell off the mechanical bull. Maybe Cort was better off just heading home. If Katie didn't want to be found, he was pretty certain she wouldn't be. He just hoped she was somewhere safe. Maybe she was at her apartment. He'd tried there first, but she hadn't answered. Maybe she'd just ignored his repeated knocks. Maybe she was already in bed. He just hoped she realized the sun was no joke. She had to avoid it.

Let Johnny's death be a lesson on that one, although Katie had no idea that's how Johnny died.

"You know I like to be a supportive friend and all, but man, I'm getting tired. I need a drink or something." Drake stopped walking and leaned against the side of the bar as if he were ancient. Which he was, but vampires didn't get tired. Not physically anyway.

Cort had to admit he felt tired, too, but he was emotionally drained. Man, this had been one stressful night. He would have thought last night was going to be the stressful one, what with dealing with the death of a friend and bandmate, but this night had managed to overshadow that one.

Sorry, Johnny.

"Okay, let's get a drink."

Drake levered himself away from the wall, eyebrows raised. "Really?"

"Yeah, it's going to be impossible to find her. Let's go to Fahy's."

"We already went there and didn't find out much of anything," Drake said.

"That's why I want to go there," Cort said. "I'm tired of looking for clues."

"Me, too, brother, me, too."

It was on the tip of Cort's tongue to point out the only drama Drake went through during their drunken debacle was losing his tooth. That didn't quite stack up to crossing someone over and a supposed marriage. But that would probably open up a conversation he didn't feel like having. Drake already sensed Cort had more than protective feelings for Katie. Not that Cort cared if the guys knew how strongly he felt. Well, as long as Katie returned those same feelings, otherwise Cort planned to play it cool.

They turned down Bourbon and headed the several blocks toward Fahy's.

"Hey, there's Raven," Drake said, pointing to the corner where a tall, bald man dressed in all black stood smoking a cigarette.

"Yippee," Cort said.

"I was just thinking," Drake started, then shook his head. "Never mind."

"What?"

"I was just thinking that"—he paused again, really not wanting to finish his thought, but took one look at Cort's impatient expression and continued—"maybe Raven has seen Katie. He always seemed to pay a lot of attention to her. He'd definitely notice her if she was around."

Cort gritted his teeth. Yeah, that was the last thing he wanted to think about right now. Another man's interest. Especially given he had no idea where he stood with Katie.

But Drake did have a point.

"It can't hurt to ask," Cort said, trying to sound casual. After all, it couldn't hurt to ask, but it could piss him off. Royally.

They crossed the street, walking over to Raven. As soon as he saw them coming, Raven shook his head, looking decidedly displeased about seeing them. He tossed down his cigarette.

"What do you guys want?"

Drake glanced at Cort, waiting for him to speak, but when he didn't, he asked, "Have you seen Katie Lambert?"

"Jesus, what is it with you Impalers and women?"

"What's that supposed to mean?" Cort said, frowning.

"Nothing," Raven said, shaking his head. "No, I have not seen your blushing bride."

Cort gritted his teeth. From Raven's sarcastic tone, it seemed he knew they weren't really married, too. And as much as Cort didn't want to talk to him, Raven might know some other things about last night as well.

"That's right," Cort said, trying to sound conversational, almost friendly, which was no easy feat with this man. "You were at our 'reception.' Did you notice anything weird last night?"

"Weirder than the fact that sweet, beautiful Katie Lambert was interested in you?" The bald, tattooed man rubbed his chin, pretending to think. "Nope, I can't say that I do."

Cort's teeth ached and he knew he had to leave before he reacted more, but before he could even turn away from the man, Raven added, "I can tell you this much though, if I'd turned over that sweet thing, I'd be taking a lot better care of her. Not letting her roam the streets without me."

"Oh, really?" Cort said, that common desire to punch this twit filling him, full force.

"Damned right. If I was going to make the effort to cross her over, I'd also make the effort to keep her close."

Drake stepped forward, as if he could sense that Cort wanted to throw this poser with his silly tattoos and Goth clothing against the side of the bar.

But Cort managed to keep himself composed, except for his hands, which were painfully balled into fists at his sides.

"Oh, yeah, I wouldn't think you could make that kind of commitment, Raven."

"To sweet, lovely Katie?" Raven made a face that could only be described as lascivious. "I'd give it a shot. One thing is for sure, I'd definitely keep her in my bed for a good long time. After all, she is a brand-new vampire, and she has a lot to learn."

Cort stepped forward, even as he told himself to ignore the asshole's taunts. Common sense told him that Raven was just trying to get him going, because he'd wanted Katie for himself, but still he wanted to hurt the dickhead for even thinking about taking his Katie to bed. Much less keeping her there.

You hadn't been able to keep her there.

Even that made him want to hit Raven. But Drake stepped directly between them.

"No point wasting your energy," Drake said, meeting Cort's eyes, trying to get him focused elsewhere rather than on Raven's damned smug face.

Cort glared past Drake anyway, but eventually calmed. "You're right. Let's go."

"Good luck finding her," Raven called after them. "Here's hoping someone else doesn't beat you to her."

Cort spun back, ready to fight again at the implication of his words.

"Don't bother, man," Drake said. "He's just pissed because Katie never noticed him. He's playing stupid mind games. It's all he's got."

Cort pulled in a deep breath and nodded. They headed down the street again, and Cort pretended he couldn't hear Raven's arrogant laughter as they walked away.

"What do you want to do?" Drake asked when they had a good block between them and Raven.

"Let's just go to Fahy's," Cort said. "I'll call Wyatt and see what's going on with them. Maybe they've seen Katie."

"Okay," Drake said, clearly willing to go anywhere as long as a drink was involved.

"Jack and Coke. Jack and Coke."

And the parrot felt the same way. For once, everyone was in agreement.

"CRACKED MY HEAD open?" Katie automatically touched her fingers to her head. She was startled to feel a rather large indentation on the back of her skull. She dropped her hand.

"Yes, you were onstage performing with the band, and you and Cort were singing . . . 'Don't Go Breaking My Heart,' I believe it was."

"As in Elton John?"

"Yes."

Katie pondered that. "Don't Go Breaking My Heart" was hardly the usual Bourbon Street fare. She was surprised the band even knew it. But it did go right along with all the other weirdness.

"Somehow you backed up and got caught on some of the wires on the stage. You fell and hit your noggin just right on the corner of one of the amps. Blood everywhere. It was really quite gruesome."

Gruesome? To a vampire? That was saying something.

"I died from hitting my head on an amp?" Now talk about a death you didn't want to brag about at the Pearly Gates.

"Like I said, you most certainly would have died. Or worse, if Cort hadn't scooped you up and taken care of you."

"Or worse?"

Nigel smiled indulgently. "Not all vampires are as sensitive as Cort and his gang. There were vamps on that boat that might have seen you as an unexpected smorgasbord."

Katie grimaced.

"Not all vampires are as decorous as I am."

It was good to know Nigel hadn't seen her as a free appetizer either.

"We couldn't have made it back to the shore and gotten you to a hospital before you'd have passed. You were bleeding too heavily. Cort made a judgment call, because he cares for you. I hope you aren't angry with him."

"No," she said automatically. No, she wasn't angry with him about the bite, she never had been. She knew some people might be, but she'd known deep down inside that if it had been Cort who'd bitten her, he'd have done it only for a very good reason.

She had trusted that.

But that wasn't what grabbed Katie's attention. It was another thing Nigel said.

"What do you mean, he cares about me?"

Nigel gave her another indulgent smile. "Girl, surely you have seen the way Cort has been pining for you. Everyone who works on Bourbon Street knows it."

Katie shook her head, stunned by his words. She could have understood if he said she'd been the one pining and everyone knew it, because, boy, had she ever pined.

"And you've carried a torch for him, too, haven't you, Katie-Katie?"

She found herself nodding, just because she was stupefied by his insight.

"So you could imagine how pleased many of us were to see him willing to save you. That's a strong bond, you know."

Katie continued to gape at him, unable to do anything else.

Nigel stared at her for a moment, then shrugged. "I guess the people involved are sometimes the last to know."

Could that be true? Could she have misunderstood his reaction to the news of their nonexistent marriage? She certainly had trusted Cort with her life and her undeath. Yet she hadn't even given him a chance to explain his feelings. Just because he didn't want to be married, didn't mean he didn't have feelings for her. After all, most people did explore their feelings before the bonds of matrimony.

"You know, maybe I should go find Cort," she said suddenly, feeling like a childish fool for running off like she had.

"That's probably a good idea," Nigel said. "I'm sure he's fretting about you."

"Maybe," she said, allowing herself to believe Cort could have feelings, true romantic feelings.

She stood, then suddenly remembered she didn't have her wallet.

"I'm sorry," she started, but Nigel cut her off.

"The beer and conversation are on me tonight. I'm just glad you are still with us, girl."

Katie grinned. "Me, too."

She headed to the bar door, only to have it open before she could do so herself.

In front of her appeared the Dancing Vagrant, and as usual her natural instinct was to back away. That smell really was too much. Maybe when she returned the man's parrot, she should also give him a bar of soap. The poor guy probably had no idea how he smelled.

He smiled widely when he saw her, revealing her assessment was very likely correct.

"Here you are," he said, then looked past her into the bar. "Do you have Winston?"

"No, not yet."

His face fell, but almost immediately lifted back into a smile. "I got ahold of Annalese for you."

"You did?" Katie wasn't quite sure if she should believe this man. He seemed perfectly harmless, but definitely a little out-there.

"Yes, she's going to meet us. At Erin Rose."

Erin Rose, another of the band's usual hangouts. That made her feel better about leaving with him. He wasn't taking her somewhere she'd never heard of. Of course she could defend herself anyway.

"But we could stop here for a minute," he said, cocking his head to the side, listening. His hips began to move a little, along with his feet. "I love this song."

He started to step into the bar, but Nigel's voice stopped him.

"We're not having any dancing in here tonight, buddy. Sorry."

Katie glanced at Nigel, who gave her a pained shrug. She understood Nigel's stance. No matter how nice and jovial this guy seemed to be, he was still a dirty, stinky homeless guy and his presence would affect business. A harsh truth, sadly.

"Katie, could you come here for a moment?" Nigel said, waving to her.

Katie raised a finger, then turned to the Dancing Vagrant. "Wait right here." She started over to the bar, then turned back to him and added for good measure, "I'll have Cort meet us at Erin Rose with Winston."

She didn't want him dancing off again.

He nodded, perking up again at her mention of his best friend.

"I know this guy is harmless, but please be careful," Nigel said as she approached the bar. He pushed a plastic cup of beer toward her, nodding to the vagrant. "Give that to him."

Katie took the cup. Nigel was really a nice guy. So much for this whole "vampires being monsters" thing.

"I will be careful," Katie assured him. "I just need to find out if Cort and I actually got married last night. And this guy says he knew the person who married us."

Nigel looked surprised, then impressed. "Attending a wake, having a fatal accident, crossing over, discovering you are in love, and a marriage all in one night. And none of you remember it. That has to be a record, even for Bourbon Street."

Katie laughed. "Definitely not the work of your average girl next door."

"Ah, Katie-Katie," Nigel said, patting her hand again. "I definitely don't think anyone would ever consider you an average girl next door. You're a stunner."

Katie beamed. Maybe she really was. Maybe she always had been and just didn't know it.

"This is good," the Dancing Vagrant said, grinning down at his beer, any hurt feelings soothed by free alcohol. "That bartender never lets me in the bar, you know, because of Winston. Some bars have really strict policies about animals."

Katie and Cort certainly hadn't helped this man's chances of getting into bars with that bird. Or rather, the bird had hurt his own chances.

But in this case, since Winston wasn't even with him, she didn't think the bird was Nigel's issue. But since the man was happy with his beer and his rationalization, Katie wasn't about to ruin that for him by pointing out the truth.

"So how do you know Annalese Bonvieux?"

"Everyone knows Annalese." He frowned as if she was mad. Maybe she was, and he was the sane one. Who knows.

"I'm sorry, I don't."

"She married you and your man last night. Of course you know her."

He had a point there. She should know her.

"Well, I was so excited, I guess everything is a bit of a blur," she told him.

He nodded. "Life is exciting."

Katie had to give this guy credit, he did put a good spin on everything. Then again, he was the Dancing Vagrant.

They reached Erin Rose, pushing aside the plastic strips that covered the doorway to keep the air-conditioning in and the humid, Louisiana air out of the bar.

"Hey," the bartender at the front bar called immediately as soon as he saw them enter. The burly man with a goatee and tattooed sleeves covering his bulky muscles pointed at the vagrant. "You can't come in here."

Dancing Vagrant gave Katie an "I told you so" look. "See, Winston again."

And again, Katie accepted his rationalization with a smile and a nod.

"Annalese is probably in the back bar. If not, I'll send her back there when I see her."

Katie nodded again. The Dancing Vagrant waved quite merrily to the grouchy-looking bartender and slipped back out of the bar.

Katie sighed, wishing she had her purse. She'd buy the poor guy another beer and bring it out to him, so he at least had something to do while he waited around outside. She supposed that he might wander off to enjoy more music and dance, but she also knew he did love his bird, and he was waiting for Winston as much as she was waiting for this Annalese Bonvieux.

And maybe this lady was already there. She glanced back once more to see the Vagrant Dancer just outside the window. He'd bummed a cigarette, or at least she assumed he'd bummed a cigarette off someone, and he was jigging slightly to some of the music that wafted outside from Erin Rose's loud jukebox.

She shook her head, again amazed at what a truly happy guy he was, and she headed into the back room.

The back bar of Erin Rose was a small square room, two of the walls lined with a nicked, worn bar and equally worn wooden stools. A few tables littered the limited floor space, but for some reason, Katie had always found the place more homey than cramped and shabby.

Maybe because it was one of the favorite spots of the locals, and whenever she walked back there, she knew she was going to know someone.

And sure enough, she recognized one of the patrons seated at the bar immediately.

"Raven," she said, greeting the bald guitarist with a cool familiarity.

Raven either didn't notice, or didn't care, because he smiled broadly.

"Katie Lambert. How are you feeling tonight?"

Katie knew that he had to know she was now one of them, since he'd been at the wake and in the pictures she'd seen.

"I feel fine," she said, looking toward the other patron, a woman who looked a little mussed and frazzled. If the way she was knocking back her drink was any indication, she was.

Could this be Annalese Bonvieux? And if it was, did she want to have the conversation she was about to have in front of Raven? Not really.

But Katie approached her, a little timidly, partly because she felt nervous and because the woman really did look more than a little stressed.

"Pardon me," Katie said softly, but the woman whipped around like Katie had shouted at her. The woman eyed Katie up and down.

"I'm sorry to bother you, but are you Annalese?"

The woman studied her a moment longer, then shook her head no, and Katie quickly realized she wasn't going to volunteer anything more. Katie thanked her, wondering what the heck happened to her tonight to make her so tense.

Katie frowned. It couldn't be anything weirder than what had happened to her.

Katie turned around, surveying the room again. Of course Raven watched her, and she felt obligated to wander back toward him. Why couldn't that woman have been Annalese? Or at least friendly so Katie would have felt comfortable sitting down with her. Instead she took a seat a couple down from Raven.

He immediately got up and sat down beside her. Of course. She should have told him she wanted to just sit here by herself, surely being a vampire should give her the ability to be a little bitchy, but still she couldn't be overtly rude. Those darn ingrained manners.

"You look lovely. Your new state suits you."

"Thank you." She really wished someone else was back here with them. As if in answer to her wish, Peter, the back-room bartender, appeared. Peter was in exact opposition to the front-room bartender. He was average height, with somewhat broad shoulders, but overall an average build. His ever-present cowboy hat was perched on his shaggy hair that was a color somewhere between light brown and gray.

He nodded at Katie and asked her what she'd like to drink. Katie hesitated, not certain that Peter would extend her a brief line of credit like she knew Nigel would have.

"Let me buy you a drink," Raven said.

Katie hesitated again, then nodded. "I'll have a vodka and tonic with extra lime."

Peter moved over to the other bar to fix her drink.

"So I guess I should tell you that your man Cort is looking for you."

Katie turned slightly on her barstool. "He is?"

Raven nodded, taking a sip of his own drink. Red wine.

"And I also have to admit, I couldn't resist ribbing him."

"How and why?"

"I gotta tell you, Katie, I'm pretty damned sick of losing all the good ladies to the damned Impalers."

She frowned, not totally following him.

"Stella Malone to Wyatt Axelrod."

Really? Katie supposed that made sense. Stella and Wyatt would make a great and truly stunning couple. In fact, now that she thought about it, she had sensed something between them on occasion, but she'd always been so focused on Cort that she hadn't given it much thought. But apparently they were together now? Good for them.

"And of course, I've lost you to Berto Cortez."

Peter appeared, placing her drink on the bar in front of her. Katie thanked him and took a long sip before responding to Raven.

"I don't think you can really say you lost me to Cort. You never had me and he always did."

His eyeliner-darkened eyes widened, and he actually looked stunned, but then he chuckled, shaking his head. "Damn, you know what, you have a good point."

Katie smiled, too.

Raven laughed again. "You have a very good point."

And he took a sip of his wine.

"SHE JUST LEFT."

Cort stared at his friend.

Nigel stopped wiping the bar and repeated himself, this time slower.

Since Cort had pretty much made up his mind that finding Katie wasn't going to happen tonight, Nigel's words didn't make sense right away.

"Do you know where she was headed?"

It was actually Drake who asked.

Cort just felt too relieved that maybe they were close to finding her. Maybe he could talk to her and tell her exactly how he felt.

"She's headed to Erin Rose to meet with a woman who apparently married you last night."

Cort looked at Drake. "But I thought you said that Katie and I didn't really get married."

Drake gave him a puzzled look. "All I know is you weren't married by the priest from the bathtub. He's a stripper who works at Bounce."

It was Nigel's turn to look baffled as he looked from Cort to Drake and back to Cort again.

"Alrighty, I'm not even going to try to follow that, but apparently Katie got some information that maybe you really did get married. Granted, she got this information from a local homeless man, but who knows."

"A local homeless man?" Cort said.

"Yes, the Dancing Vagrant. He tends to hang around Frenchmen Street more than Bourbon, but he does come down this way occasionally."

The Dancing Vagrant? Cort racked his brain. He remembered hearing that name before. Wait, that's right. That couple from earlier, Betty and Ed, they'd had pictures of a man they'd called that name. But he didn't recall them saying this guy had also been a part of their wedding party. Damn, more confusion.

Whatever. He knew where Katie was.

"Thanks," Cort said, smacking Drake on the shoulder just as he was about to settle on a barstool.

"What?" Drake said, giving him an innocently confused look.

"We're going to another bar—get a drink there."

"Jack and Coke. Jack and Coke."

"You, too," Cort muttered to the bird.

"Oh, and by the way, that parrot belongs to the homeless man with Katie."

Damn, that was almost as good news as the fact they were going to find Katie. Almost.

Cort waved to Nigel. "Hallelujah. Thanks, man."

"You bet. Go get your lady."

Cort planned on it.

"SO IF YOU don't like The Impalers, why did you go to Johnny's wake?" Katie asked.

Raven didn't answer for a moment. "I never said I didn't like The Impalers. In fact, I really admire them. Just somehow since the moment I came to Bourbon and started with my band at Famous Door, we've had this rivalry."

Katie pondered that, knowing that a few of the bands had rivalries, but for the most part they were friendly rivalries.

"Yet, last night you were hanging out with all of them, bonding, having a great time," Katie pointed out. "I mean I saw a picture of you and Cort giving each other bunny ears for heaven's sake. If that isn't bonding, I don't know what is."

Raven nodded, but his expression grew sober, even almost disappointed. "The problem is, none of the guys remember that."

Katie stared at him, realizing that all of Raven's persona—his angst and arrogance and Goth look—was just that, a persona. A front. He wanted to be accepted just as much as anyone.

Wow. Suddenly Katie felt rather sorry for him. He just wanted to be liked, just like everyone else.

She found herself reaching out to rub his back, wanting to offer him comfort.

"They did forget last night," she agreed. "I did, too, but I think if you tried a little harder to show the guys your softer, gentler side, they'd react well to it. They really are nice."

The woman at the other bar snorted, although Katie decided it couldn't be a reaction to what she'd said.

Raven sighed and took a drink. "Well, I was pretty rude to Cort earlier, trying to get his goat. But like I said, it is pretty damned irritating that The Impalers get all the good girls."

"I'm not a good girl," Katie said, again annoyed that everyone saw her as sweet. And as a girl.

"Oh yes, you are. You are a good girl and that's what makes you so appealing. You're sweet, kind, and beautiful. You have no idea how special that makes you. Cort is a very lucky man. And I'll tell you right now, that dude is crazy about you."

Tears welled in Katie's eyes, but she hid them by taking a sip of her drink.

It was funny, it took a night she couldn't remember to finally see the truth. And to see what others saw. It also took starting a new life to see that her past life had been exactly what it should have been. She was the person she was supposed to be. The person she would be for an eternity. And that was a good thing.

But most importantly, she was going to be with the man she was supposed to be with. And she was going to make sure that was for an eternity, too.

"Thank you, Raven," she said, leaning forward to hug the man who she would have never considered hugging even fifteen minutes ago.

He shifted on his barstool and hugged her back.

"Thank you for the talk, and for the advice. I'm going to take you up on it."

Katie smiled at him, pleased with their talk, too.

But the moment was interrupted by a shout.

"You fuckin' asshole! Get your hands off her."

Katie moved away from Raven instantly, shocked to see Cort come barging into the back room. Before Katie even realized what he intended to do, he grabbed the back of Raven's black coat and was lifting the man to his feet.

From the other side of the bar she vaguely heard Peter mutter, "Jesus Christ, what the hell is going on with everyone tonight?"

Raven jerked away and spun toward Cort, the movement blindingly fast, but Cort was just as fast, popping Raven in the face before the other man could even get his hands fisted. Raven's head jerked to the side, the sound of Cort's fist against his jaw, loud and sickening. And Cort was ready to hit again, drawing back.

But Raven didn't allow the second punch to make contact, landing a brutal hit himself. Cort's head snapped back, blood instantly gushing from his nose.

Katie screamed, finally snapping out of her shock to stand, to speak.

"Stop," she cried. "Stop it!"

But Cort wasn't listening. He grabbed Raven's lapels and shoved the man hard into the tables. Raven nearly fell, but caught himself, glaring at Cort.

At that point, Katie stepped between them. She faced Cort, trying to get his attention focused on her.

"Cort, Raven wasn't doing anything wrong."

Cort didn't respond to her. In fact, he seemed to stare right through her.

"Listen to your woman, man. We were just talking," Raven said.

"I didn't see any talking. I saw your hands on her. And that's not going to happen again."

"Cort." Katie moved closer to him, rising up on her tiptoes to block his view of Raven. When he still didn't meet her gaze, she grabbed his jaw, forcing him to look at her. "Cort. Raven and I were talking, nothing more."

Cort's eyes calmed slightly, some of the flashing anger fading. His gaze searched her face. "Why was he touching you?"

"I gave him a hug because he said kind and supportive things to me. Things that made me realize I need to believe in myself and go after what I want. Which is you."

Cort frowned, clearly not expecting to hear that.

"Yeah, man, I was telling her that you were damned lucky to have her." Raven rubbed his swollen jaw. "But I was acknowledging that you do have her."

Cort's expression grew even more perplexed, then a little suspicious.

Raven lifted his hands. "Listen, I'm telling you the truth. You are wasting your time attacking me, you already won the girl."

Cort stared at him a moment longer, then looked back to Katie.

"You have already won me—if you want me."

Cort didn't hesitate. His mouth captured hers, his kiss hungry, possessive, filled with pure desire.

She groaned, her chest swelling with joy, longing, and love.

"This is all fabulously romantic," a voice said from beside them, and they parted to see Peter standing next to them. "But I've already had a shitty night, and you two guys need to leave."

Chapter Twenty-one

VAMPIRES DON'T DIE
(Duh)

STELLA held hands with Wyatt as they approached his apartment, feeling giddy and girly and achy with anticipation. She had said, out loud no less, that she loved Wyatt. And she had meant it. It was amazing. More than a hundred years without ever experiencing love and here it had been, right in front of her face for years. But maybe that's why she loved Wyatt. She wasn't the impulsive type, really. She needed to let her emotions simmer and rise to a boil. Over four decades, apparently. Thank God she had eternity, because she was no quick decision maker.

But there was one thing she wanted to get to quickly now, and that was his bed. "I'm glad you live so close."

Wyatt laughed. "Me, too. And I'm also glad I don't have a roommate. I don't know how Cort and Drake stand living together."

"I think they play a lot of Guitar Hero." Stella watched Wyatt stick his key in the lock and push the door open. "You have a nice place, you know. Johnny was such a slob."

Saying her brother's name still caused a stab of pain in her heart, but she didn't want to stop talking about him, especially not with Wyatt, who had cared about Johnny as well. Who had been there for her the minute her grief had exploded.

"He was totally a slob." Wyatt pulled her inside. "But I like things clean. I left the dust behind when I left the Wild West. I've been in this place ten years and you're the first woman to set foot in my bedroom."

"I'm not there yet." Stella kicked off her shoes by the front door and closed it behind her. She set her flowers down on his coffee table. "And your bedroom leads to your courtyard. A lot of women we know have walked through at parties." It was being nitpicky, but she wanted to clarify. She was fishing for compliments and he seemed to know it.

"That's true. A few women have used it as a hallway, but no one has ever been in my bed." His palm cupped her cheek and she turned into him, her skin sensitive to his touch. "No other woman ever will be."

She sucked in a breath. He was talking forever. That should scare her. But at the moment all it did was thrill and arouse her. She reached out and tugged Wyatt's T-shirt up so that she could run her hands across the hard planes of his sculpted chest. Five nights a week she watched him play his bass guitar and she never tired of it, the way he mastered the instrument, the way he kept his arms low and relaxed. Bass was sexy and Wyatt was even sexier, and she was very much aware of that at the moment. He helped her take his shirt up over his head, then he shook his hair loose. It was just the right length, brushing the shoulders, perfect for musicians and models alike.

Wyatt's jaw was too square, his nose a little hooked, for the perfection of the runway, but as a musician he was perfect. And he was hers.

His gun medallion fell against his chest and she toyed with it before letting her fingers trail down past his pectorals to the smooth skin of his abdomen. She popped the snap on his jeans.

Fingers stilled her before she could take down his zipper. "You're overdressed," he told her.

"I can fix that." Stella dropped her purse on the hardwood floor. Then she peeled off her own shirt and tossed it on top of his.

Wyatt reached forward and traced the top of her black bra with one finger. "You're beautiful."

She was average for a vampire, but with him, she felt beautiful. "You're not so bad yourself."

"Come here and kiss me."

But he didn't wait for her answer or for her action. Wyatt ate up the space between them and buried his hands in her hair. His mouth took hers in a passionate kiss that had her inner thighs aching and her nipples beading, desperate for attention.

"Oh!" she said, stunned at how shattering the impact of skin on skin, lips on lips, hips pressed against hips was.

It was like the volume had been turned up, like their acknowledgment of what they felt had stripped down any barriers of reserve that had remained and allowed their passion to scream at its highest setting. Desire amplified.

"Stella, God, I want you," he murmured, his teeth nipping at her earlobe before reclaiming her lips.

His hands were everywhere, caressing from her shoulder blades to her ass, giving it a thorough squeeze, then slinking around to the front to tease at the seam of her jeans before heading north to taunt her nipples. Just when she adjusted, accepted his touch somewhere, he retreated, and she moved restlessly, unable to keep up, his sensual assault setting her body and nerves on edge. It felt decadent and urgent and out of control. Normally she didn't like out of control, but this . . . this was divine.

He popped her bra open.

She yanked his zipper down.

But before they could go any further, he scooped her up into his arms and swung toward the kitchen. "I promised you a bed."

A wall, the floor, a bed. She wasn't sure at the moment she cared, but she did have to admit, being carried was a novelty. A hot one. Stella put her arms around his neck and flicked her tongue across his nipple.

There was a brief pause in his step while he cursed, but then he continued to move through the kitchen to the bedroom. His bed wasn't made. He dropped her down onto the rumpled blankets. She turned her head and buried her face in the cool cotton sheet. It smelled like him, masculine and earthy. Whiskey. With a tug, she stripped off her unhooked bra with her hand between her breasts and tossed it aside.

Wyatt descended on her, taking a nipple into his mouth with enough ferocity that she yelped in both pleasure and near pain. Then he went to the other one, plucking at it like the strings of his bass with his fingers, then his tongue. Somehow he managed to slide into her jeans at the same time, wiggling his way into the dewy dampness of her inner thighs.

"That feels good," she breathed, figuring she was stating the obvious but not really caring. The bed was soft beneath her and he was hard over her and she was in love.

The moment needed words, even small ones.

"I'm glad you like it. I think you'll like it even better with your jeans off."

She wasn't going to argue with that. Or the skill with which he divested her of the pants. Before she could do much more than nod, she was bare before him. Wyatt nuzzled up the inner side of her knee, his lips and nose teasing and tickling her. Gripping the bedsheet, she waited in deep anticipation, her womb aching with the need for him. For him deep inside her.

But that wasn't what he had in mind and she knew it. After a leisurely route up her thigh, Wyatt stroked her curls with both thumbs, staring at her most intimate spot with a great deal of intensity. She didn't mind him looking. She would just prefer he were touching. He blew on her clitoris and she jerked on the bed, her backside tightening in reaction.

Stella lifted her hips a little in invitation to urge him to put her out of her misery, because she was starting to think this was one of the very few ways a vampire could die, and her number was just about up. "Wyatt . . ."

"Yes?" He spread her folds and brushed his lips lightly over her.

"I don't know." She honestly wasn't sure if she had been meaning to say anything or not. All she could think about was his tongue and the delicious strokes it was now making across her clitoris. "Yes, yes."

Letting her eyes drift shut, she gave herself over to the sensations that were swamping her, the tight pressure of his hands on her thighs, his hair tickling her pelvis, his breath coming in short, hot bursts on her sensitive flesh. His mouth licking and sucking and eating her. Moisture flooded her and she groaned in ecstasy.

She thought he might tease her, take her to the edge and pull back, but he didn't. He just kept doing those delicious things to her, his tongue darting inside her moist opening, and back again, until she felt the orgasm building up, higher and higher. Still she held it back, not trusting it, but Wyatt urged her on.

"Go ahead, I can feel how close you are. Let go."

So she did. She let go of everything. The past. Her inhibitions. The need for order. She just gave in to her body, to Wyatt, to the love she felt for him.

With a yell, she came in the most freeing orgasm she'd ever had, the waves of pleasure not tumultuous, but sweeping and fluid. "Yes, yes, yes," she chanted.

Then Wyatt was shucking his own jeans and moving in between her legs. His erection teased at her warmth, triggering little aftershocks of delight. Catching her under the knee, Wyatt drew her right foot up to his shoulder. She wasn't sure why it surprised her but it did, in a good way. She knew he was going to be deep, deep inside her and that was such a wonderful thing. He held her gaze, waiting, drawing out the mutual suspense.

Stella knew how to change that. Letting go of the sheet, she rolled her palm over her nipple, biting her bottom lip on the gasp the movement elicited.

It worked. Wyatt groaned and thrust into her, burying himself to the hilt.

Oh, yeah. That's what she was talking about. Stella lay back and dropped her free hip farther open. For him. She wanted to take him as deep as she possibly could, feel the immense pleasure that the man she loved could give her with his cock fully inside her warmth.

"Make me come again," she demanded.

"I'm happy to." Wyatt struggled to maintain his composure. Stella had no idea what she did to him. She turned him inside out. Took him to the very edge of his control.

Her body wrapped around his cock in a warm, tight embrace

and he could feel the pulsations of her building orgasm. He was barely moving, just a slow slide in and out, not pulling out all the way, and she was already reacting to him like she was going to come. That he could do that to her so easily made him want to come. Her taste lingered on his tongue and her body was lithe and sexy beneath him. Her taut nipples rose toward him and he turned his head to kiss her smooth delicate calf.

Wyatt set a hard rhythm, knowing that's the way she would want it. Stella liked to take it. And he was determined to give it to her.

Pumping faster, he bit back a groan, meeting her gaze as her eyes widened in pleasure.

"Oh, yes. That feels so good."

"Good?" he asked. "That's it?" He wanted to hear her say it. He wanted her to beg for it.

So he pulled all the way out of her, gritting his teeth on a silent curse as his cock throbbed in protest. Stella yelled out, her hand coming toward him.

"Wyatt, no! Don't stop."

That's all he needed to hear. He fisted in her hair and plunged deep inside her.

Stella's body stiffened, then she broke apart in a gorgeous, big, no-holds-barred orgasm, a frantic yell of ecstasy breaking past her lips. Wyatt had thought to hold off on his own release, but when he saw her, heard her, there was no way he could stop himself.

With his own groan he came in a ball-draining explosion that wiped his mind clean and shook him to the core.

So that's what it was like to have sex with the woman you loved.

It was the hottest damn thing he'd ever encountered.

"Holy moly," was Stella's opinion.

He couldn't have said it better. "Babe. Damn." He'd find better words when his blood returned to his brain. At the moment he was nothing but shaky arms and deep gut-grinding satisfaction.

Pulling out with a sigh, Wyatt collapsed on the bed next to her. "I love you."

She gave a giggle, which made him laugh. "I love you, too."

She did. He could see it in her eyes when he looked down at her. They were glassy and filled with softness. "You're beautiful."

Her finger reached out and traced his bottom lip. "Together feels better than alone."

"That it does."

With a sigh, she snuggled up against him. "I'm sleepy."

"So sleep. I'll be here when you wake up."

He would be there forever.

WYATT WATCHED STELLA sleeping from the step to his courtyard, inordinately pleased with having her in his bed, and with the fact that he had completely worn her out. She needed the sleep, even if it was just a short nap. The last few nights had been eventful, to say the least.

The moonlight was flooding his room from the open windows and door, glancing off of Stella's curled-up body. Her face was tucked in the shadows, her hair falling over her cheek, a soft crisp breeze drifting over him, bringing the scent of flowers to mingle with the tangy aftereffects of their lovemaking. He had pulled the sheet over her lower half and put on jeans before lounging on the bricks, bare chest and feet. He loved his little courtyard, a private oasis in the crowded and noisy Quarter. Now he loved it even more that he wasn't there alone.

Stella filled the space nicely and he didn't want her to leave.

But that was a discussion for another night sometime in the future, when they'd gotten their relationship legs steady beneath them. For now, he was content to share his space whenever she liked.

A *thump* in the back of the courtyard had his eyes straining to see into the dark. There were a number of stray cats who liked to visit and he didn't mind. Most wouldn't get too close to him since he gave off an undead vibe, but there was one tiger who was bold enough to offer his ears for a rub. But this sounded like something bigger than a cat and Wyatt stood up, suddenly on alert.

"Hey," came a whispered, urgent voice from the corner behind a banana plant.

Wyatt pulled the door closed behind him in one swift motion, protective instincts kicking in. "Who's there? Step into the open so I can see you."

The person obliged, moving into the middle of the courtyard, full moonlight shining on him and his AC/DC T-shirt.

Wyatt almost had a heart attack. "Johnny?" he whispered. Oh, my God. He was fucking going crazy. Or seeing a ghost.

"Yeah." Johnny darted a glance behind him at the wall he had just leapt down from. "You've got to hide me, man. She's relentless."

Since his crossover Wyatt didn't dream. So this had to be real. But he still felt like pinching himself. "I thought you were dead!" he exclaimed, moving forward to get a closer look at his friend, a massive sense of relief flooding him.

"Well, that was the point. Only somehow she figured it out and she tracked me down." Johnny was rushing forward, right on past Wyatt. "If she shows up here, you haven't seen me."

"Who?"

"Bambi."

Wyatt's relief was replaced by utter astonishment. "You faked your death to hide from a woman?"

"Yes."

"Are you fucking kidding me?" Wyatt was going to kill him. Johnny was alive and now Wyatt wanted him dead. "You put Stella through hell, you asshole!"

"It was unavoidable. She'll get over it. But now is not the time to chat about it. Now is the time to hide." Johnny opened the door and slipped into Wyatt's bedroom.

Where Stella was sleeping naked. Shit. Wyatt moved to follow him when another thump alerted him to a potential problem. He turned around and saw a mortal woman on the bricks of his courtyard cursing and swiping at her hair as she stood up, shaking out her leg like the drop had injured her. Which it probably had, given it was a five-foot drop and she was clearly mortal, since Wyatt could smell her blood.

"Um, can I help you?" he asked, because what the fuck else was he supposed to say?

"You can tell me where that lying deadbeat dad Johnny Malone is."

Wyatt's brain froze for a second and he stared through the murky darkness at a very angry-looking blonde woman in the tiniest denim shorts he'd ever seen in his life. That couldn't be good for her health. "Uh . . . what was the question again?"

She cracked her knuckle and bounded toward him. "Never mind. I know he's here. I saw him go over the wall. Faking his death, I mean, really? That's not going to get his sorry ass out of paying child support."

Wyatt was more than a little confused. Last time he'd checked, vampires couldn't procreate. So why did this woman think Johnny owed her child support? He wasn't exactly sure what to say but he did manage, "I think there must be a mistake."

She stopped in her march on him and snorted. She was a pretty girl, in an overblown sort of way. Lots of bouncing cleavage and swinging hair. "Are you going to stand there and defend him? I don't think so. Who the hell are you anyway?"

"I'm Wyatt Axelrod." He stuck his hand out, which she ignored. "Bambi, I presume?"

Her eyes widened. "So you do know. Don't cover for him. I'll still find him and it will just piss me off. You don't want to piss me off."

No, he suspected he really didn't want to do that.

But he was saved from having to reply by the ear-piercing scream Stella gave from his bedroom.

For the second time today Wyatt figured that was the sound of the shit hitting the fan.

Chapter Twenty-two

WHEN BAMBI BECOMES THE HUNTER

STELLA was yanked out of a sound sleep when a loud *slam* happened somewhere behind her head. Jerking her eyes open, she half sat up, searching for Wyatt and the source of the noise. The door was closed; the wind must have blown it shut.

But it wasn't Wyatt staring down at her, holding a finger to his mouth to indicate she should be quiet.

It was her brother.

Stella opened her mouth and let loose with a scream. Oh, my God, she was seeing her dead brother. Did that mean she was dead, too? She patted her legs and bit her lips, drawing blood. She felt alive. But did dead people feel dead? She didn't know because she'd never been dead.

"Stella," Johnny groaned, looking and sounding exactly like he had when he was alive. "Not cool. She's going to—"

Whatever his dead self was going to say was cut off when the door flew open, slamming hard into the wall, and a wild-eyed blonde with a big chest came barreling into the bedroom. Stella blinked, clutching the sheet to her own flat chest, and wondered if she had lost her mind. Because she was starting to think she wasn't dead. Which meant that Johnny wasn't dead.

"You're alive?" she asked him, brain firing a little slowly from sleep and shock.

"Kind of obvious, isn't it?" was his response.

Wyatt came in behind the blonde and came over to her. "Stella, are you okay?"

She nodded. She wasn't sure she was okay, really, but it was an automatic response. "Johnny's alive."

"So it seems."

And her live brother was rolling his eyes at the blonde who had walked straight up to him and slapped him cleanly across the face. "You're going to accept your responsibility," she told him scathingly.

"Bambi," Johnny said in a soothing voice.

So this was the infamous Bambi.

"It's not my responsibility."

"What the hell is going on here?" Stella asked.

Bambi rounded on her. "Who are you?" She whirled back to Johnny. "You've been hiding out with this ginger slut? Did you get her pregnant, too?" Her hand went up to deliver another slap but Johnny caught it this time and held her still.

Ginger slut? Stella felt her mouth fall open. What had she done to deserve that? Besides being naked in Wyatt's bed at the moment, but she hadn't been expecting company. Certainly not her dead brother. Who apparently wasn't dead.

"You faked your death?" she asked Johnny, relief that he was actually alive hitting her full force, followed by pure rage. "You motherfucker."

"Tell me about it," was Bambi's opinion. "But no one asked you, slut."

"Hey!" Johnny protested. "This is my sister, Stella. Don't be calling her a slut."

"Why the hell would you fake your death?" Stella said, picking up the bed pillow and hurling it at him. It bounced off his knee. "You selfish prick! I was devastated."

"Wait a minute." Johnny looked at her like he was seeing her for the first time. "Why are you naked in Wyatt's bed?" He looked over at Wyatt, who was standing in the doorway without a shirt or shoes on. "Did you have sex with my sister? What's wrong with you? You're my best friend! I'm barely cold in the grave and you're banging my sister? God!"

Oh, no, he didn't. Stella was so furious she couldn't form words. Her lips just sputtered as she searched the bed for another pillow to throw.

Wyatt moved to his dresser and yanked open a drawer. "Johnny, don't even go there with me. And you're changing the subject. The real question is how could you do this to us? Let us think you're dead? That sucks, man."

"No, the real question is how he can look himself in the mirror and not throw up in his mouth?" Bambi asked. "He's refusing to accept responsibility for his child!"

"I told you, it's not my baby."

"Are you accusing me of sleeping around?"

"I'm not accusing you of anything. I'm just saying that it can't be my baby. I'm sterile."

There was truth to that. Stella had never heard of a vampire impregnating a mortal. Maybe once in like ten million vampires. But that still didn't explain her brother's ludicrous need to write a made up suicide note.

"Oh, if I had a dollar for every man who handed me that line when he didn't want to wear a condom. I wasn't born yesterday, you know."

"I wore a condom," Johnny protested. "I'm not the father."

"So take a DNA test. I offered you that option and instead you pretended to be *dead*. That's fucked-up, Johnny."

Stella had to agree with Bambi on that one. "What was that pile of ashes?" she asked her brother. "There was a pile of ashes in your apartment."

He shrugged. "Cigarette ash. Took me all damn week to collect that many. They don't accumulate as much as you'd think. I spent forty bucks on cigarettes, twice my weekly budget."

Cigarette ash. Stella shook her head, wishing she wasn't naked so she could jump out of bed and beat the living shit out of him. "You're an ass," she told him.

"Don't be mean," he told her. "And I'm not taking a DNA test."

Stella imagined that he didn't want to hand over his blood for testing because vampires didn't exactly have the same genetic makeup as mortals. But no one was going to be doing a full analysis on his blood. They were going to do a paternity test, end of story. This seemed like a ridiculous way to maneuver around that. Or hell, he could have just paid Bambi child support and played daddy, even if the kid clearly wasn't his.

Anything would have made more sense than letting your loved ones think you were dead.

She was going to kill him.

Wyatt had pulled a T-shirt and pajama pants out of his dresser and he handed them to her, smoothing her hair back off her face. "It's okay," he whispered to her. "Remember the positive. Johnny's alive, after all."

She wasn't sure that was such a positive at the moment, but she appreciated the reassurance. Nodding, she said, "Thank you," and pulled the shirt on over her head.

Wyatt stood up and turned to Johnny. "You owe Stella an apology. What you did was cruel."

"Sorry." Johnny didn't sound particularly sorry. "I didn't mean to upset you, Stell. I figured Wyatt would tell you last night and you'd think it was funny. Good wake, by the way. I liked the music and there was a good turnout."

Stella wiggled into the pants under the covers, falling onto her elbow, trying to process her idiot brother's statements. He was making even less sense than Saxon, and God knew that was saying a lot. "What do you mean, you thought Wyatt would tell me last night?"

If Wyatt knew her brother was alive and he didn't tell her, well, then the body count was going to rise even higher.

"I was spying on you guys. Well, you weren't there, but all the band was, and Wyatt spotted me in a doorway. We talked, and I gave him my necklace for safekeeping. It's my blood, you know, didn't want that falling into the wrong hands." He shot a side glance at Bambi, who was clearly the DNA thief he was referring to.

"Wyatt, you saw Johnny?" she asked, astonished.

"No." Wyatt looked as flabbergasted as she felt. "Though I don't remember anything, remember? I very well could have had a whole conversation with him and would have no clue."

"Oh, my God." Stella finally got herself into the pajama pants and shoved back the covers. "That would explain where you got the necklace from."

"You're right." Wyatt groaned. "This is ridiculous."

"Johnny, where did you get the necklace?"

"I went back to my place and took it off the kitchen counter. It's my necklace."

The kitchen counter. Right where Wyatt had said all along it was. Before the night had gone black and all hell had apparently broken loose.

"So are you going to give me DNA or do I have to serve you in court?" Bambi asked, hands on her hips.

Stella felt a great deal of sympathy for the woman, and figured she should be happy that Johnny couldn't have children. His idiocy should not be passed on to a future generation.

Wyatt left the room. Stella climbed out of bed, intending to follow him. She was done with this conversation.

But he came back immediately.

Johnny was saying, "No. I'm not doing it. You can't force my hand, Bambi."

Stella didn't see it coming. Johnny clearly didn't either. Because he didn't have time to react or block it when Wyatt came behind him and shoved a Q-tip into Johnny's mouth. There was some gurgling and Johnny's arm coming up in reaction, but Wyatt had it back out before Johnny could grab his hand.

"Here." He held the Q-tip out to Bambi. "Do what you need to do."

"Hey!' Johnny protested.

"I don't want to hear it," Wyatt told him.

Bambi took the offering delicately, holding the swab up between two fingers, and said, "Thanks."

"Front door is this way." Wyatt took her through the kitchen and living room to the front door of his apartment.

Bambi followed without a backward glance at Johnny.

"I'm not at all comfortable with that," Johnny said, frowning.

"I'm not at all comfortable with you at the moment. And if you want to prove it's not your kid, this is the only way to do that. It's certainly easier than faking your death."

Stella went over to Johnny and whacked him in the arm. "How could you do that to me?" Then she burst into tears. Johnny wasn't dead. He was alive and well and driving her crazy and she was absolutely grateful for that fact.

"Hey, Stell, it's okay." Johnny pulled her into his arms.

It felt good to have her big brother hold her. She closed her eyes and breathed in his scent of tobacco and cologne. He'd been a thorn in her side for over a hundred years and she sincerely hoped he would be a thorn for hundreds more. She hugged him tightly.

"If you ever do anything like that again, I will string you up. I'll never forgive you."

"So you forgive me now?" Johnny grinned, his charming smile, one that had affected many women over the years. His dark hair fell across his forehead and there was his customary twinkle in his blue eyes. They didn't look like siblings, but he was her blood.

"I don't think I forgive you as much as I'm just glad you're alive."

"I don't forgive you," Wyatt said, coming back into the bedroom. "That was the crappiest thing you've ever done, Malone."

Johnny's eyes narrowed as he dropped his arms from around her. "I'm not too thrilled with you either, Axelrod. You've got a lot of nerve taking advantage of my sister in her time of grief."

Uh. Stella pictured her hands yanking down Wyatt's zipper in Johnny's kitchen. "Johnny, that's not what happened." In fact, it might have been the other way around.

"Stella and I are together. This wasn't about sex. We're in a relationship and I love her, so get over it."

He loved her. The sound of that, coming so easily from his lips, made her giddy. Stella hugged her arms to her chest. Her arms in his T-shirt. His pajama pants. Call her a complete dork, but wearing his sleepwear made her happy.

"For real? You love Stella." Johnny looked incredulous.

"Don't sound so surprised," she said. "It is possible for a man to care about me."

"Of course it is, don't be a harpy."

How was she being a harpy?

"Don't call Stella a harpy."

Johnny broke out into a grin. "You do love her. Man, I didn't see that one coming." He reached out and clapped Wyatt on the shoulder. "That's awesome. Hey, if my sister has to be in a relationship, I couldn't ask for anyone better than you to take care of her."

Wyatt broke into a smile, too. "Thanks, bro. I plan on making her very happy."

Hello. Stella standing over here. She was glad that they were making up, so to speak, but she would also appreciate it if someone noticed she was still in the room. "Can I say something here?"

They both turned and looked at her expectantly, but then she found she had no idea what she wanted to say.

Johnny said, "Cat got your tongue?"

"I just wanted to say that I love you both." She did. Her heart suddenly swelled and she realized that she was one lucky vampire. She had family and friends and the man she wanted to spend eternity with.

"Aw," Johnny said. "I love you, too. Group hug." He threw his arms around her and Wyatt both, pulling them in close.

Stella wound up with her head buried between two chests since she was a foot shorter than them. Wyatt was laughing. Then Johnny was rubbing his knuckles across her hair like she was ten.

"You still owe me fifty bucks, Johnny. I didn't forget."

Johnny grinned at Wyatt. "You still sure you want to be with her? Stella never forgets anything, man."

"Oh, I'm sure."

The look he shot her was so hot and loving, that Stella said, "Johnny, you know the way out. Wyatt and I will see you tomorrow night."

"Gross," was her brother's opinion on the matter.

But he left.

Wyatt came over to her and pulled her into his arms and gave her a soft kiss. "You okay?"

"Yeah. That was unexpected. But good. Even if I want to kill him."

"Agreed." Wyatt shook his head with a laugh. "Man, what a couple of nights. But hey, it brought us together and I wouldn't trade that for anything."

"Me either. Me either." Stella closed her eyes and lost herself in the kiss of the man she loved.

Chapter Twenty-three

THAT VOODOO YOU DO

CORT didn't need to be asked twice. He found Katie. She'd told him her feelings, and he wanted nothing more than to be alone with her.

"Why do I have to leave?" Raven complained. "After all, he attacked me."

"It's true. Let Raven stay. I will leave."

Peter rolled his eyes, exasperated. "Whatever. Just no more fuckin' fighting tonight. Damn it, I thought the full moon didn't affect your kind."

Katie shot Cort a look. "Did everyone but me know what you guys are?"

Cort laughed and placed a hand on the small of her back. "Sorry, man," he said to both Raven and Peter, then led Katie out of the back room and through the bar.

At the front bar, Drake sat leisurely sipping a drink and tapping his fingers along with an Eagles song playing on the jukebox. He didn't appear to have noticed the commotion in the back room

"Thanks for the backup, man," Cort said as he passed. Not that he'd needed it, but it was just the principle of the thing. A bandmate should be there to back up a fellow bandmate.

"I'm a lover, not a fighter," Drake stated. "Besides, I knew you had things under control."

"Yeah, sure," Cort said.

"I wasn't talking to you," Drake said. "I was talking to Katie."

Katie laughed, the sound joyous and lovely. "Yes, I did."

Cort rolled his eyes, even though he really did agree, she did have it in control. "You were just worried you'd lose another fang."

"Totally," Drake agreed without hesitation, then took another sip of his drink. "See you back at the apartment."

Cort laughed and he and Katie left the bar.

Outside, they were immediately greeted by the Dancing Vagrant and Winston. Both seemed very happy to be reunited. The man jigged on the sidewalk, his moves surprisingly agile and rhythmic. The bird bobbed its head along with the man's movements, quite content to be back with its owner.

"I got him back," the man said to Katie as soon as he saw her.

"I see." Katie smiled. "I'm glad."

"You have no idea how glad," Cort added wryly, and Katie elbowed him.

"Shake your groove thing. Shake your groove thing," the bird crowed, and the Dancing Vagrant did.

Both Cort and Katie laughed. Cort supposed in a weird way they were a rather cute couple.

"Well, good night," Cort said to the man.

The man stopped dancing. "Oh, you can't go. Annalese will be here any moment."

"Annalese?"

"The woman who married us last night."

"Oh," Cort said, "right."

He looked at Katie. The last thing he wanted to do right now was wait for some woman, the friend of the Vagrant Dancer's, who was probably as slightly off as he was.

"Do you really think this woman married us?" he whispered to Katie.

Katie shrugged. "I guess we could wait and see."

Cort debated trying to convince her to leave, but decided that they had searched for answers all night, what could waiting a bit longer hurt?

Aside from his erection, which pressed uncomfortably against the fly of his jeans.

"Okay," he said.

She rose up on her toes to kiss him, and very quickly it didn't seem to matter that they were out on the sidewalk. Their desire overtook them.

Only when the bird began singing Barry White again, did Cort have the sense to realize where they were. But instead of waiting, he took Katie's hand and pulled her toward an alleyway just past the bar.

"What are you doing?" she asked with a giggle.

"Taking you somewhere where I can kiss you senseless."

"Okay," she said readily, and he laughed.

Once in the shadows of the alley, away from the lights and few die-hard, late-night partiers, he pulled her back in his arms.

But instead of kissing her, he asked, "Why did you run away from the apartment?"

Katie looked up at him, her blue eyes wide. "I heard you talking to Drake about the fact that we weren't married, and you sounded so relieved, that I just thought—well, I thought you didn't want to be with me, period. It was silly of me to jump to conclusions without talking to you."

"It was," he agreed, but quickly added, "but I think we've both been doing that for a long time."

Katie nodded. Then she reached up and touched his still bloodied nose. "Does it hurt?"

He shook his head.

She looked down at her fingers, then sucked his blood off her fingertips, the action so incredibly erotic.

He leaned in to kiss her. Their kiss quickly became as frantic and needy as it had been on the street, only now there was no winged chaperone to keep them in check. Soon they had their clothing yanked and askew, their hands roaming over each other's bare flesh.

Cort reached for the zipper of her jeans, yanking it down. He shoved at the waistband, getting it down so he could sink his fingers between her thighs and stroke her wetness, her heat burning his fingers.

She gasped, dropping her head back against the brick wall.

"Why the hell did we wait so long to do this? To reveal to each other how we feel?"

Katie shook her head, half answering him, half responding to his touch.

"I don't know. But I'm so glad we finally told each other."

Cort made a low noise of agreement. He kissed her again. Stroking her lips with his, stroking her clitoris with his thumb as his fingers penetrated her.

She cried out, the hoarse sound so sexy, he groaned, too.

Without breaking their kiss, he reached for his own zipper, releasing his hard, aching cock.

"I want to go slow, but I can't, baby," he murmured against her lips.

He felt her smile. "We're in an alley. I don't think we are supposed to be going slow. I think it's supposed to be hard and fast and dirty."

He chuckled, thrilled by her words. "Oh, you are a bad girl, Katie Lambert."

"Only for you."

He growled, loving that fact. He positioned her and took her just as she said, thrusting into her hard and deep and fast.

Soon they were both panting and making low noises of their impending release. He filled her over and over, her body writhing between him and the wall. Then he felt her body tense, her muscles clamping around him, her orgasm holding her, and him, in its powerful grip.

"God, yes, baby. Come for me."

She cried out, giving into it, and he rocked forward, deeper, preparing for his own orgasm.

And just as he thrust to the hilt and he felt his cock throb and his come filling her, he shouted, his ecstasy increased a hundred times as her fangs penetrated the fragile flesh of his neck.

She sucked, drawing his blood deep into her body. His cock inside her, her fangs in his, and his blood filling her.

It was heaven, pure heavenly bliss, beyond anything he'd ever felt. And this time he didn't try to stop her. He wanted to give himself to her in this way. He wanted to feed her, satisfy her desire, her lust, her hunger. He wanted to be her everything.

She was his, and he was so very much hers.

So she drank and they both came again from the rapture of it.

And when he knew he had to muster the strength to stop her, she lifted her head on her own. She licked her red lips, regarding him with a combination of guilt and pleasure.

"I wasn't supposed to do that," she whispered.

He cupped her cheek, rubbing his thumb across her lips. "I wanted you to do that. I wanted you to feed from me."

"And I want you to feed from me," she said.

"I have. And I will again. But right now, I just want to get you home." He looked up at the sky. "In fact, we need to get home."

She looked up, too. "Okay."

They straightened their clothing and tried to compose themselves as best they could. Not an easy task, given the intensity of what they just experienced.

"You know," Katie said as they reached the street, "I don't think either of us has really said exactly how we feel about each other."

Cort stopped, reaching for both of her hands.

"That one is easy for me. I'm falling in love with you. I have been for years."

Katie's gaze moved over his face, and he could see tears glistening in her gorgeous blue eyes.

"I'm falling in love with you, too."

They kissed, and Cort couldn't recall ever feeling this damned good.

"Here they are."

They parted to find the Dancing Vagrant standing beside a short woman in colorful flowing skirts. Her lovely skin was smooth and the color of café au lait. Her hair fell in cornrows around her face, and she had the most piercing blue eyes Cort had ever seen.

Cort didn't need her to say a word to know she was a voodoo priestess. But that didn't mean a marriage performed by her would be recognized as valid.

"My friend here says you wanted to talk with me about your marriage last night," Annalese said, her voice as lovely and smooth as her skin.

"Yes," Cort said. "We don't know exactly what happened to us last night. In fact, we can't remember much, or anything really about what happened, and we wanted to know if we are truly married."

Annalese raised an eyebrow, but then nodded. "Yes. You are."

Cort nodded, looking at Katie, trying to read her reaction to the news. She regarded him, clearly trying to do the very same thing.

But before he could state his feelings, the voodoo priestess continued, "But my marriage isn't the bond that brings you together. You should know that. What has joined you is far more binding than a religious ritual."

Cort frowned, not quite sure what she meant. Was this another mystery that would have them searching for more answers?

But to his surprise, Katie squeezed his hand. She seemed to understand what this lady meant.

"Thank you," she said to the voodoo priestess and to the homeless man.

Both nodded and left them.

"Okay," Cort said, frowning at Katie, "I'm totally lost. What just happened?"

"You were the one who crossed me over," Katie said, and then explained the story of her accident and how he'd saved her by giving her immortality.

"That has to be an unbreakable bond, right?" she said.

Cort nodded, suddenly realizing that was exactly why he'd been feeling so possessive and protective of her. They were bonded. They were a joined couple as surely as any wedded couple.

"Wow," he said, shaking his head, amazed.

"Are you freaked out by that idea?" she asked, worry still lingering in her eyes.

But he didn't hesitate. "Not in the least."

She smiled then.

They started down the sidewalk, heading back to his apartment.

"I have to say, I feel really awful about the loss of Johnny," Cort said after a moment. "But that was sure one hell of a wake."

Katie nodded. "I think Johnny would be happy for us."

So true. That was one thing about Johnny, he enjoyed a good story with lots of twists and turns. And he would love this one.

"You are totally right," Cort said. "I wish he was here to hear about this."

Katie squeezed his hand again. "I'm sure he knows."

Cort nodded. He'd miss his friend, but in a weird way, his passing had given him the love of his life.

And he couldn't be sad about that.

"But we still don't know why we blacked out," Cort said.

"True, maybe we should go find Wyatt and the others. Maybe they have some answers."

"Yeah." Cort pulled out his cell phone and dialed Wyatt's number. It went right to voicemail. He hung up and shoved it back in his pocket.

"You know what?" he said, moving closer to Katie. "I've had enough searching for clues tonight."

"You have?" she said, smiling in a way that was sweet and seductive all at once.

"Yeah, I think we have more important things to do now."

She raised an eyebrow, her sexy little smile not slipping. "Oh yeah, what's that?"

"Well," he said slowly, pretending to think, "we do have a marriage to consummate."

She laughed. "I think we already did that."

"But not nearly enough." He pulled her against him, and kissed her hard.

When they parted, she pursed her lips. "I suppose it is going to get light soon. Maybe we should head home."

"Oh really, that's the only reason, huh? The threat of impending sunrise?"

She tried to look serious as she nodded, but she couldn't, instead laughing again.

"Okay, I might want to get my new husband naked, too."

He caught her hand and started walking. He didn't need to be told that twice.

"Do you think we should try to find the others?" she asked.

"I'm sure they are fine," Cort said, being serious for a moment. "We'll see them tomorrow."

Katie nodded.

After a moment, Katie squeezed his hand and said, "I have to admit, no matter what happened to us, I think last night was the best night I don't remember."

He stopped and looked down at his amazing wife. "I think so, too." He kissed her. "I think so, too."

Chapter Twenty-four

A GOOD BARTENDER IS HARD TO FIND

(And They All Lived Happily Ever After. And After. And After.)

JOHNNY sat behind his drum kit and pounded away, watching his sister ogle Wyatt from the deejay booth and vice versa, glad his plan had worked. Okay, so maybe it hadn't been the nicest thing in the universe to fake his own death, but hey, it had worked, hadn't it? Stella had finally stopped ignoring the nose on her face and had fallen into Wyatt's arms.

For years he'd been waiting for those two to make a move on each other and they hadn't so Johnny had stepped in and taken matters into his own hands. Plus, it had neatly gotten him off the hook with Bambi. He hadn't really been that worried about giving her his DNA because he knew he couldn't be the father and he knew Bambi had a number of studs in her stable at any given time. He had been more worried about the fact that she seemed to have decided she wanted to be with him in some kind of family relationship and she was a tenacious chick. Who was good in bed, not so good otherwise.

So it had all worked out, if not exactly according to plan.

There had been no predicting everyone blacking out. He couldn't explain that any more than they could and he wasn't taking any flak for it.

The plus side of faking his death was that he had a renewed sense of how lucky he was to have the friends and sister that he did. Seeing that they had been genuinely torn up was touching. He figured he had an obligation to make sure he was a better friend and brother from here on out. He'd even paid Stella the fifty bucks he'd owed her.

At the end of the Bon Jovi song, Cort called a break. Johnny still couldn't believe Cort had married the washboard girl. But they, too, were making eyes at each other and there was a lot of cuddling going on in the bar. Johnny put down his sticks and reflected that maybe they were on to something. It wouldn't be a bad thing to have a woman who loved him to come home to every night.

Which meant maybe he was actually maturing. Crazy.

"I still can't believe you're alive," Cort said, giving him a grin as they climbed down off the stage. "You're such a bastard."

"You should be grateful to me. If it wasn't for my wake, you wouldn't have bagged Katie."

"Good call. Man, I'm stupidly happy. Who would have thought?"

"Not me," Johnny said in all sincerity.

The whole band gathered around a table in the back of the bar and Johnny ordered them a round of drinks from Jacob, the bartender. He was feeling generous. Katie snuggled up next to Cort, and Stella took a stool next to Wyatt. Drake was messing with his fang implant. Saxon was smearing ChapStick on his lips.

"I can't believe you guys were hanging with Raven the other night. I was like, seriously?" Johnny said, shaking his head. It had been highly entertaining following his friends throughout their night of drunken ridiculousness.

"What?" Drake stopped messing with his tooth. "What do you mean?"

"I'd have thought he was your long-lost brother the way you were cutting up with him. Cracked me up. He was with you most of the night, at the casino, at the Bourbon Cowboy, the wedding chapel . . ."

Astonished faces met him. "You mean Raven wasn't trying to kill Saxon?" Wyatt asked.

"No, though Saxon did borrow five hundred bucks from him. He seemed to think he knew how to play blackjack." Johnny gave Saxon a look. "Word to the wise. Don't play blackjack. But yeah, you were the five amigos, having a great time. Six, actually, if you count the priest. I was kind of jealous, I'm not going to lie. I think Raven was flattered actually. The guy doesn't have a lot of friends."

"How did Benny end up with us?" Stella asked.

"Who the hell is Benny?"

"The priest. The stripper priest." She waved her hand around. "You know, the guy in the robe."

Johnny shrugged. "He was just walking down the street and Cort grabbed him and asked him to marry him and Katie." He turned to Katie. "Beautiful ceremony, by the way. The rings were a nice touch."

She flushed. "Thanks."

"Though I can't believe you gave away my Elvis cookie jar. I loved that thing and it wasn't cheap."

"eBay, dude, eBay. Buy yourself another one," was all the sympathy he got from Cort.

Jacob brought over their drinks, juggling them all with consummate bartender skill. He was distributing beers all around.

"So I guess the only question that's left is who drugged us? Why did we all black out?" Wyatt asked.

Jacob didn't miss a beat. "I did."

"What?" Cort's foot fell off his stool to the floor and he gaped at Jacob.

"Yeah, you were all so broken up over jackass here dying." He shot his thumb at Johnny.

"Hey." Johnny knew he deserved it, but still.

"So I slipped you all a little happy drug. I had no idea you were going to black out. That doesn't happen to werewolves." He put the final beer down. "My bad."

Johnny let out a crack of laughter. Now that was some funny shit.

"Living on a prayer, dude," Saxon said.

As usual no one seemed to know what the hell Saxon was talking about. So Johnny raised his beer. "To friends."

"To sex, blood, and rock 'n' roll," Drake said.

"Cheers." Stella raised her beer. "Wait, this isn't drugged, is it?"

Half of them were already drinking.

Jacob paused. Then he grinned and shook his head. "Nah. I don't think it is."

Johnny drank it anyway, not worried about it.

You only lived once. And forever.